Praise for Toni Leland

"...all great reads that I could hardly put down. I just wanted you to know how much I enjoy your books..."

–MP at ArabianExperts.com, 2006

Gambling With the Enemy ~ "...a gripping, 'can't put it down' novel, with unforgettable characters and one of the most terrifying scenarios a modern-day American could imagine."

–Marilyn Fisher, author of *The Case of the Three Dead Horses*

"...I could not put it down...I really felt the story unfolding in what astrologers call a 'conspiracy of energy'..."

–Robbie Hueseth, Blue Ribbon Books

"...a fast paced book that's part romance, part thriller, and part the kind of horsey book you grew up reading."

–Carolyn Banks, best-selling author of *A Horse To Die For*

Hearts Over Fences~"...a charming and clean love story set in the heart of horse country and the horse industry. .."

–*Midwest Book Review*, June 2005

"...Ms. Leland weaves a fascinating tale of horses, business, and romance...*Hearts Over Fences* is a great read that I highly recommend."

–*Coffee Time Review*, June 2005

Winning Ways~"...this book took me on an exciting journey of how cutthroat the show world can be...a roller coaster ride from start to finish..."

–Rebecca, *Horsemen's Yankee Pedlar*, June 2004

"...Toni Leland presents us with a sensitive, well written story. Her knowledge of horses and the people who care for them is impressive."

–Luvada White, *Ohioana Quarterly*, Fall 2004

Titles by
TONI LELAND

Deadly Heritage
Gambling With the Enemy
Hearts Over Fences
Winning Ways

Deadly Heritage

TONI LELAND

ISBN 978-1-887932-20-2

Printed in U.S.A.

Parallel Press is the fiction imprint of the Equine Graphics Publishing Group

Acknowledgments

I owe sincere thanks to those who dug deep for answers to my many questions. The devil is always in the details, and without the help of these supportive folks, this story would never have been told.

Thank you: Candy M. Ford at the Guthrie Public Library, Logan County Commissioner Mark Sharpton, the Guthrie Fire Department, and the Guthrie Chamber of Commerce for helping me fine-tune the regional details. Georgia veterinarian Dr. Kenneth Marcella "vetted" the equine health sections, Mary Ann Kean at Markel Insurance advised me on equine liability policies, and Kirsten Johnson of KESMARC in Lexington, Kentucky provided fascinating in-depth information about equine hyperbaric oxygen therapy. Manager Marsha Glass gave us a deluxe tour of the facility.

More thanks go to author Judie Aitken for insight into "horse sticks," Pat Elder for guidance on Quarter Horses, and advance readers Art & Holly, author Carolyn Banks, and "the horse book lady," Robbee Hueseth, for catching all the glitches.

Last, but not least, thank you, Bob, for humoring me as I investigated every alley and historic building in Guthrie, Oklahoma.

1

A sickening odor clung to the still morning air and fear curled through Kellie Sutton's chest.

Dr. Hyde Browning's eyes darkened with compassion. "I won't kid you–he's going downhill fast."

Taking a deep breath to quell the nausea churning through her stomach, Kellie forced herself to look down, and another wave of revulsion rolled through her. The stallion's left front foot was a volcano of angry red flesh, with thick yellow pus oozing from the ruptured skin.

Her voice cracked. "Do you have anything else that might work better?"

"Without knowing what happened to him, I can only make guesses on treatment. Based on the extensive tissue damage, I'd say it's a staph infection, but he doesn't seem to be responding to the antibiotic. I can try a different type, but..."

The unfinished sentence held little optimism.

Kellie stroked Dancer's sleek coat, brilliant as a newly minted penny. His skin quivered beneath her touch, the elegant head hung low, and his large brown eyes, usually so alert and curious, were dull as dry river pebbles. In the space of three days, what she'd thought was a simple stone bruise had escalated into a nightmare.

"Would an x-ray show anything? Could it be a fracture? Or something embedded in his foot?"

The veterinarian shook his head. "I've ruled those out, plus a few you haven't thought of." He touched her arm. "I know this is hard for you, but the medication needs time to work."

She struggled with emotions that threatened to overwhelm her. "You do whatever it takes to save him." Her voice broke again. "He's my best stallion."

Hyde depressed the plunger on a syringe and a tiny drop of liquid squirted from the tip of the needle. "I'll photograph the wound, and take a tissue sample over to Stillwater. Maybe the university lab can give us some answers."

"What about a spider bite? Or a scorpion–I got stung once when I was a kid, and it hurt like hell!"

"Neither of those would cause this much damage."

He deftly slipped the long needle into the horse's bulging heel, and Kellie flinched. Focusing on the vet's ministrations, she pushed away all thoughts of the possible outcome of the disaster in her barn.

A few minutes later, she followed Hyde out into the morning sun. His expression revealed nothing, but his tone was cautious.

"I gave him a shot of Bute to keep him comfortable. You can dose him again with the paste in eight hours. I'll be back in the morning–hopefully, with some answers. If anything changes in the meantime, call me." He walked toward his truck, then turned back. "I checked the palomino mare. She should deliver her foal tonight."

A cloud of red dust churned behind his tailgate all the way to the end of the lane. The strong spring sun beat down on Kellie's bare head, but despite the temperature, she shivered with apprehension. Nothing in Hyde's demeanor gave her any confidence that world champion Docs Dirty Dancing would recover.

For long moments after the truck had disappeared from view, she stared at the endless pale yellow fields spreading across acres of flat land. A cobalt sky slammed into the horizon and a few wispy clouds drifted above, with no promise of rain. Scattered mesquite trees punctuated the skyline, and the steady up-and-down movements of several oil pumps brought to mind the image of giant birds pulling the rich black treasure from beneath Oklahoma's parched crust. Her home. Her heritage. Red soil that flowed through her veins.

She turned and stared at the round corral behind the barn. *Dancer might have injured his foot on something while he was turned out.* Resolve lengthened her stride as she headed that direction. Her life and livelihood depended on the stallion's recovery, and she couldn't idly stand by, waiting for someone else to come up with answers. She slowly walked the inside fence perimeter, examining the base of each post and scanning the ground for anything that could have caused the horse's wound.

Fifteen minutes later, she'd made the full circle, finding only a beer bottle top. She leaned against the rail, running her thumb over the sharp ridges of the metal cap, trying to imagine how it might have caused Dancer's wound. She shook her head and pushed away from the fence, stuffing the cap into her pocket as she walked toward the main barn. The university lab would have answers.

Inside the spacious office, she passed by the ranch manager's desk. His papers were neatly stacked, pens and pencils tucked into a mug, his to-do list squared up with the edge of the desk. A sharp contrast to her own jumbled workspace in the corner. Once upon a time, Frank Frazier's attention to detail had made him the perfect choice for ranch manager, leaving her free to pursue the business of building her Quarter Horse herd. She set her jaw. Once upon a time, a *lot* of things had been different.

She settled into the comfortable leather chair behind a dark mahogany desk, an ornate relic from her Grandfather Sutton's ranching days. The antique seemed out of place in the new modern building, but she didn't care. History and family heritage were precious commodities to be guarded with a passion.

A ranch hand rapped on the doorjamb.

"Boots is limping."

Kellie jumped up and followed him down the barn aisle. At the stall door, she closed her eyes tightly.

"Aw, you have to be kidding!"

Boot Scootin Doc, the best reining horse on Rocking S Ranch, stood in a corner of the stall, holding his left front foot off the ground.

Kellie smoothed her hand over his shoulder, then kneeled in the wood shavings to get a closer look. Angry red skin glowed through the sparkling white hair on the horse's ankle, and swelling had forced the flesh into a puffy ridge along the top edge of the hoof. She touched the foot lightly to confirm the heat of infection.

"Where was he yesterday?"

"In the east grazing pen." The young man sounded nervous, and hastened to add, "He seemed fine when I brought him in last night."

Rocking back on her heels, Kellie focused again on the distorted foot. *Could* they be dealing with a bite? She knew nothing about spiders, but she'd grown up sharing the land with scorpions and had always given them the respect they deserved.

She pulled out her cell phone and dialed Hyde's number. "We have another one. Same foot, same beginning signs."

"I have two more farm calls to make, then I'll swing back. In the meantime, check all your horses' feet, see if any others have similar symptoms."

She snapped the phone shut and turned to the ranch hand. "Find Frank and tell him I need him."

Kellie had checked three horses by the time Frank appeared.

He leaned against an upright and shoved a hand in his pocket. "What's up?"

"We have another lame horse. I want you to check the

outside stock."

"Can't–I'm headed into the city."

Kellie mentally took a deep breath. "This won't take long."

Frank pushed away from the post, his features hardening. "We pay the hired help to do this stuff, so let's get our money's worth."

She carefully controlled her tone. "Frank, this is serious. Please do your job."

Anger darkened his hazel eyes and a muscle twitched along his jaw line. "Yes, *Ma'am!*" He turned on a heel and strode down the barn aisle.

The unpleasant exchange burned through Kellie's thoughts. His nonchalance about the critical situation bothered her deeply. She glanced toward the doorway where he stood talking to the stable manager. What had triggered this sudden attitude?

Putting the troubling thoughts out of her mind, she worked her way down the row of stalls, further considering the idea of scorpions as the source of her problem. During the past few severe drought years, the population of strange-looking-but-timid creatures had exploded. Normally, the creepy little spider relatives were considered harmless, but hidden in the dark corners of a stall, they most certainly could attack a poorly placed foot.

An hour later, Hyde picked up Boots's foot and leaned in close, brushing his fingers lightly over the heel area. He released the hoof and straightened up.

"I don't like what I'm seeing here."

~ ~

Anger still snapped through Frank's thoughts as he barged through the squeaky door of the Sooner café and headed for the corner booth where his coffee pals waited. He slid across the cracked red vinyl seat, wedging his thick thighs under the edge of the low table, settling himself into the morning din of the popular meeting place. No women, just the guys catching up, savoring the brief chance to be themselves. Ranchers, merchants, retired men with nothing to do–all equal for an hour each morning.

Across the table, an overall-clad man grinned and stubbed out his cigarette. "Yer late, Frankie. Boss Lady got you doing extra chores this morning?"

"Fuck you."

The local mechanic cackled and shook his head. "Boy, I sure don't understand how you can work with her."

"Business is business."

"I guess...Did ya hear the fire department's havin' equipment problems again? That damned old military brush tanker keeps breakin' down. Bad timing, too, what with the dry weather." He stopped to wheeze and clear his throat. "I'm tellin' ya, we're gonna get caught with our pants down one of these days."

The café door creaked and Sheriff Ed Campbell ducked through. He greeted a couple of patrons, then his gaze drifted to Frank, and the pleasant expression disappeared. He nodded, then turned back to the waitress and paid for a cup of coffee to go.

Frank scowled. *Pompous sonofabitch.*

A moment later, Campbell left the café and the mechanic chuckled. "Whoo-ee! No love lost between *you* two!"

Frank bit back a nasty retort and grinned smugly. "Only on his part. I got the girl, remember?"

"Yeah, but *that* didn't last long...I wonder who convinced ol' Ed to come back to Guthrie."

Frank carefully controlled his expression. Campbell's recent return bothered the hell out of him, but he'd be damned if he'd let anyone know it.

Beside him, a portly man stirred three sugars into a cup

of coffee. "Frank, you ever buy another racehorse after that accident at the track?"

Another path Frank didn't want to follow. "No, I'm still looking at prospects."

"Sure was a shame. I couldn't friggin' believe it when I heard. That was some nice looking horse."

Frank's gut tightened at the recollection. Nice looking and worth half-a-million dollars. Gone in a heartbeat.

The mechanic chimed in. "I heard some Texan offered to buy him before the race."

For about the millionth time in the past two years, Frank kicked himself for not accepting the generous pre-race offer to buy the colt. Greed had commandeered *that* decision. But on the up side, the horse's death had set the wheels in motion for something much bigger, a business operation now earning a hell of a lot more money than racing.

He ignored his friend's fishing expedition, and glanced at the clock above the door. "Gotta go, I have an important meeting."

"Break a leg. Oops–sorry!"

~~

Kellie could not control the waver in her voice. "Deputy White, please."

She chewed her lip while she waited, Hyde's words looping over and over in her head. *Who would do such a thing? And why?*

A soft drawl hummed through the phone. "Sheriff Campbell. Can I help you?"

Stunned recognition snapped through her brain and familiar images crowded in, forming a vise-grip around her chest.

The voice took on more authority. "Hello? This is Sheriff Ed Campbell."

She took a deep breath. "It's Kellie Sutton. I have an emergency out here."

A taut silence filled the line. "What's going on?"

"Please, just send someone out."

She closed the cell phone and swallowed hard, struggling with the echo of Ed Campbell's voice in her head. How could fifteen years have evaporated in the space of a phone call?

Hyde stepped out of the stall and latched the door. "I'll drop this sample off at OSU this afternoon. We'd better get some answers soon–this stuff is moving like wildfire." He stopped and peered into her face. "Hey, what's wrong?"

"I just got off the phone with the new sheriff."

Hyde raised an eyebrow. "And...?"

"I wasn't ready to talk to him yet."

Hyde patted her arm. "That's ancient history–time heals most wounds. Let's go take a look at your young stock."

Outside, Hyde moved to the center of a grazing pen filled with yearlings, and the youngsters crowded up close, eager for his attention. He raised his arms to shoulder height and the milling crowd melded into an attentive group, all ears pricked forward. The way he communicated with horses seemed almost mystical, a subtle body language that only the animals recognized. The talent had never ceased to amaze Kellie, but Hyde shrugged off the skills as being part of his Osage heritage. Squatting beside each horse, he carefully examined the small feet. The young horses stood quietly while he worked and, when he'd finished, the formation dissolved into playful pushing and rearing. Class was dismissed.

He strode across the grass toward her, his long legs covering the distance quickly. Dark eyes gazed from beneath heavy eyebrows, and his wide high cheekbones accentuated a rugged classic face. Kellie's heart warmed. He'd been the best friend anyone could have–loyal and sympathetic, supporting her in everything she tried, and always there to pick up the pieces when she failed.

He pushed his hat back off his forehead. "The kids are fine." He gestured toward two sheep dogs stretched out in the sun. "You oughta get some watchdogs instead of those worthless mutts."

The old dog, Buck, raised his head to stare indignantly at Hyde, and Kellie laughed.

"Working dogs need their sleep."

Hyde's phone beeped and he turned away, lowering his voice. Within minutes, he closed the phone and shook his head.

"Your neighbor's horse has a swollen foot. Sounds like the same symptoms."

~~

Kellie sat in her office, lost in thought about Dancer. More than all his national and world championships, or his prowess in the breeding barn, she treasured his friendship. They'd been a team for over ten years. Her eyes misted at the terrifying possibility he might die. The emotional tussle lasted only seconds. *It will not happen. It* can't. *Hyde will save him.*

In moments, her usual calm confidence returned and she reached across the desk for a scheduling calendar. A shiny reflection caught her eye and she picked up a snapshot from amongst the papers strewn over the desktop. The scene was almost ethereal, looking as though it might have been taken from outside a stall, since the only light in the photo came through a small screened window in the background. She stared with growing curiosity at her own image standing next to Dancer, her cheek resting against his large jaw, her red hair almost the same color as his coat. She drew the photograph closer to inspect the details. *Must be a shot for one of the farm ads.* The phone rang and she set the picture aside.

Her brother's hearty greeting sounded a little too cheerful.

"Hey, Sis, how ya doin'?"

She pursed her lips. "I'm good, Cliff–and you?"

"Can't complain, other than Houston's a steam bath again today." He cleared his throat. "I'm gonna be up to Guthrie next week on business. Thought I'd come by and catch up on the news."

An alarm sounded in Kellie's head. Cliff Sutton wouldn't just drop by from Texas unless he wanted something.

"I'm judging a horse show this weekend, but I should be around after that."

"I'll give a holler when I get to town. See ya."

The line went dead, and Kellie set the portable phone back into the base. *I hope this isn't about the land developers again.*

She glanced once more at the snapshot, then pushed it out of the way to make room for a three-panel calendar. June, July, and August were booked with competitions almost every weekend, and she'd blocked out the first three weeks in October for the American Quarter Horse Congress–the largest breed show in the world, and one that had been the setting for many of Dancer's triumphs.

Her index finger trailed down the list of horses slated to go to Congress, and an uneasy thought formed. She'd planned to take Boots, but unless his injury was unrelated to Dancer's, he wouldn't be competing. She leaned back in the chair and stared at the raftered ceiling. Why did things seem to be going sour lately? Ever since the blow up with her brothers, she'd felt as though she controlled nothing. Now this with the horses.

"Mama?"

Kellie's dismal thoughts evaporated as her nine-year-old daughter stepped into the office.

"Hey, Sara Baby, what are you up to?"

The little girl's green eyes sparkled and a rosy flush covered her freckled cheeks. "I'm gonna work Juicy on the lunge line. Can you come and watch?"

"Sure, give me a sec."

Kellie closed the scheduling calendar, and Sara reached across the desk to pick up the snapshot.

"Where'd this come from?" She peered at the image, then giggled. "Your hair was really short!"

"It sure was–hey, are you coming to the show with me on Saturday?"

Sara laid the picture back on the desk and rolled her eyes. "Oh, duh!"

Kellie laughed, emotion crowding into her heart as they moved out into the barn aisle.

Sara fell into step beside her mother. "Why does Dancer's stall stink so awful?"

"He has a bad infection, honey."

Sara stopped mid-step, her eyes suddenly big and glistening with fear. "Is he gonna die?"

Kellie's dread bubbled up, clamoring for release, but she pushed it away. "Doc Browning's taking good care of him. We just have to hope he gets well soon."

Sara nodded solemnly, then opened a stall door and stepped inside to put a halter on a flashy sorrel and white pinto. After setting the horse up in crossties, she deftly applied splint boots, and gave the horse a quick once-over with a brush. Kellie's own childhood memories freshened as she followed Sara and her horse out into the sunshine.

"When I was your age, I spent every possible waking hour with horses. I dreamed about them at night, and drew pictures of them during school." She chuckled. "Your granddad was pretty worried about my one-track mind."

"Did your brothers like horses too?"

"Only my older brother–your Uncle Randy."

"What about Uncle Cliff and Uncle Clarke?"

Frick and Frack. The twins' attitude about horses had

always been a sore spot.

"They taunted me constantly about my obsession. Horses were nothing more than work animals to those two. When I turned twelve, Randy started letting me ride with him. We spent hours on horseback, playing rodeo and practicing our roping skills on fence posts. He was fantastic. He advanced to High School Rodeo and won all the titles."

Sara stopped walking and looked up with sympathy. "Do you miss him?"

Well-remembered sorrow moved into Kellie's heart. "Yes, I do. Very much."

She turned to gaze toward the rambling ranch house where they'd all grown up. The memories seemed like only yesterday. While her brothers and school chums had abandoned the sticks for the excitement of the world outside ranch life, she had settled in, knowing she belonged right where she'd come into the world. The painful memories deepened–the choice had cost her dearly.

In her peripheral vision, a county patrol car turned into the lane and she closed her eyes. *Please let that be anyone but Ed.*

~~

Kellie waited inside the barn, trying to calm her jumping pulse by listening to the background sounds. A country beat thrummed from a radio, someone laughed, a tractor rumbled outside. A silhouette appeared in the doorway, then Ed Campbell stepped into the light. His long legs quickly closed the distance between them, and breath-stopping thuds hammered through her chest.

He tipped his brown Stetson and offered a large tanned hand. "How are you, Kellie?"

His steely gray eyes glinted like mica at the bottom of a mountain stream, and his firm grip sent a familiar stutter through her heartbeat.

Unable to deal with the rush of memories, she looked away. "Not good. Two of my horses have come up seriously lame."

His tone rang with surprise. "Sounds like Doctor Browning could help more than I can. Why'd you call *us*?"

"Come down to the office and I'll fill you in."

She headed across the aisle, intensely aware of his nearness.

He stopped for a moment in front of the awards display. "Looks like the Suttons are doing pretty well for themselves."

Spiraling into the magic of his strong baritone, Kellie caught her breath at the burst of excitement coursing through her. A flashback rushed into her head. After all these years, could he deny his own history here?

He eased into one of the chairs beside her desk, and she focused on the way his crisp uniform shirt hugged the contours of his chest and shoulders.

He leaned forward, elbows on knees, a serious expression sharpening his chiseled features. "Okay, what's the deal here?"

Unfamiliar indecision grabbed her. Had she called the authorities too soon? What if...no, it was the right thing to do. Still horrified at what she was about to say, she swallowed hard.

"Hyde says...he thinks someone purposely injected something into my horses' feet."

Ed straightened up in the chair, his eyebrows coming together. "Why does he think that?"

"Both horses have identical symptoms in the same foot, and the most recently injured horse has a round puncture wound, like it was made by a needle. Swelling and infection haven't camouflaged it yet."

Ed reached into his shirt pocket and removed a small brown notebook, then looked up. "Could be an insect bite."

She looked away from his impersonal expression. "Hyde collected tissue and blood samples, and took them over to the university lab, but we won't know anything until tomorrow."

"Assuming this *is* a deliberate attack, do you have any idea who might want to cause some trouble?"

Disbelief snapped Kellie's somber mood. "*Trouble?* Ed, you don't seem to understand–this is disastrous! My horses could *die* from whatever's in their systems!"

He looked startled at the outburst, and apology surged into her thoughts. She rose and headed toward the door. "I'll show you what I'm talking about."

A minute later, Ed took a quick step back from Dancer's stall door. "Holy cow, what's that smell?"

"Rotting dead flesh."

Her throat constricted to the point where she couldn't say anything more, and tears threatened behind her lids, intensifying her feelings of helplessness. Worse, Ed's nearness made her long to erase the past, step into his arms, let him make everything right again–the way it used to be.

His tone was grim. "I'll get a deputy on it right away."

His boots echoed on the concrete barn floor, then faded, leaving Kellie with a familiar sense of loss. She gazed at Dancer for a moment, then turned away, squaring her shoulders with resolve.

"Roy?" Her voice resonated through the cavernous building. "You in here?"

A lid slammed shut on a grain bin in the feed room, and a grizzled old man stepped into the aisle. Kellie walked swiftly toward him, gathering her thoughts.

"Get the staff together in my office in fifteen minutes."

He nodded and moved toward the barn door, and Kellie began to compose what she would say to her employees.

Shortly, six men and three women crowded into the office, their faces forming a collage of curiosity and apprehension.

"It appears we've had an intruder in the barn–Dancer and Boots have been viciously attacked."

A collective gasp echoed in the small room, but no one spoke.

"I want each one of you to think back over the past week. Tell me if you saw anything unusual, no matter how insignificant it might seem."

A newly hired stall cleaner spoke up. "I found a half-smoked cigarette by the door to your office one morning." The young woman glanced around nervously. "I didn't say nothing, 'cause I didn't want to get anyone in trouble...me being new here an' all."

Kellie narrowed her eyes, controlling her annoyance. She'd remind everyone later about smoking in the barn.

"What did you do with it?"

The girl's voice wavered. "I threw it in the manure pile."

"Okay, we'll discuss that later. Someone from the sheriff's office will be coming around. Please cooperate so we can catch whoever did this horrible thing."

"Are the horses going to be okay?"

"Yes."

Her voice sounded hollow, but maybe if she said it enough times, it would be so.

~ ~

Water pounded the top of Kellie's head and streamed down her body, encasing her in a cocoon of heat. She inhaled deeply, letting the steam filter through her lungs to cleanse away the dust of the day while she focused on a glob of soap bubbles sliding down the tiles. Today had been the longest day of her life and, as usual, she'd handled it on her own. But this time, her aloneness held a sharper edge. Seeing Ed had severed an emotional artery, spilling the past into the present with painful force. He hadn't even seemed glad to see her.

Polite, but distant. She closed her eyes tightly, denying the painful admission of youthful error.

Stepping out onto the soft bath mat, she shivered as the change in temperature prickled over her body. Ed's handsome face materialized again, and another flood of memories washed over her. She swiped the condensation from the mirror, then leaned on the sink and stared at her forlorn expression.

"You can't do this to yourself."

An hour later, she leaned back in the porch swing and nibbled a piece of cheese as Frank approached the front steps.

She brushed a crumb off her lap. "Have you been to see the horses yet?"

His boots thumped on the old planks, then he dropped into a wicker chair. "Nope."

An angry retort teetered on her tongue, stayed only by the chime of her cell phone and the appearance of Hyde's number on the screen.

"Kellie, the Anderson horse has the same puncture wound as your horses. Same foot, same symptoms. We're up against a real sick-o."

"I've already talked to Sheriff Campbell, but you should give him a call too. And please let me know the minute you hear from the lab."

She closed the phone, instantly aware of Frank's frown.

He crossed his arms. "*Now* what's going on?"

"Hyde hasn't figured out the cause, but he found a similar puncture wound on the neighbor's horse. The injuries were intentional."

Frank snorted. "Jesus, Kellie, you have one hell of an imagination!" His eyes narrowed and a nasty smile curled his thin lips. "Or maybe you were just looking for a chance to reconnect with ol' Ed."

She rose from the swing and stalked toward the front door. "Go to hell, Frank."

"Guess you shoulda married him instead of me."

2

The chilly dawn air raised a flush of goose bumps over Kellie's bare arms as she walked briskly toward the barn, wrestling again with Frank's cruel words. Yes, she should have married Ed, but youthful ignorance entertains the fantasy that there'll always be plenty of time. She'd thought she could make choices on her own terms, manage pride and passion as she controlled everything else, only to lose the one thing she'd ever really wanted.

Stopping inside the door, she inhaled deeply, letting the unique aroma of horses and hay salve her inner turmoil. Horses were in her blood, had been from her earliest childhood, and nothing had ever affected her the way these magnificent animals did.

Her step faltered as she neared Dancer's stall. The horrible odor drenched her with apprehension, but the stallion's deep nickered greeting filled her heart with hope.

She opened the door, then closed her eyes for a second. "Oh my God."

The big horse leaned heavily against the wall, holding his left foot above the bedding. Kellie forced herself to look at the gauze-wrapped hoof. A dark yellow patch stained the bandage, and a bright red center formed a bull's-eye. The ankle had swollen to twice its normal size, and the distention encompassed the foreleg to the knee. The antibiotics weren't working.

Dancer let out a heavy sigh, and sympathy seared Kellie's heart. The horse was exhausted from keeping the weight off his foot, knowing instinctively that, if he lay down, he'd never be able to get back on his feet.

Her despair fed her sense of helplessness. Hyde wasn't due for another thirty minutes. Would he find a solution before Dancer ran out of time?

~~

Ed Campbell doodled along the edge of the desk mat while he listened to the soft-spoken man on the cell phone. Several thoughts vied for attention, the strongest being how good Kellie Sutton looked–even better than his memories. A prick of disappointment quickly popped the warm feeling. She hadn't acted happy to see him, in fact, had never made more than brief eye contact during their conversation. He scratched an X over the heart he'd just drawn. Who was he kidding? The past was just that, and she'd moved on without looking back. Coming home to Guthrie had been a mistake.

The voice on the phone sharpened. "Campbell! Did you hear me?"

Ed straightened in the chair, pressing the small white phone closer. "Sorry, say again."

"The subjects have accelerated their activity. It's time to move into phase two. Everything from here on out is strictly dark–including discussions with the commissioners. Make something up if you have to, but report only to me." The man paused, then his tone changed. "You having any problems down there?"

"No, there's some town stuff going on, but I have it covered."

The phone screen faded and Ed scowled. Kellie Sutton's problems were not going to screw this up–not after all these years.

"Morning, Chief." Deputy Danielle White's husky voice preceded her voluptuous six-foot body into the office. She flashed a wide smile and leaned a shoulder against the doorjamb. "Got time for breakfast?"

Ed slipped the cell phone into his pocket and shook his head. "Can't, I have a ton of paperwork, and a new situation is brewing out at Rocking S. They've had some mysterious attacks on the horses. I want either you or Jimmy to go out there this morning and start asking questions."

Danielle's smile disappeared and she gazed at him for a moment, then nodded and left the room. He exhaled slowly, wondering again why he'd thought accepting this assignment had been a good idea.

~ ~

A creamy yellow foal pranced around the stall, swishing her sassy little white tail, her bright eyes glowing with curiosity about her new world. Kellie leaned on the door and offered a hand. The tiny filly came forward to sniff the fingers, then snorted and tossed her head.

Hyde's soft voice resonated in the quiet morning air. "Born in the full moon. My grandmother would say that brings good temperament."

Kellie cast a sidelong glance at her friend's serene expression. "Oh, puh-leez! Temperament comes from genes, not planetary positioning. All Dancer's babies are like this."

Hyde's expression darkened, and Kellie hastened to soften her retort. "But I'm sure the timing helped."

The filly uttered a throaty nicker and moved nearer the stall door to peer up at Hyde. She bobbed her head as though a silent message had passed between them, then squealed and pivoted on her hind legs to dive beneath her dam's belly.

"She has come at the right time, to fill the void."

His words hung on the warm air, and Kellie whirled to face him. "What void? What do you mean?"

"My grandmother would say, 'For every death, a birth'."

The breath froze in Kellie's lungs. *Whose death? Not Dancer!* She began to shake her head, trying to break the paralysis that kept her from speaking.

Hyde slipped an arm around her shoulders and squeezed. "The guy at the lab called. The culture didn't grow staph. He tried a couple of different tests, but got no identifiable results. I asked him to send some of the sample over to the state forensic pathology lab. Maybe they can tell us something." He released her and stepped back, shaking his head. "I can't fight what I don't know."

Kellie almost choked on the tightness in her throat. "What do we do in the meantime?"

"One of my colleagues suggested hyperbaric oxygen therapy after we clean out the dead tissue. The treatment is relatively new and I don't know much about it, but apparently it is highly effective for speeding new tissue growth and healing. It's also quite expensive." He paused a little too long before continuing. "The real danger here is laminitis. Dancer's good leg is beginning to swell from the excess weight he's putting on it. I brought along some special heel pads that should relieve the strain. It might give us some time."

"Anything. Just do it."

She watched him leave the barn, then turned her attention back to the newest addition to the herd. With a full tummy, the foal now rested in the straw with her eyes closed.

"Hey, new baby!"

Kellie spun around at Frank's voice close behind her. For a moment, she was happy to see him, wanted someone to soothe her pain and hold her close. The impulse passed immediately, and she stepped aside while he inspected the new arrival.

Years of playing high school and college football had built muscular shoulders and a thick neck, but more years of beer and cigarettes had allowed those muscles to go soft. In the beginning, she'd thought he was sexy, but that notion had disappeared quickly the first few times they made love. Frank's sex drive was strong, but basic–every man for himself, as they say. Kellie's salvation on that front had been her pregnancy. With the announcement, her new husband's libido had veered in other directions, leaving her to savor, undisturbed, her impending motherhood.

Frank straightened up and faced her, his eyes without emotion, his unshaven jaw tightening. "Okay, show me the horses you *think* were vandalized."

His patent disbelief sent a flush of anger up Kellie's neck. "I can't believe you haven't been to see them yet."

His patronizing stare reminded her that fighting with him was unproductive. He always managed to maneuver her into a position that made her feel ineffectual. Without a word, he turned and strode down the aisle toward Dancer's stall.

A moment later, he grimaced. "Jee-zus! What a stink!" His eyebrows formed a dark line. "Is Boots this bad?"

"Not yet, but he will be if Doc Browning can't identify the cause of the infection."

Frank stepped into the stallion's stall, talking in a low voice. "Hey, big guy, how ya doin'?"

The horse didn't respond, and Frank dropped to a knee to inspect the bandaged foot. When he rose, his dark expression was heart stopping.

"I'd better call the insurance company and get permission to have him put down."

"No! Frank, it's too–"

"Kellie! Wake up! Look at this swelling–he's in a lot of pain and he's not getting better."

He turned away, his footsteps tapping across the concrete aisle. She slumped against the stall wall, her throat constricting as panic spread through her body and a deep shudder convulsed her. She could not–would not–accept the grim promise of

Dancer's death.

"Kellie, what's wrong?"

Hyde's voice curled around her, hooking the edges of her near-hysteria and drawing it back. He stepped into the stall and laid a hand on her arm.

She drew a deep breath. "Frank thinks we should have him destroyed."

Hyde dropped his bag into the shavings, and moved to the stallion's shoulder.

"Frank's not the vet, and I haven't given up on this."

~~

Half an hour later, Sara bounced into the spacious country kitchen, her sunny disposition the perfect tonic for Kellie's fragile mental health. Hugging the child tightly, Kellie buried her nose in the soft curly hair and inhaled the light floral scent of shampoo, gathering strength from the love bond between them.

"Morning, Baby. You'll have to settle for cold cereal–I'm getting ready to leave."

Sara wriggled out of the embrace. "Mama, let me come with you. I just love watching you be the judge."

Kellie gave her a stern look. "You have school, remember?"

The child's pink lips puffed into a pout. "Pleeeze, Mama? We aren't doing anything important today, and I–"

"Absolutely not." Sara's smile faded, and Kellie softened her tone. "Ask your dad to bring you down after school."

Sara flounced over to the refrigerator and yanked open the door. "I *never* get to do anything fun!"

Kellie chuckled and grabbed her jacket. "Don't forget to take your vitamin."

Easing her dark green Silverado onto Sutton Corners Road, she almost relented. *What would it hurt to miss one day of school? She's such a joy to have around, and she loves horses so much, and...*

"No, I'm already a big pushover."

She pressed the accelerator and headed toward the highway. A quarter mile down the road, she pulled onto the shoulder and squinted against the sun, trying to get a good look at the neighboring farm that abutted Sutton property. Waist high weeds surrounded the small drab house, and the original barn had finally succumbed to gravity. A scraggly oak tree grew inside the roofless corn silo, and rusted equipment dotted the property. One lone length of barbed wire fence remained upright.

The elderly owners had clearly given up, and it was only a matter of time before they would sell out. Kellie frowned. Too many things were changing too fast, and she didn't like it one bit. Rather than wait until it was out of her hands, perhaps she should make them an offer. The property wasn't a full section, but it did have the advantage of being right on the road. *I'll call the bank on Monday.*

As she put the truck in gear, a vehicle appeared farther up the road and she recognized the light bar on the roof of the cab. A jolt of anticipation shot through her. Glancing in the rearview mirror, she pushed a renegade strand of hair off her forehead, suddenly feeling ridiculous about her reaction to the prospect of seeing Ed. *Like a silly young girl.*

The cruiser pulled up beside her, and Deputy White unfolded from the front seat.

Kellie swallowed her disappointment and rolled down the window. "Hey, Dani, you're certainly the early bird!"

The woman shook her head. "New sheriff is a hard task-master." She grinned wickedly. "But he sure is easy on the eyes. Anyway, I'm supposed to question your staff about this thing with your horses. What happened, anyway? Campbell didn't say."

Kellie hesitated, distracted by the woman's personal

observation about Ed. "We don't know for sure, but it's serious...I'm judging a horse show today at the Lazy E, but I told the staff to cooperate fully. I'll call the stable manager and tell him you'll be there shortly."

Danielle straightened up and shook her head. "I'd rather you go with me to get things started." She stepped away from the window. "I'll follow you."

Kellie turned the truck around and started back toward the ranch, disturbed by her reaction to Danielle's frank appreciation of Ed. Glancing in the rearview mirror, she felt the beginnings of a new concern. The woman was drop dead gorgeous.

Danielle's friendly manner put the barn staff immediately at ease, and Kellie watched, wondering what it would be like to have the woman for a close friend. Many times during her adult life, she'd wished for a female confidante to share her secrets and joys. Her sorrows. Someone who'd understand. Hyde had been wonderful, but there were things she'd never been able to discuss with him. A stall latch chunked and Kellie turned to watch him walk toward her, his features composed, as always.

He stopped beside her and shoved his hat back off his forehead. "I think those pads will help."

Danielle's husky voice interrupted. "Your turn, Doc."

A deep flush darkened his burnished cheeks and he snatched off his hat, then strode across the aisle to where the deputy waited. Kellie shook her head. The woman was a man magnet.

Thirty minutes later, Kellie's truck cruised down the highway toward Guthrie, and her thoughts centered on the situation in the barn. Hyde had spent over two hours fitting the corrective pads to both horses, but his cautious optimism made her nervous. While he'd never been one to pull punches, he'd also never dealt with such dire circumstances in *her* barn.

Would their long friendship keep him from telling her the truth? She *had* to believe he thought the horses would recover.

Outside town, the highway curved and her thoughts derailed. Red dust boiled behind a bulldozer, and several dump trucks were parked just beyond a construction site entrance. A large sign posted the bad news. *"Available Soon–Westview Homes at Red Creek Farms."*

"Dammit! That was prime pasture a week ago!"

An angry knot formed in her gut and she clenched her jaw. Urban sprawl relentlessly crawled north from Oklahoma City, obliterating the beautiful historic land of her ancestors–land they'd starved for, fought over, died on. And for what? So the newly affluent could talk about their country estates over martinis? She stared grimly at the yellow line threading down the center of the highway. They'd only get Sutton land over her dead body.

When she pulled through the gates of the Lazy E Arena, she squinted up at the huge structure. She'd grown up showing her horses at the old county fairgrounds south of Guthrie, and had never understood why the region needed another facility, much less one that seated seven thousand people. But when Randy had reached the top echelon of High School Rodeo, she'd understood–the seats were always filled and, as the years passed, the Lazy E hosted more national events, not all of them horse-related. Another questionable advantage of living only thirty-five minutes from a major city.

Inside the cavernous building, she strode past the dirt-floored arena, glancing briefly at the riders practicing their patterns. Show volunteers were setting up the announcer's booth and hanging banners. Somewhere, a horse whinnied and another answered. *Thank God, some things never change.* She climbed the stairs to the second floor and entered the judges' lounge.

"Kellie! Good to see you again!"

"Pete Dayton! What are *you* doing back in town?"

Her high school pal shuffled forward, dragging a stiff leg, and packing about twenty pounds more than the last time she'd seen him.

His ruddy face beamed. "I never miss a chance to come home."

She hugged him, then stepped back. "I guess we old timers are doomed to spectate instead of ride."

Pete pulled himself up to a full five-feet-four-inches. "I like to think they want our superb expertise."

"Yeah, I like that concept better. How's the leg?"

"Pretty good, still gives out occasionally." He grinned. "Doc says no more bronc riding."

She tried to smile, but the joking comment only reminded her of another tragic ride.

He touched her arm, and his voice grew thick. "Aw Kellie, I'm sorry. Not a day goes by that I don't miss him too."

She smiled sadly and shook her head. "Don't apologize–Randy would kick our butts for being morose."

"He could do it too. Remember the time I stole his award buckle?"

Memories bubbled up, smoothing away her sadness. "I could never figure out why you took such a chance."

Pete's face colored with embarrassment. "Man, I wanted that buckle so bad I could taste it. Figured if I couldn't have one, my best friend didn't need one either...boy, did I pay for *that* joke!" The mirth faded from his eyes. "Whatever happened to it?"

"I don't know–it disappeared."

Pete threw his hands up. "Don't look at me!" He suddenly stopped clowning and took her hand. "What's wrong?"

She regarded him for a moment, grateful for a sympathetic ear. "Two of my horses were attacked a few days ago."

"*Attacked*? Holy cow! Cougars?"

"Worse–humans...but we don't know that for sure. Both horses are in serious condition." A painful lump grew in her throat. "The vet doesn't know how to treat them."

Pete put his arm around her shoulders and squeezed. "When did this happen?"

"Dancer came up lame early this week. The other horse began limping yesterday."

Pete's face crinkled into a sorrowful mask. "*Dancer?* Oh man, I'm really sorry. Anything I can do?"

The sympathy almost unraveled her composure, but she lifted her chin. "No, we just have to wait it out, but thanks for asking."

"Any idea who'd do something like that? Could it be related to the land deal you killed?"

"How would you know about *that*?"

He looked sheepish. "I still get the *Daily Leader*...stupid, huh?"

"Not at all. Staying connected with your roots is important." She frowned. "I hadn't given a thought to the land developers, but I guess anything's possible. I'll mention it to the new sheriff."

"How is ol' Ed? Still smitten as ever?"

Kellie's cheeks burned and she looked away. "We broke up after he returned from the Gulf War."

"But you two were the perfect couple."

The familiar heartache unfurled and Kellie's voice softened. "Yes, we were, but the timing was wrong. Real life stepped in and I set my own needs aside."

"Maybe, but you were always so definite about getting what you wanted. Marrying Frank Frazier seemed out of character."

Kellie smiled wryly. "I guess if you still read the town newspaper, you also know we ended up getting divorced."

Pete's face reddened and he picked up a clipboard.

"Sorry–I didn't mean to pry."

"It's okay–I'll tell you about it later."

~~

Kellie dropped into a chair on the sideline. After staring at riders for three hours, her shoulders ached, her feet hurt, and her throat felt dry and scratchy from breathing dust. A ground crew hurried into the arena to begin setting up for the pole bending class, and she took a long swig of bottled water, dreading another three hours of classes. At least the show kept her from dwelling on the situation at home.

The announcer called the next division, and Kellie observed while Pete judged the class. He'd been such a good horseman when they were teenagers, but his daredevil spirit had channeled him into rodeo, and one bad ride had ended his chance at a trophy buckle forever. A shiver ran up the back of her neck and warm moisture blurred her vision. Blinking hard, she tried to erase the images of her own brother lying mangled and bleeding in the dust. She leaned forward, fighting off the gruesome memory. Lately, the past had been her constant companion.

The last exhibitor raced through the poles, bumping one, but still riding against the clock. Disappointment clouded the girl's face as her horse cantered toward the out-gate. The announcer called for a fifteen-minute break, and Pete dropped heavily into the other folding chair.

He winced as he stretched his bad leg. "So, what's Frank up to these days?"

She glanced at Pete's face, open with curiosity. "He still manages the ranch...when he's around." She gazed at the tractor dragging the arena floor. "When Dad had his heart attack, I had too much to do by myself. Frank came back to town, looking for a job...He'd studied business management in college, and seemed a natural."

"Maybe so, but you didn't have to *marry* him!"

She sighed. "Yes, I did."

The PA system hummed with the announcer's voice, and she rose. "I'm up."

Striding toward the center of the arena, her cheeks burned with embarrassment at the revelation of her secret. She nodded for the ring steward to call the class, the in-gate opened, and a line of beautifully groomed horses paraded through, their heads bobbing in perfect rhythm to the ambling gait. Sterling silver fittings sparkled on bridles and saddles that had been buffed to a soft sheen. The riders wore elegant outfits in exotic color combinations. Tunics and jackets of black with shimmering copper. White with Indian turquoise. Blood red with tan. Soft leather chaps in earth tones. Crisp, perfectly blocked hats and highly polished boots. A fashion show on the hoof.

A shiny sorrel with four white socks entered the ring, and Kellie gaped at the rider's arrogant expression. *No way–I'm not going there again.* She motioned a time-out to the ring steward, then hurried across the arena.

"Pete, you have to do this one."

He lumbered to his feet, raising his eyebrows. "What's wrong?"

"I'll tell you later. Trust me–I can't judge this class."

Thirty minutes later, the lounge door opened and Pete shuffled in as Kellie unwrapped her chicken sandwich.

He pulled off his hat and dropped it on a chair. "Okay, tell me what happened out there."

"The last exhibitor in that class was the woman who harassed me last year after I disqualified her."

"The one you filed an official complaint against?"

"Yes, and I'm surprised she entered the class, knowing I'd be one of the judges."

Pete chuckled. "Maybe she was hoping for a rematch."

"That's not funny. I don't take personal threats lightly."

Kellie pushed her lunch away, unnerved by the bad memories and the chill crawling across her shoulders.

Pete reached for his soda. "You might consider adding her to your list of suspects."

"What kind of lunatic would mutilate animals because of an organizational slap on the hand? I think you're stretching here."

"You shouldn't discount *anyone*, Kellie. Today's world is full of crazies."

3

Frank leaned on a fence rail and pressed the cell phone against his ear, straining to hear over the rumble of a manure spreader in the next field.

"I'll be there, but don't keep me waiting this time."

He closed the phone and turned toward the barn. Yellow flashed in his peripheral vision and he turned to watch the school bus roll to a stop at the end of the lane. Sara jumped to the ground and ran toward him, wildly waving her arms. He grinned, watching her skinny little legs propel her along at an amazing speed, her ponytail bouncing with each step. Her happy grin sent a soft twang through his heart. She was the brightest spot in his life, and he could no longer remember why he'd been so angry with Kellie when she'd announced she was pregnant.

"Daddy, Daddy! Mommy says you'll take me over to the horseshow!"

Frank's sentimental feelings vanished. *Mommy's not running my life anymore.*

"I can't, honey. I have an important meeting in the city."

"But she promised!" Sara's eyes widened, tears pooled on her lower lashes, and her voice quivered. "You're *always* too busy."

He leaned down and thumbed a tear from her cheek. "Honey, I'm really sorry. Your mom should have told me early this morning so I could rearrange my schedule."

Her sad little face turned away and, for one second, he considered canceling the appointment.

"Tell you what–tomorrow, you and I will ride out to check on the cattle."

Her radiant smile sent a shaft of guilt through his head. The day might come when she would hate him. Was there any way he could prevent that? He watched her skip across the grass toward the house. How had his life disintegrated in such a short time?

He walked slowly across the lane, stopping briefly to admire the black HumVee parked by the barn door. Though Kellie had been disparaging about him spending money on such an ostentatious vehicle, he'd ignored her. It was *his* money, and the sucker made him feel fantastic. He wiped a patch of dust from the hood and grinned at his distorted reflection in the shiny paint. *Fuck her.* He might even buy himself another one.

A short while later, he steered his old Jeep Wrangler onto one of the section roads of the ranch. A cloud of dust appeared in the rearview mirror, then a kid on a dirt bike with no muffler roared past on the right shoulder of the road. The two dogs jostled each other for the window, barking at the intruder. Frank scowled as the biker disappeared into the red fog he'd stirred up. The off-roaders loved it back here, and didn't care that they were trespassing on private land. But this particular road was buried deep in Sutton property, and Frank's thoughts escalated to the possibilities and risks. All he needed was some stupid kid showing up where he didn't belong.

The dust cloud drifted down the road, and Frank turned left onto another less defined lane with grass growing in the center between the wheel ruts. A hundred yards ahead, the silhouette of a winter hay storage barn loomed against the brilliant blue sky.

Frank grinned at the dogs. "What do you think, boys?

Pretty soon we can buy us a big spread in Dallas, an' you guys can work cattle all day while I drink margaritas."

Stumpy tails wiggled and both dogs licked their chops.

~ ~

Hyde's truck moved up the lane toward the barn and Kellie steeled herself. No matter how much she wanted to believe otherwise, her horses were losing their race against time. She tried to read the vet's expression as he walked toward her, but his years of dealing with life and death in rural Oklahoma had set his features into a perpetually neutral mask.

"Thanks for coming back, Hyde. I expect you've had a long day."

"No problem. I don't have anyone waiting on me at home. How are the patients doing?"

She fell into step beside him. "Dancer isn't eating, but Boots seems to be in a little better condition."

"I think he might have been given a smaller dose...How was the horse show?"

Kellie's anxiety level increased. Was he being evasive? Or was he just trying to reassure her?

"The classes these days are huge–nothing like when we were kids."

"Uh-oh, the famous good ol' days."

He stepped into Dancer's stall and the mirth faded from his eyes. Silently, he examined the horse's legs and the bandaged wound. Dancer didn't flinch as the skilled hands gently touched and probed.

Kellie's voice rattled in her throat. "Can you–"

"I need to get some x-rays before I know where we stand."

While Hyde returned to his truck, Kellie stroked Dancer's warm neck and battled the crushing pressure in her chest that made every breath an effort. A soft nicker rumbled from deep in the stallion's throat, and he rested his chin heavily on her shoulder. She pressed her face against his cheek, soaking up his familiar scent and struggling to keep fear from conquering her.

Hyde returned with a portable x-ray unit slung over his shoulder, and Kellie stepped away from the horse, trying to steady her emotions.

Hyde's manner was brisk and professional. "You'll need to hold his head."

Relieved for the distraction, she grabbed a soft leather work halter and slipped it gently over Dancer's ears.

Hyde fiddled with the dials on the unit. "See if you can swing him around about forty-five degrees so I can get behind that good foot."

For the next twenty minutes, the x-ray unit clicked and hummed, the only sound in the still air. When Hyde finished, Kellie ventured a question.

"Any word yet from the forensics lab?"

Her friend's dark eyes softened with sympathy and he shook his head.

"They've never seen anything like this, but they're going to run some other tests."

He closed up the x-ray unit, then turned to her, puzzlement furrowing his forehead. "I was wondering...why wouldn't your dogs bark if a stranger came on the property?"

"Frank takes them home with him every night, except when he's, uh...with his girlfriend."

"I think you should install some security cameras."

Her chest thumped. "You think this person might come back?"

"If he or she does, wouldn't you like to find out who it is?"

~~

The morning newspaper landed with a plop on top of Kellie's work schedule, sending several sheets of paper spiraling to the floor. She jerked at Frank's ugly tone.

"What the hell is *this?*"

He towered over the desk, his square jaw knotted, his eyes glinting with anger.

She stared hard at the dark headline. "Champion Quarter Horses Vandalized."

"Oh, boy," she muttered, reading on.

> *"Who says small towns don't have any excitement? In a classic Dick Francis whodunit scenario, Rocking S Quarter Horse Ranch is the scene of apparent malicious vandalism that has crippled two of Kellie Sutton's finest horses. According to our sources, sometime last week, an intruder allegedly entered the barns at the historic ranch and injected an unknown substance into world champion Docs Dirty Dancing and state champion Boot Scootin' Doc. The Logan County Sheriff's Department is investigating."*

Frank's irritation clogged the air. "Jesus, we don't need this kind of publicity. Why did you talk to the press?"

Kellie shoved the paper aside and rose from her chair. "I had nothing to do with it. The editor is *your* friend."

She strode out into the barn aisle, anger crawling over her skin and confusion fracturing her thoughts. *What's his problem, anyway? He doesn't seem to give a darn about the horses.* Frank's boots thumped behind her and she braced herself for more of his tirade.

"Kellie, hold up. I feel as bad about this as you do, but I can't believe it was an intentional act–that's ridiculous. The horses probably tangled with some insect, or maybe rats. Certainly nothing that warrants a headline on the front page."

She whirled to face him. The lame ideas sounded defensive. And why was he so concerned about the publicity? Wouldn't he want the culprit caught? His expression revealed only irritation.

Keeping her tone level, she said, "If you can't be supportive in this, why don't you look for another job?"

He opened his mouth to retort, then frowned, his gaze diverting to the barn door. Two men in tan work overalls walked toward them, and Kellie glanced at her watch.

"That's the crew to install security cameras."

Frank's stunned expression hardened into sharp planes. "Pretty damned hard to be supportive in a one-woman show." He turned and clumped away.

Kellie instructed the installers to place a camera at each of the four main barn doors and two in the mare barn. The office phone rang and she hurried across the aisle, feeling as though she'd been swept into a movie set where the bad guys were winning.

Ed Campbell's tone was all business. "I trust you've seen the morning paper."

"Will the article hurt the case?"

"Can't really say. If the culprit is still around and knows we're looking, he or she might disappear. Any idea how the story got out?"

"At first, I thought Frank was responsible, but we had a major blow up over it a few minutes ago and now I'm not so sure." She moved to the window and closed her eyes, pushing away the altercation with Frank, and trying to absorb Ed's presence at the other end of the conversation.

He remained silent for a moment before continuing. "What do you think about offering a reward? It might encourage anyone with information to come forward."

"Good idea." She pressed the phone against her ear, not wanting the connection to end yet. "I'm also having surveillance cameras installed today."

"Excellent. We don't want anyone slipping in there again. I'll be out later to ask you some more questions."

"Wait, did Dani find out anything yesterday?"

"She took everyone's statement, but I haven't had a chance to look at them yet."

For long moments after she hung up, Kellie gazed out the window, trying to fathom why, after twenty-four hours, Ed still hadn't read Danielle's report. Shaken by the thought of a lunatic returning to the barn, she reached for the phone to call him back, then changed her mind. *I can ask him about it when he gets here.* She shuddered and moved back to her desk, trying to obliterate her increasing fear that more horses might be attacked. She dropped to one knee and began gathering the scattered papers from the floor. As she retrieved the last one, she spotted the mystery photograph wedged beneath the leg of the desk. Examining the picture again, she squinted, trying to figure out where or when it had been taken. In the dim background–out of focus, but still readable–a banner stretched across a stall door. *A horse show.* And her hair–she'd cut it very short over a year ago. *Before or after I had the run-in with that exhibitor?* Why did this image bother her so much, and why didn't she remember it? How had it appeared on her desk? Had Frank put it there? Had he taken it? The dizzying parade of questions bombarded her, but no answers followed. Could the snapshot be connected to the attacks on the horses? Should she have mentioned it to Ed? She closed her eyes, fighting the paranoia that threatened to destroy any vestige of clear thinking.

The confusion pressed her into action. How much money would be enough to entice someone to speak up? She pulled the checkbook from Frank's desk drawer, and dropped into his chair. As she focused on his precise handwriting and neat numbers, his nasty remarks echoed in her head. Clearly, if she wanted any cooperation, she'd have to start including him in the plans–or eliminate him from her life. Easier said than done.

"Ma'am? Where do you want the monitor screen?" A

short man wearing a baseball cap stood in the doorway.

"Does someone need to watch it all the time?"

He grinned and shook his head. "Only in the movies. These here cameras are on twenty-four hours around the clock and are triggered by motion sensors. If you get any intruders, they'll show up on the tapes."

She gestured toward a file cabinet in the corner. "Put it over there."

The installer picked up a small black monitor. "Hear you've had some bad stuff going on here." He placed the screen on the cabinet. "I'm real sorry–I like horses. Rode my granddad's nag when I was a kid. Always wanted to be in a rodeo."

He squatted down and reached behind the file cabinet to find the electrical outlet and, in seconds, the dark screen brightened, giving Kellie a view of the main barn aisle. The unfamiliar downward angle of the camera distorted the stall doors somewhat, but she recognized the view from the north entrance. The silent scene flicked to another angle as a different camera sent its image to the monitor. A ranch hand stepped out of the tack room and closed the door behind him. The screen changed again and Kellie shook her head, struggling with the surreal circumstances, and wondering what misstep she'd taken to bring on such vengeance. Who could hate her so much?

The previous day's mail lay unopened on the corner of the desk, and she idly leafed through it, thinking about how fast disaster could strike. She snatched up an envelope from the state unemployment board. *Of course! Tina Brown!* The obnoxious stall cleaner had gone ballistic about being fired. No doubt, this mess was revenge.

The camera installer stepped into her line of vision. "Ma'am? This picture was on the floor in the corner. It must've fallen off your bulletin board."

Kellie plucked the photograph from the man's hand. The snapshot was grainy and underexposed, but not so much that she couldn't identify the subjects–she and Hyde standing beside a fence rail. They both wore their usual barn garb, but nothing in the picture gave a clue as to when it had been taken.

~ ~

Travis Mack shifted his lanky body on the lumpy mattress, trying to find a comfortable position, then pulled his knees up and buried his face in the pillow to sink back into the depths of tormented sleep.

The old house creaked with night noises and shadows stretched up the stained walls to crisscross the cracked ceiling of the small room. The bedroom door opened and she *stepped in. Her blouse was unbuttoned, exposing her immense breasts. He tore his gaze from the bobbling brown nipples to focus on her bright red gash of a mouth forming words thick with alcohol.*

"Your daddy's making a mess in the living room."

The strong odor of whiskey drifted on the air and he looked down at the broken toys scattered around his feet.

When he looked up at her again, she was wearing a black chiffon negligee, draped off her shoulders. A wide-brimmed black hat, adorned with a large red rose, covered her bleached blonde hair.

"We're waiting for you at the cemetery." She turned and walked away, her voluptuous curves visible through the transparent garment. The hinge on the old door creaked as she left the room.

He looked down again, and screamed. His father lay amongst the toys, a dark pool of blood oozing across the floor, creeping slowly toward his bare feet.

Travis bolted straight up in the bed, gulping for air, his heartbeat thundering in his ears. Beside him, the girl's plump ass shifted against his thigh, and he jerked away from the sweaty contact. Swinging his long legs over the edge of the bed, he took a deep breath, his pulse slowly receding to a dull thump. He pulled on his jeans, glanced at the sleeping mound in the bed, then padded down the hall and flopped onto a low-slung fifties-era couch. The match shook as he lit a cigarette. He took a long drag, waiting for the nicotine to work its magic while he focused on sending the nightmares back into the dark recesses of his mind.

A green neon sign across the street throbbed through the window of the girl's tiny apartment, flooding the cheap furnishings with a ghoulish glow. He stared without seeing, his thoughts far away, his head filled with memories of slinking through dark fields, a long bus ride, a shattered life.

"You okay, hon?"

He jumped up, adrenaline screaming through his body as he fought the urge to tell the stupid bitch to get the hell out of his face. "Yeah, can't sleep. You go on back to bed. I'm headed out."

"See you after work today?"

"Dunno, got some business to take care of." He stubbed out the cigarette. "I'll call ya."

Tina Brown's round face puddled into a pout, and he wanted to smack her. *Fuckin' pushy broad.*

As he drove north, he flicked on the radio, paying little attention until an early morning call-in talk show came on. A report of a vicious attack on innocent animals was the hot topic, and he listened intently to the indignation and anger voiced by the many callers and the moderator. At one point, someone mentioned security cameras, and Travis boosted the volume again.

"My neighbor's husband works for Acme Security and they're gonna install cameras at all the barn doors at the Sutton place. That should stop anyone from doing any more damage."

Travis snapped off the radio.

~~

Ed pulled into a parking spot halfway down the block from the Sooner Café, then glanced up the street. The town hadn't changed much while he'd been away, but he could see the restoration efforts for many of the original buildings. In keeping with tradition of the annual 89er Celebration, red-white-and-blue flags adorned the elaborate minarets and spires on the beautiful red stone Gaffney Building, and banners hung from the streetlights, proclaiming the start of the event. In a few days, Guthrie would swell with thousands of tourists, and he'd have his hands full. Timing certainly wasn't on his side these days.

A shiny black Hummer pulled into a spot in front of the café, and Frank climbed out. Ed snorted. How a military vehicle could have so charmed the civilian population was a real mystery. These yahoos had no clue what they were driving. His thoughts briefly reverted to a vision of dust and heat and noise, but he pushed it away. Frank entered the café, and Ed strode down the sidewalk after him. Through the big window, Ed saw Frank slide into a booth with the newspaper editor and the local grease monkey.

Ed pushed through the café door and headed for the counter, where he settled onto a stool and reached for a menu.

The local editor's voice carried in the small room. "Frank, what in the world is goin' on out at your place?"

Frank's voice rumbled with anger. "Chaos, no thanks to *you*. Why the hell didn't you talk to me before you printed that story?"

"News is news. I figured I'd do a more in-depth piece after I interviewed you."

"Where did you hear about it?"

Ed turned to watch the exchange.

"My cousin's sister-in-law works over at the vet's office.

The information came straight from the horse's mouth, so to speak."

Frank's exasperation exploded. "Jesus, isn't there some rule about client privilege?"

The mechanic laughed, his bushy white eyebrows stood out against his flushed face and his bright blue eyes twinkled with amusement. "Not in Podunk Guthrie, there ain't!"

The news editor pushed a Meerschaum pipe to the corner of his mouth and narrowed his eyes. "Frank, let me remind you that the *Daily Leader* has been keeping Guthrie up to date since before the big land rush. No holds barred. As editor, I have the right–and the responsibility–to keep the town informed of everything that goes on." He pulled a small spiral notebook from his shirt pocket, then licked the end of his pencil. "Do you have any new information yet?"

"Nope, and I'm not convinced this was deliberate. Kellie's too theatrical sometimes. And I don't appreciate your timing, either–we're trying to get the ranch ready for tours this weekend, and she's got her panties in a twist."

"Sheriff have any ideas?"

"Not that he's shared."

Ed slid off the stool and stepped over to the booth. "Actually, Frank, I was hoping you'd share *your* ideas with *me*."

Frank's jaw rippled with anger as he rose from the bench. "Don't you have robbers or killers to catch? This whole thing is ridiculous!" He dropped a dollar bill on the table and glared at the newsman. "How about a heads up before you put any more of your surprises in the paper?"

The mechanic gestured toward the window. "I see you're drivin' that tank today. Why the hell would you buy something like that?"

"Because I can."

Frank stalked out of the café, and Ed turned to the men.

"Might be a good idea to soft-peddle this story for a while... give us a chance to investigate."

The editor glowered. "Perhaps you weren't eavesdropping close enough. This is news and not even *you* can keep me from letting the public know what's going on."

Back out on the sidewalk, irritation crawled over Ed's shoulders. He had yet to meet anyone who didn't resent his return to Guthrie. He scanned the street and caught a glimpse of the Hummer's taillights turning the corner. Animosity rippled through his chest. *Frank Frazier isn't good enough to clean Kellie's boots, yet he acts like she's a nobody.* The emotional thought startled the hell out of him, that he could become so instantly distracted at a time when he needed all his wits about him.

He climbed into the cruiser and headed after Frank. Three blocks away, he spotted the Hummer parked in front of a row of businesses. He pulled into a parking spot and waited, making a list of every visible license plate on the street. A few minutes later, Frank emerged from a building and headed down the sidewalk toward the old Santa Fé depot. A dark skinned man appeared from an alley and approached Frank on the corner. Ed whipped out his camera and, as the two men came into focus, he began to smile. He zoomed to full power to confirm who he was seeing, then pressed the burst button. Maybe timing wasn't working against him, after all.

~~

Sara skipped into the office and Kellie smiled. "You're just the person I need to see. Help me decide who to ride in the parade."

"Oh Mommy, I forgot about Dancer."

Her face crumpled, and Kellie gathered her up, hugging her fiercely, unable to murmur even one reassuring word. Sara finally pushed back and gazed up through brimming eyes.

"You can ride Juicy."

"That's very sweet of you, honey, but then who would *you* ride?"

The child's eyes widened and her small mouth formed a perfect "O".

"I get to be in the parade?" She squealed and launched herself back into Kellie's arms, wriggling like a puppy. "Thank you, thank you, thank you!" She stepped back and solemnly took her mother's hand. "C'mon, I know the perfect horse for you."

Kellie chuckled as she was pulled out the door and into the sunshine. "Where are you taking me?"

A dimpled grin sparkled over Sara's shoulder. "You'll see."

Minutes later, Kellie stood in front of a stall in the mare barn, hearing tenderness threading through Sara's voice.

"Mama, she's so lonely since her baby died. You should ride her in the parade so she'll feel wanted again."

Kellie gazed at the aged bay horse staring balefully at the two visitors. The mare had a beautiful head, wide chest, firm barrel, and a perfect straight back. Bits of straw hung in her tail, and a damp spot on her hock revealed she'd been lying down not long ago.

"Hey Belle. How's my girl?"

The mare nickered softly and stepped up to nuzzle Kellie's outstretched hand.

"I think you're right, Sara. She certainly deserves a little reward."

"Daddy!" Sara raced across the aisle. "Are we going riding now?"

Sara's delighted squeals and Frank's laughter bounced off the rafters and, for one instant, Kellie wished things had turned out differently.

Frank straightened up from tickling Sara. "How's Belle doing?"

"She's physically fine, but she *is* depressed."

"Then let's get her bred back right away. It sure as hell doesn't make sense to feed her through another open season."

Kellie gritted her teeth. Frank was always about the money, but this wasn't a good time to challenge him, nor to bring up the idea of offering a reward.

"Listen, Kellie, I'm sorry about what I said earlier. You're probably right to install some security. We have too much at stake here to be careless."

She recognized the sincerity in his eyes and accepted the truce. "I should have mentioned it to you."

~ ~

Frank watched his daughter lead her horse out into the sunshine. Her eyes sparkled with anticipation, and it struck him how little it took to make her happy. *I'll spend more time with her as soon as things settle down.* A flashback to that morning sent a sickening roll through his gut. He'd nearly peed himself when that Mexican walked right up to him. *I need to get a grip. Maybe the big doings in town will overshadow all the local interest in the news about the horses.*

Sara trotted Juicy toward the pasture gate, then reined him around so that he stood parallel to the fence. She leaned down and flipped the latch to let the gate swing open.

Frank let out a low whistle. "Where'd you learn to do *that*?"

She threw him a proud grin. "Roy taught me."

Regret tugged at Frank's heart. His little girl was growing up fast, and he was missing most of it.

Their horses ambled through the tall grass in the empty field, and his thoughts shifted to business. By July, he could move his herd of beef cattle to this sector for a couple of months, then down to the feedlot. If beef prices held steady, he'd get a hefty return on his investment.

"Dad! Did you hear me?"

"Sorry, I'm listening."

"Mom's letting me ride in the parade on Saturday. Is that too cool?"

He grinned. "It's about time. Aren't you almost sixteen?"

Sara giggled hysterically. "No! I'm going on ten!" She sobered. "I don't know why she treats me like such a baby."

"You're *her* baby and she'll always look out for you. Don't ever forget that."

Sara rolled her eyes, and Frank caught a glimpse of the headstrong young woman she'd grow to be. Kellie would definitely have her hands full. Could he be of any help? Considering the fractious relationship they'd been two stepping through for the past couple of years, probably not.

Sara opened another gate, and they struck off on a diagonal through a pasture filled with sleek Black Angus. The two dogs immediately started working, circling and dropping back, moving the herd without spooking them. Several of the cattle stood knee deep in a muddy waterhole rimmed in red dirt, and Buck splashed in after them.

Frank chuckled. "They're having a ball–nothing worse than a bored work dog."

Sara steered her horse around a large pile of cow dung. "Eeeww, why are cows so messy? Why don't you raise horses, like Mom?"

"Can't eat horses. I make money on beef."

She didn't respond, and he took it as acceptance of his answer. They rode on in companionable silence, skirting the perimeter of the field. The roof of the winter hay barn came into view and his thoughts turned again to his precarious situation.

Sara threw him a mischievous grin. "I'll race ya."

"No, I have to get back."

"Aw c'mon, that old barn is really neat. I love climbing

around on the hay bales, especially when it's full to the rafters."

A lead weight plummeted through the pit of his stomach, and the reaction sharpened his tone. "Don't you *ever* go out there alone! Jesus, what if you got hurt? No one would be around to help!"

Her face paled and her lower lip began to tremble. "You don't have to yell at me."

He sidled his horse up beside her and patted her knee. "I'm sorry, but I just don't want anything to happen to you. You're *my* baby too, you know."

The happy glow had faded from the outing, and Sara rode quietly beside him as they headed back toward the ranch. Frank's adrenaline rush disappeared, his head reeling with all the problems that had suddenly become a way of life. Where was he headed? And who was in control?

"Will you take me to the racetrack with you sometime?"

"Where did you hear about *that*?"

She gazed at him for a moment. "It's no secret. I've known for a long time. But you never talk about it." Sarcasm edged her soft voice. "Like you're ever around."

He shook his head. "The track is no place for a chil– young lady."

"So tell me something about it. Mom said you lost your shirt–what does that mean?"

He paused, searching for the right response. "I had a fantastic Thoroughbred colt. He was worth a lot of money, but he broke his leg during a race and had to be destroyed."

A sob bubbled into Sara's voice. "Ohmygod, Daddy! That's so horrible! The poor horse!"

Frank gazed across the wide expanse of land that had held him hostage for so long. He felt isolated from the real world. Everything he'd ever tried to do had turned to shit. A fucked up football career. A short-lived farce of a marriage. A racing business gone bad.

And then he'd dived into the cesspool.

4

Kellie closed the breeding ledger and set it aside. Ten of thirteen broodmares were safely foaled out, and she could rest easy for a while. Voices echoed through the barn, and Sara's laughter brought a warm glow into Kellie's heart.

Frank stepped into the office. "One of the guys brought in a couple of mares from the west graze. I think they're okay, but–"

Kellie leaped up. "Oh my God! When is this going to stop?"

"Put your imagination away for a minute. This looks more like a hormonal altercation–they're both in heat."

"I'll call Hyde."

"I said they're *fine!* Give it a rest! What's the matter with you?"

She stared at his hard expression. "A better question is, what's the matter with *you?*" She grabbed the two snapshots and held them up. "Did you take these? Or leave them on my desk?"

He flicked a glance at them. "Never saw them before. Why?"

"Just wondering. I don't remember them either." She gazed at him for a moment, wondering whether to pursue it. Their recent clashes made her think better of starting another argument.

The minute he was out of earshot, she dialed Hyde's number.

His strong voice calmed her. "Slow down, Kellie, I'm on my way over."

Thirty minutes later, he settled into the chair next to her desk. "The mares are fine–they only have a couple of scrapes." He cocked his head. "But are *you* okay?"

She nodded, then her shoulders sagged. "What kind of sick person would attack innocent animals?"

Hyde remained silent for a moment, then laced his arms across his chest. A dark fire burned in his eyes.

"Whoever did it has knowledge of the ways of a horse. First, this person knows exactly where to inject to do the most damage. Second, Dancer would never allow someone to touch him who didn't have confidence and authority, and your dogs wouldn't bark at someone they know–the criminal could be right here in your own back yard."

Stunned by the simplicity of truth, Kellie stared at her friend. In the panic and emotion of the past two days, she'd wracked her brain trying to think of any outsider who might have it in for her. The thoughts had dead-ended with the more likely idea that these were random acts by a crazy person. Now, Hyde's assessment opened up a new and frightening array of suspects. Someone in her barn. *Including Frank, which could explain his strange behavior lately.*

After Hyde left, she dialed Ed's number, tapping her foot against the chair leg while she waited. How naive could she be? Frank would never admit to knowing about the mystery snapshots if they were part of a plan. She closed her eyes. He couldn't possibly be involved. If he was, she didn't think she could stand it.

Ed's rich voice curled intimately against her ear, but she pushed away the heady distraction. "I just talked to Hyde and he–what?" She hung up, then hurried out of the barn as Ed climbed out of a plain dark brown vehicle.

He grinned. "Now, where were we?"

His intense gaze sent a double thump through her chest. She took a deep breath and began to reiterate Hyde's observations.

While she talked, Ed nodded slowly, his features hardening in the shadow of his hat. "Unfortunately, he's probably right. We've questioned all your employees, but I've also asked for lie detector tests." He pursed his lips. "I'll talk to Frank later this afternoon."

"I can't believe Frank would do this. We've had our problems, but he's not cruel."

Ed considered her for a moment. "Jealousy is a powerful emotion." He gestured toward the building. "Can we go inside? I need to get some more information from you."

Kellie's thoughts reeled as they walked toward the office. The jealousy comment had rung with conviction. Had he ever been jealous of her? She searched the memories. If he had, she'd never known about it. So in love and consumed with each other, they'd been oblivious to anyone else. She glanced at him as he pulled a chair up next to the desk, and warmth radiated beneath her shirt. The almost forgotten physical reaction to his presence startled her.

He opened his notebook and thumbed through the pages, his easy manner bringing on another flood of memories. The two of them, laughing and breathless, racing their horses across the fields. The senior prom, and how he'd been all thumbs trying to pin the gardenia corsage on her strapless gown. Heavy necking in the warm hay nest they'd carved out in the winter hay barn. A stir moved through her belly, and she struggled to quell the pain building in her heart.

He looked up. "Think hard–who might have a grudge against you?"

"I fired a stall cleaner last month–her name's Tina Brown and she's a local. She was furious the day she left."

"Did you notice anything out of the ordinary after she'd

gone?

"No, but a new employee just informed me about finding a cigarette butt by the office door. We don't allow–"

"What did she do with it? Could be evidence."

"Manure pile. I doubt you could even find it now."

He made several notations, then looked up. "Anyone else here at the ranch?"

She shook her head. "The land developers weren't too happy when I put the kibosh on their plans to buy part of the estate."

"They'd be insane to jeopardize their business with something like this, but I'll put it on the list."

"Pete Dayton thought an angry exhibitor might want to cause me some grief. I filed a formal complaint against her last year, and she was suspended for three months."

"How is ol' Pete? I hear he's raising Thoroughbreds down around Lawton."

"Seems to be doing fine...he's put on a lot of weight since the accident."

Ed shook his head. "Damned rodeo games. I used to nearly go crazy when you–" A muscle in his jaw rippled and he quickly looked down at his notebook.

Kellie's thoughts reeled. The quick side trip into the past had clearly jolted him. She gazed at the silver glints scattered through his short brown hair, remembering its silky texture beneath her fingers. Longing washed over her. Would it be possible to close the door on the past and start over? Was the decision even hers to make?

Ed cleared his throat and his gray eyes darkened. "What about Cliff and Clarke? I understand you all had a falling out over this property."

Her heart thumped hard, and she stared at him for a full minute, unable to respond. Her own flesh and blood couldn't possibly do such a horrendous thing.

Ed's tone softened. "When was the last time you saw your brothers?"

"About six months ago...I can't believe they'd stoop so low over a piece of land."

"Families do more damage to each other than a stranger could ever dream up–land hunger didn't end in 1889."

Cliff's recent phone call surfaced in Kellie's thoughts. Clearly, the property dispute still simmered on a back burner.

Ed studied his notes for a minute, then looked up. "Let's talk about Frank."

"You're serious, aren't you?"

A veiled flicker passed through his eyes, and she recognized the unmistakable animosity. The meaning of his jealousy remark crystallized. Did a spark of love still burn in his heart? Did she have the nerve to find out?

He stood up. "We have to question everyone. Meanwhile, I'll have a couple of my deputies come out and search the surrounding area. The person who did this might have been careless and left something behind."

"Oh wait a minute." Kellie pulled the bottle cap from a cup of paperclips. "I found this in the corral. Do you think it's important?"

"Everything's important. It could carry fingerprints or DNA."

He pulled out a small plastic bag and she dropped the cap into it, intrigued that the trail to the culprit might start with ordinary litter.

He peered at the cap. "Huh, light beer. Only about a million of these around." He wrote something on the label, then tucked the evidence bag into his shirt pocket. Kellie watched him, wondering again if they could leave the past behind them.

Boots scuffed on concrete and Frank stepped into the office, then stopped abruptly. Kellie shivered in the chill that suddenly pervaded the warm room. A scowl darkened his face as he stepped over to the desk to pick up a file folder.

"I'm headed for Tulsa."

Ed turned to Kellie. "Let me know about the reward." He strode from the office, leaving a heavy silence in his wake.

Frank crossed his arms. "This is gettin' *real* old."

She didn't blink. "Yes, it is."

~~

About a quarter mile down the road from Rocking S, Ed backed his vehicle into the overgrown driveway of a shabby farm, then sat back and stared out the windshield at the far horizon. The soft browns and pale greens formed a watercolor memory, and regret settled into his heart. This land was his home and he'd been away too long. For what? Foolish pride. His dreams had sequestered themselves into a hidden part of him, never daring to surface over the years. But the few minutes with Kellie had taken him right back to where he'd started. Crazy about her. How could all the pain and slights disappear with just a glance? And what a mess the whole thing was turning into. Four months ago, the plum undercover assignment with the Drug Enforcement Agency task force had seemed a dream come true, giving him a chance to be near her, maybe see if anything had changed. How the hell could he tell with all the shit going down? Maybe when this was over...

The white cell phone vibrated against his chest and he turned his attention to business. "You get an ID on those pictures I sent? Is it who I think it is?"

"Yup, Jesus Hermano–contractor to the cartel. Good work, Agent Campbell."

"What I don't understand is what he'd be doing in a place like Guthrie."

"That's what you're going to find out. Keep me posted."

A black Hummer roared past, and Ed reached for the ignition. "Roger that."

Pulling onto the road a minute later, he settled back in the seat to see exactly where Mr. Franklin Frazier was headed in such a hurry. At the crossroads, the Hummer turned south on Route 35 and Ed scowled.

"Tulsa, my ass."

~ ~

"Un-fucking-believable."

Frank glared through the windshield as he sped down the highway toward Edmond. Kellie's arrogant independent attitude was beginning to piss him off. And every time he turned around, Ed Campbell was there, pretending to be professionally involved. *Hah. The only thing he's interested in is crawling back into Kellie's good graces. Lotsa luck, chump. The Ice Queen melts for no one.*

Frank shook off the disturbing thoughts and concentrated on the serious consequences of the events at the ranch. In the space of a few days, Rocking S had taken center stage in the news, and the attention would only intensify with the offer of a reward. If Kellie wouldn't keep him in the loop, maybe it was time to take things into his own hands.

The Edmond city sign appeared and he grinned, relaxing his grip on the wheel. *Right now, I'm gonna get something else into my hands.*

His long-time girlfriend owned an elegant home in a select part of Edmond. The porch lights came on as he pulled into the driveway and activated the garage door remote. The Hummer eased to a stop beside a shiny red Mercedes convertible.

Celeste Harding appeared at the door before he'd even climbed out of his vehicle.

"Hey Baby, you're early."

The luscious blonde's smile sent a thump through his pulse and lust into his loins.

He gathered her perfect body into his arms and nuzzled her ear. "The early bird gets the nookie."

She pulled him into the kitchen and pressed close, kissing him and making little whimpering noises that tickled his lips. All his disappointment and worries vanished as Celeste's tongue explored the contour of his ear.

Her husky voice hummed with invitation. "What time do we have to be at the club?"

He slipped the silk robe off her shoulders and gazed at her beautiful naked body. "Later. *Much* later."

Sprawled in the jumble of satin sheets, Frank stared at the ceiling and listened to Celeste humming in the shower. His thoughts wandered far from the cozy bedroom. An intentional attack on Dancer and Boots was a far-fetched possibility, and for what purpose? Who would be a reasonable suspect? Someone with an axe to grind. He clenched his jaw. That damned lazy stall cleaner was just the kind of lowlife loser to pull a stunt like this.

The bed jiggled as Celeste slithered her naked body across the sheets. She touched his face, her violet blue eyes dark with concern. "What's the matter, honey?"

He ran his fingers over her full breast. "Nothing. Just all the bullshit with the horses."

"I saw the newspaper. How's Kellie taking it?"

He sat up and shook his head. "I dunno. We aren't even on the same playing field anymore."

She moved closer and slipped her arms around him. "I'd never let you be so miserable."

He savored her embrace for a moment, wondering if she'd stick with him if she knew the truth.

"Frankie, I have more money than even Kellie–we could go somewhere, do anything you want."

He didn't trust himself to respond. From one "kept man"

situation to another–would her love make a difference?

~~

Kellie leaned on the porch rail and stared at nothing, willing her weary brain to take a break. To the west, a smooth band of black clouds hovered just above the sinking dark orange sun, a storm bank that would bring either rain or destruction. She closed her eyes. Mother Nature's wrath couldn't come close to what was happening at Rocking S.

The background sounds of a television show drifted from an open window, punctuated by Sara's giggles. A pair of mockingbirds barked and meowed from a branch in the massive pecan tree shading the house. Kellie exhaled long and slow, abandoning her attempts to stop thinking about the conversation with Ed. Through the years, he'd remained in her heart, secure and familiar, loving and vulnerable. The man who'd sat in her office today seemed a stranger. Why had she expected an older version of the softhearted teen who'd vowed to do anything she ever wanted? Had the willingness to compromise always been only his? Recognition of her blunder was a dagger through the heart. She straightened up and crossed her arms, pushing away the pointless self-recriminations. She'd think about it later.

Mentally, she cross-examined each possible suspect to see if anything new occurred to her. Someone close, someone with access and familiarity. Roy was the only employee who still lived at the ranch, but the old man would lay down his life for the horses–not maim them. Frank came and went as he pleased, but she still couldn't seriously consider him as the culprit. What would he gain? Nothing. In fact, he had almost as much to lose as she did. His financial investment in the business had been pivotal in their success, he leased Sutton land for his cattle, and he drew a good salary as ranch manager. Would he do something like this simply to hurt her? Doubtful–Frank had never loved her, and he worried only about himself and what would be in his best interests. Yet his seeming lack of concern about the injured horses was a strange reaction, considering the seriousness of the attacks. She couldn't rule him out completely.

She straightened up and stretched the tension from her shoulders. Ed was right–the developers might want the land, but not enough to face criminal charges. She frowned. Would the attacks even *be* considered criminal acts? What category would cover vandalizing farm stock? Property damage? Trespassing? She shook her head sadly. Whatever the proper term, it was enough to destroy everything she'd worked for.

She glanced at her watch, then stepped over to the screen door. "Sara...bedtime."

A whiney "Aw Mom" drifted back. She grinned, then returned to the process of elimination. Grudgingly, she acknowledged that the suspended exhibitor would no more retaliate like this than sprout wings and fly. A big legal hassle would be no trade-off for three months out of the show circuit, no matter how prestigious the trophy she'd been chasing.

A light breeze wafted around the corner of the house and Kellie looked again toward the fading sunset. The clouds were breaking up, moving in different directions, leaving only a dark azure sky with a soft pink stripe above the horizon. Soon the land would plunge into a darkness that only a rancher knew–starry skies unspoiled by man-made lights. With that image came the unsettling certainty that whoever was stalking her not only felt safe in the cover of those black skies, but also was comfortable and confident in the open and wild land.

The unthinkable suspicion she'd been avoiding surged into her conscious thoughts. Her brothers had spent their young lives in this environment, had done their share of ranch chores, and would certainly know every inch of the property. She closed her eyes tightly. What needs could they possibly have that would warrant destroying her livelihood to get their money out of the land?

Sara came out on the porch and wrapped her arms around Kellie's waist, pressing her pajama-clad body close. "'Night, Mama."

Kellie kissed the top of her head and stroked her shoulder, gazing through the dusk. "See you in the morning, hon."

~~

Slipping through the partially open barn door half an hour later, Kellie took care not to make any noise. The aroma of warm bodies and alfalfa drifted on the still air, and she stopped to listen. Only the occasional sigh or snuffle broke the silence. Walking softly, she moved down the aisle toward Dancer's stall, acutely aware that none of the horses paid any attention–her confident familiar presence gave them no cause for alarm. Hyde's words reverberated in her head. She'd just proven him right. At the stallion's stall door, her throat constricted at the sight of the once vibrant stud, now only a shadow of his former self. Whoever did this would pay dearly–she'd see to that.

She moved on to the office and her attention immediately focused on the surveillance monitor and its steady parade of gray images from each of the barns. What good would it do to have the culprit on tape if another horse suffered? For no distinct reason, she had a feeling the intruder would return. If nothing else, she wanted to feel as though she was doing something constructive toward catching this person. She strode back into the barn aisle and out the rear door, a surge of adrenaline prickling her skin. The rush felt good as she hurried across the grass toward the mare barn.

She stopped to peek at the palomino filly, then continued on to the foal-watch room at the end of the barn. The bunk had been stripped, the bedding washed, folded, and stacked on the chair, ready for the next round of deliveries. She grabbed a blanket from the cupboard and headed back to the main barn. After putting together a makeshift bed on the couch in the tack room, she wandered restlessly about, her senses on full alert, her thoughts racing. The soft aroma of leather polish cooled her agitation and she focused on the array of fine saddlery, gleaming in the soft light. Dancer's show halter hung next to an ornately tooled saddle with sterling fittings. Her heart almost shattered at the memories.

She turned away and her gaze stopped on a small chest of drawers in the corner. She hesitated, then kneeled to open the bottom drawer. Her pulse thumped and she took a deep breath, then set aside a small worn saddle blanket to gaze at a scrapbook in the bottom of the drawer. How long had it been since she'd looked through that record of joy and sorrow? Indecision crowded her thoughts, but the desire to revisit the past was stronger, and she lifted the book from its hiding place.

Curled up on the couch with the blanket covering her legs, she leafed through the first few pages, smiling at the gangly red-haired girl on horseback, holding ribbons or trophies. Details in the yellowed newspaper clippings supported the photos and, on one frayed page, a blue ribbon had come unglued. She picked it up and squinted at the faded gold printing, then shook her head sadly. The ribbon was from the year she met Ed Campbell. How important it had been, that she would sequester this bit of fabric away from the trophy case. She leaned her head back and thought about the changes in her life after that year. Swallowing the hard lump rising in her throat, she leafed through the next ten pages until she came to one that had nothing to do with riding.

Private Edward Campbell gazed back at her from the official Army photograph. His expression was properly solemn, but even now, Kellie could see the message to her in his eyes. In the lower corner, his bold scrawl proclaimed his love. "To my darling Kellie." She turned the page and scanned the various snapshots of Eddie and his class of recruits doing all the corny things young men do for the camera. As she turned the pages, she saw for the first time the change in Eddie's physique, as he ground through boot camp and muscled up. The journey through the scrapbook began to take its toll, and her eyes burned.

She turned a page and was transported from photos of a happy-go-lucky young man to newspaper clippings of a sober faced hometown hero. A tear rolled down her cheek and splashed on the page. She closed the scrapbook and set it aside.

~~

Barking echoed through the dream and Kellie bolted upright, confusion slashing through her thoughts as she struggled to untangle the blanket from her legs. Outside, Buck's deep bark had a warning edge to it, then Pal's voice joined in. Kellie raced toward the barn doors. *God, what time is it?* She dashed into the night and stopped abruptly, stunned by the brilliant white wash of moonlight that painted everything with eerie shadows. The dogs were running along the pasture fence, and she ran toward them, squinting into the moonscape field to see what had upset them. She called out, commanding them to stay. If a cougar was prowling through the pasture, she didn't want the dogs to tangle with it.

They stopped running, but continued to bark, looking back at her expectantly. Her eyes adjusted to the strange light, and she saw a shadow moving along the fence on the east side of the pasture. A human shadow. She started forward, then stopped. What could she do? She'd never catch him. She reached for her cell phone, then swore. She'd left it on the floor beside the couch. She darted forward, racing along the fence line, keeping her eyes on the shadowy form, trying to see where it headed. Barking like mad, the dogs ranged far ahead of her and ducked under the fence. The running shadow merged with the dark trees along the section road, and Kellie stopped, gasping for breath. An engine roared to life and gravel ricocheted against metal. She ran forward again, straining to see through the trees. Taillights careened down the section road before disappearing around a corner. Tires squealed, the sound echoing through the night air, a hollow background to her thundering heartbeat.

5

The deep ache of a sleepless night complained through Kellie's shoulders as she eased into the desk chair and reached for the phone. Ed picked up on the first ring, and she glanced at her watch, surprised he would be in the office so early. His voice calmed her fractured thoughts.

"Logan County Sheriff Department, Ed Campbell speaking."

She smiled at the familiar cadence of each syllable.

"It's me, Kellie. Someone came on my property last night."

"I'll send someone right out to pick up the surveillance tapes."

"Whoever it was didn't get that far–I only saw a shadow out in the pasture."

"At what time?"

She frowned. "I'm not sure–after midnight, I think."

His tone hardened. "What were you doing out there in the middle of the night?"

"I slept in the barn last night, just in case."

"Kellie...never mind. I'll be out shortly."

She listened to the dial tone for a moment, then hung up. The conversation hadn't gone the way she'd expected. Why did he sound so annoyed? She hadn't done anything wrong, yet his tone made her feel as though she had. If she could just put this whole mess on hold and talk to him, maybe they could close the yawning gap between them. Her shoulders sagged and, with a resigned sigh, she picked up the schedule of activities for the 89er weekend. The opening ceremonies, her heritage speech, a chuck wagon dinner...and the parade. Stinging tears burned her eyes. She and Dancer had been part of the Grand Parade for the past eight years. She pushed back from the desk. *I will* not *let this cripple me.*

Before pointing a finger at Frank, she needed to locate Tina. She was exactly the type who'd seek revenge for being fired. Kellie dug through a drawer and found the girl's work file. She reached for the phone, and it jangled beneath her fingers.

"Rocking S Ranch."

A heavy voice rumbled through the receiver. "Kellie? What the hell's going on up there?"

Oh great. "Darrell, how are you?"

"I'll be better if you tell me my mare is okay. Your story is all over the news down here."

She kept her anxiety from coloring her reply. "She's just fine. In fact, Doctor Browning just confirmed that she's settled. Congratulations–you'll have a Dancer foal on the ground next spring."

"I'll be up to collect her in the morning. Sorry I was so gruff...hope your horses will be okay."

Kellie nodded and hung up as the gush of adrenaline subsided, leaving a wash of tremors in its wake. She opened Tina's folder, and picked up the phone again.

"Mrs. Brown, this is Kellie Sutton. May I speak to Tina?"

The woman's gravelly voice oozed contempt. "I seen in the paper you got yerself in a bind. Whadaya need her for?"

"I just want to ask her a question."

The woman wheezed into a phlegm-choked coughing fit, and Kellie considered hanging up.

"She ain't here. Tina's got a real job now, working in

Okee City. She's a vet'narian assistant–she don't need you no more."

The line went dead and Kellie shook her head. How could Tina possibly be any help to a vet? She could barely get out of her own way.

The Oklahoma City yellow pages listed over a hundred and forty veterinarians, plus twelve display advertisements for clinics. Starting with the ads, Kellie made eight calls before she connected with the right one. She hung up before Tina came to the phone.

Skyline Equine Clinic. She printed the name and phone number on a scrap of paper and stuffed it into her back pocket. On her way out of the office, she stopped to examine the breeding roster posted on the wall. She still had eight outside mares in residence–five confirmed in foal and three awaiting a second cover. Worry rippled through her head. Dancer was in no shape to breed a mare–they'd have to use artificial insemination. *Thank God we collected him over the winter. At least enough to last until he's recovered.*

The phone rang and Kellie stopped to listen as the answering machine picked up. Her heart sank at the panic in another mare owner's message. Unable to deal with it right then, she headed down the aisle toward the barn door. She had to do something–anything–that would make this go away.

The rising sun bathed the dewy fields in glistening shades of pink and yellow, and the air was crisp and lightly scented with spring. Her mood lightened. Buck and Pal fell into step beside her.

"How are my fierce watchdogs this morning?"

Stumpy tails wiggled, and Buck stopped to stare expectantly toward the site of their nocturnal adventure. Three broodmares milled about a paddock where an employee was tossing out flakes of hay. A shot of adrenaline jerked through Kellie's gut and she stopped in mid-stride.

One of the mares was limping.

~ ~

Ed closed the desk drawer with a snap. "Boy howdy, she hasn't changed one bit–still determined to do everything *her* way."

He rocked back in the chair and scrubbed his hands over his face. After a long night on stakeout, he'd managed only three hours of sleep–an uneasy, frustrating night of mixed dreams peppered with gangs of drug dealers, the desert, and Kellie. An elixir of gut wrenching images. This job might kill him yet.

He opened the Sutton case report to review each of the possible suspects so far. He crossed the veterinarian and the horseshow exhibitor off the list. Tina Brown still seemed the most likely suspect, although after the scene in town yesterday, Frank's name had drifted nearer the top of the list. Ed sat back in his chair, pursing his lips. What possible motive could Kellie's ex-husband have for doing something like this? On the surface, they seemed to get along all right. Did some dark secret lurk beneath that benign facade? Time to do some digging.

As he headed down the hall, irritation crackled through his mind at the thought of Kellie playing detective in the middle of the night. At first consideration, the attacks on her horses seemed to be either a warning or an attempt to destroy her business, and he hadn't considered her personal safety. But now...

"Sheriff? What do you want me to do with this stuff?" A young deputy held out two plastic evidence bags. "We didn't find much."

Ed took the bags and examined the contents. The first one held a soggy half-smoked cigarette. The label indicated it had been found by the manure pile. The second bag sent his instincts racing. A disposable syringe with a small drop of brown goop inside.

"Where did you find this?"

"One of the stalls in the big barn."

"Which one?"

The man's face sagged with embarrassment. "I don't remember."

Ed shoved the bags back into the deputy's hands. "Get these down to the lab ASAP and tell them I want a report *right now.*"

He turned and strode down the hall, stopping briefly at the dispatch window. "I'm headed out to the Sutton place. See if you can locate a local girl named Tina Brown."

The dispatcher nodded. "I know who she is. I'll put the information on your desk...Don't forget your meeting with the commissioner."

"Ah! Thanks for reminding me. I'll be back in time."

He stepped out into the fresh morning air and started down the steps. On the sidewalk below, Deputy White leaned against the handrail and grinned up at him.

"Morning, Chief. Ready for decadent doughnuts and caffeine?"

Danielle's pristine uniform hugged every womanly curve, and the sun glinted off the shiny badge rising and falling on her ample breast. In another time and place, she'd be just what his tormented heart needed, but this duty was too important to chance a FUBAR situation. In a small town, any indiscretion would be on the grapevine before Noon.

"Sorry, I'm on my way out to the Sutton place."

She pivoted on her heel and fell in beside him. "I'll come along. I don't have anything going right now."

He stopped abruptly and pinned her with a hard look. "Dispatch is searching for the address of a local suspect. When she gets it, you go do some digging. And call me as soon as the lab has something on the new evidence."

A dark flare of anger crackled in Danielle's dark brown eyes and she lifted her chin. "Yes, *Sir*!"

~ ~

Fighting the panic rising in her chest, Kellie led the chestnut mare into the barn, trying to convince herself the limp was unrelated to the night visitor. She glanced over her shoulder, consumed with the thought she might be under someone's scrutiny at that very moment. Who hated her enough to do something like this? Why didn't they just confront her in person? For probably the hundredth time in the past few days, she reviewed her actions and contacts from the perspective of an antagonist and, again, frustration burned through her dead-end thoughts.

Initially, the mare's left front leg appeared normal, but Kellie gingerly lifted the hoof for a closer look. The wound was identical to the others–a small dark hole rimmed with red skin. She released the foot. *My god, what am I going to do? This isn't even my horse.*

She pressed the cell phone against her ear. "Hyde, I have another one."

"Aw Jeez. I'll be there as soon as I can. I'm at the Anderson Farm. Their kid's horse isn't responding to the medications."

Kellie slowly closed the phone. In all her mental rambling, she'd forgotten the attack on the neighbor's horse. What did *that* mean? Was the attacker simply a lunatic, and she was unfortunate enough to be in the wrong place at the wrong time? Or was the Anderson attack part of a larger plan–a diversionary ploy meant to confuse everyone?

The mare shook her head, rattling the chain on the crossties, and Kellie turned to stare at the slender ankle and fetlock that would swell to draft horse proportions before this was finished. Never in her life had she felt so helpless. Worse, now she had to call the owner with the bad news.

Outside, a vehicle door slammed and she glanced at her watch. Hyde had made record time. She strode toward the barn door and stepped into the sunshine, then sucked in her breath at the sharp quickening in the pit of her stomach.

Ed waved, sending a flood of joy and relief through her mind. Why did the mere sight of him make her believe everything would turn out all right?

His eyes reflected amusement. "You look like you just saw a ghost."

Warmth raced across her cheeks. "I thought you were Doc Browning."

The twinkle faded to concern. "What's wrong?"

Her lower lip began to quiver and she pulled it hard between her teeth before speaking. "Another attack. Out in the paddock. Right under my nose."

Ed's jaw line hardened. "Damn!" He punched a button on the radio clipped to his shirt at the shoulder. "Dispatch, get a couple of units out to the Sutton ranch. *Now.*" A response crackled and he nodded before signing off. His features softened with sympathy. "God, I'm really sorry...I should have posted someone sooner." He quickly retreated into his official capacity. "Think back, try to figure out what time you saw the intruder."

"The moon was brilliant...it lit up everything like daylight."

"Then it had to be well after midnight. Full moon was high at one a.m. Will Doctor Browning be able to pin down the time precisely?"

"I think so."

"Were you able to see if the intruder was male or female?"

"No, and I couldn't see the vehicle, either."

Ed touched her hand, sending sizzling warmth over her skin. "Kellie, I–"

The sun glinted off two patrol cars rolling up the lane, and he stepped back. Kellie shaded her eyes against the glare to watch Hyde's truck follow close behind the deputies.

Ed cleared his throat. "I'll get my men situated. Give me a call after you've talked to the vet."

He turned away, leaving her with the sense that he'd come to the ranch with more on his mind than the horses.

"Ed? Fifty thousand dollars to catch whoever did this."

~~

Hyde released the mare's foot. "I'd say this happened about four or five hours ago. I'd like to try something different–an old Indian remedy my grandmother used."

Kellie shook her head. "No Hyde, this is an outside mare, here for breeding. I can't tell the owner we're practicing on her."

Hyde gave her a hard look. "I've been talking to a friend of mine about snakebites. First aid involves opening the puncture wound, then sucking out the venom." His expression softened and he grinned. "Since I'd like to keep my teeth, I think I'll use a different method. A poultice should draw out the poison. Then we can pursue treating the wound traditionally and preventing infection."

Hyde's logic made sense. The wound was new enough to give them an advantage. Maybe.

The horse jerked and snorted as a long needle pierced the tender flesh at the back of the fetlock. Hyde released her foot and straightened up.

"A little local anesthetic. It'll take a few minutes to work." He cocked his head. "My friend at OSU came up with some interesting possibilities for these cases. A number of toxins cause tissue destruction, and leave no identifiable traces."

He glanced at his watch, then picked up the mare's foot again and pressed a thumb against the wound. The horse didn't flick an ear.

"Good, she's numb–but hold her head, just in case."

He reached into his bag and pulled out a shiny scalpel.

Kellie cringed. "What are you going to do?"

"A puncture wound closes up on itself and traps the infection inside. If I can get the toxin out, she should be okay."

Kellie held the mare's halter and looked away, trying not to visualize the razor-sharp blade slicing through flesh.

Hyde rose to his feet. "A small amount of fluid came out. I think we're early enough for this to work." He opened a plastic container, then sniffed it and chuckled.

"Smells like gin. Juniper berry is one of the ingredients."

He squatted down beside the horse's foot, and Kellie's thoughts drifted to the recent conversation with Ed. He hadn't told her anything about their progress with the investigation, and his manner had been guarded, except for that one brief personal touch. He had something on his mind–she was sure of it. She frowned. She'd forgotten to give him the clinic address. History seemed to be crippling their ability to work together. She *had* to find a way to distance herself from him, at least until this nightmare was over.

"Are you about finished? I need to catch the sheriff before he leaves."

"I thought you caught him a long time ago."

"You are so bad."

"You go on, I can finish up alone, then I'll check on Boots. This might help him too."

With another glance at the mare's foot, Kellie left the stall and hurried toward the door, but she was too late. Ed's patrol car was already turning onto the road.

Questions tumbled about in her head like lottery balls. When would he question Tina? What was taking so long? Irritation replaced her earlier calm. Perhaps no one thought this was important enough. She strode toward her truck, muttering to herself. The only way to get something done was to do it yourself.

~ ~

Ed picked up a handwritten note lying on his desk. *"Tina Brown lives in Oklahoma City now. What do you want me to do?* A phone number concluded the terse message, and he smiled wryly. Danielle's bold script matched her personality perfectly. He pressed the intercom button.

"Have Deputy White contact OCPD with Tina Brown's information. I'm leaving for the commissioner's office right now."

Outside, he walked past his vehicle and headed down Harrison toward the tracks. The five-block walk to City Hall would give him time to gather his thoughts. He'd never liked these meetings with the Chairman of the Board of Commissioners. An undercover operation had to be one-hundred-percent secret. Even one person in the loop could screw up the whole thing. He wished he knew what DEA had done to guarantee Barney McBee's silence.

Ed's footsteps echoed on the tile floor at City Hall. The walls held portraits of former mayors and town officials from Guthrie's earliest days. Serious faced men who'd struggled in the dangerous environment of land hunger, building the town from a plot of dust and scrub, constantly alert for those who would take it from them.

He strode toward the commissioners' offices at the end of the hall, mentally rehearsing the only things he would agree to talk about today. After checking in with the secretary, he turned and gazed at a display of photographs of military men from Guthrie. Two rows of faces stared back at him, many of them killed in battle through the decades. Above the top row, his own sober face stared back, a silver star pinned to his chest. A ripple of irritation moved through his head. Why would he be any different than the rest of the gallery? He'd been doing a job–nothing more.

A minute later, he stepped into Commissioner McBee's office. The rotund middle-aged man rose from behind a wide oak desk, removed a fat cigar from his mouth, and extended his hand.

"Afternoon, Sheriff. Have a seat. Already getting warm out there, huh?"

Ed nodded as he settled into a leather chair in front of the desk. "Before we get too involved, I have a request. Would you please move my photograph to a less conspicuous spot? It should be in the lineup with everyone else."

McBee pursed his lips. "You always were a humble young man. If that's what you want, I'll see to it." He made a note to himself, then sat back in his chair and laced his fingers across his expansive waist. "What's the status of your situation? Any idea when you'll be finished?"

"Absolutely none. This isn't a project with a schedule."

McBee's soft face tightened and his voice took on an edge. "Don't forget, you're only here because I got my arm twisted. This is still my town and you report to me. I want a weekly update, you understand?"

Ed kept his anger under control. "You'll have to talk to Washington about that. I have limits on what I can discuss."

The commissioner studied him for a moment, then nodded. "Fair enough." His tone became friendlier. "You making any headway on that mess out at the Sutton place?"

Ed stood up and tried to smile. "When we do, you'll be the first to know about it."

Minutes later, he strode along the sidewalk, taking deep breaths to calm his anger. This mission had put him between a rock and a hard place. McBee's good-ole-boy attitude was like a bear trap–suck you in, then rip your throat out. Kellie's face appeared in Ed's thoughts, the fear and sadness in her eyes driving a stake through his heart. If nothing else, he would catch the person responsible for her pain, and maybe that would heal some wounds.

6

City buildings appeared on the horizon, an elegant geometric pattern of angles and shadows against the brilliant sky. Kellie's brief appreciation of the scene faded quickly. The element of surprise would be in her favor, but beyond that, she didn't have much confidence in the outcome of a confrontation with Tina.

The traffic thickened on I-35 and she concentrated on finding the correct exit and getting off without being mowed down by the idiots who drove with one hand on the wheel and the other on a cell phone. She glanced in the rearview mirror at the small car dogging her bumper. The young woman chattered and laughed, oblivious to the world around her as they all flew down the interstate at eighty miles an hour. Kellie tried not to think about the hazards of slowing down or changing lanes.

She passed the interchange for I-44, then took the next exit, breathing a sigh of relief as she entered the city traffic pattern.

"Give me the country any day."

Staying in the right lane, she slowed down enough to read the street signs. Within a couple of blocks, she passed the huge memorial to the Oklahoma City Bombing–a testament to the event that had shattered so many lives and driven home the unsettling reality that safety was a precious commodity. Redbud trees surrounded by neatly mowed grass belied the horror that had once filled the space. Terror could come in large or small packages–in a vast city, or in her own backyard.

A hard lump grew in her throat and her brain flashed a vision of Dancer, grazing in the morning sun. She *would* find whoever did this to him, and make sure they suffered for it.

Skyline Equine Clinic was situated close to the road, flanked by a small barn with a turnout pen. A mare and foal stood by the fence nearest the driveway. The mare's leg was bandaged to the knee. Kellie shuddered and climbed out of the truck.

Piney antiseptic cleaner mingled with animal odors and stale air. A middle-aged woman sat on a plastic bench, reading a magazine. The reception desk was deserted, but voices drifted from a room at the back. Kellie tapped the bell on the counter and Tina appeared.

Her sticky pink lips immediately formed a hard line and she leaned against the doorjamb, crossing her arms. "Y'know–I saw the news and figured it'd be just like you to think *I* did it."

Kellie hesitated. The girl didn't seem surprised by the visit, so why was she being so defensive?

"Well, *did* you?"

Tina barked a derisive laugh. "Why would I waste any more time on your nags? I have an *important* job here."

Kellie glanced at the customer on the bench, then lowered her voice. "You also have access to needles and who-knows-what drugs. And a motive for revenge. If you didn't have anything to do with it, I'm sure you won't mind talking to Sheriff Campbell."

Tina's skin paled beneath her freckles, but her tone remained cocky. "Bring him on–I have an alibi. I have a new boyfriend and he's been keeping me *real* busy." Her eyes darkened with innuendo. "If you know what I mean."

Kellie picked up a business card from the counter. "Goody for you–maybe he likes you enough to keep you out of jail."

She hurried out the door and inhaled deeply, stunned by the effect of the confrontation. What had she expected–a confession? Tina's surly confidence undermined Kellie's own, and her fingers shook as she turned the key in the ignition. What exactly had she accomplished with this visit?

At the outskirts of the city, she almost slammed on the brakes.

"Oh my God! None of this is random–these are my best horses. Even in the field, someone knows exactly which ones to target. It *has* to be her!"

Every detail of the past week roiled through Kellie's brain as she burned up the highway toward home, but no clear answers appeared. She turned onto Sutton Corners Road and, moments later, braked to a stop in front of the old Borden place. An orange-and-white rental truck was backed up to the front door, and two burly young men carried furniture and boxes up the loading ramp. A sick feeling oozed into her stomach.

She pulled into the driveway and climbed out of the car. "The owners around?"

One of the men gestured toward the house and Kellie maneuvered through the jumble on the porch, then knocked on the doorjamb.

A petite elderly woman appeared, her leathery face crinkling into a big smile. "Howdy, Miz Sutton. Come on in, pardon the mess, but we're movin', as you can see."

Kellie gazed around the shabby living room. "This is sure a surprise–I didn't see a for-sale sign in the yard."

The woman cackled. "Nope. Sold the place for cash. No bother with banks and all that carry-on. Cold, hard cash. Goin' to live in Tulsa, near our grandkids."

Dismay moved through Kellie's chest. "Must have been a really rich person to pay cash."

"Don't know. He was a furiner, but their money's as good as any."

~~

Kellie strode angrily into the office. Would *anything* ever go her way again?

Frank looked up. "I passed Hyde on the way in. Any new developments?"

She pursed her lips, resisting the urge to snarl. "Another horse came up lame. She was out in the field. The wound hasn't festered yet."

He frowned. "A pasture horse? That makes this sound even more like a natural accident than an attack. Who'd be fool enough to roam through a pasture full of horses in the dark?"

She stepped closer and glowered. "How would you know it happened in the dark? Did *you* have something to do with this?"

Startled surprise lifted his eyebrows, then he laughed out loud. "God, Kellie, you should have been a script writer! We already know that whatever is affecting the horses takes a while to show up. Stands to reason, it happened sometime during the night."

He was right. Exhaustion and despair were sending knee-jerk responses in all directions and she was falling apart, which wouldn't help anything.

"Sorry. I just wish you were around sometimes when I need you."

He was silent for a moment, then he spoke softly. "Since when did you *ever* need me?"

~~

Travis hunkered over his beer and cast an overt glance at the girl sitting beside him at the bar. Tina's round face was flushed, her eyes a little too bright. And no wonder. So far, she'd matched him beer for beer. She caught him looking at her, and ran her tongue suggestively over her pouty lips. A jolt shot through his groin–he'd get more than lucky tonight.

He threw her a lecherous grin, then waved two fingers at the bartender. Tina's throaty laugh intensified the growing pressure in his crotch.

She drained the last of her beer. "Have you seen the news? Someone tried to kill a couple of champion horses where I used to work."

Travis raised an eyebrow. "Really? Where'd you see that?"

"Channel 5, and if you can stand it, the owner thinks *I* had something to do with it!"

A thought grew in his head. "How do you know?"

"'Cause she came to see me today! Since she fired me, I've bitched to anyone who'd listen, and she just automatically assumed I was looking for revenge."

Damn. I didn't think of that. He glanced at Tina in the mirror. "Long as you have an alibi for that night, you're in the clear."

"*What* night?"

Caution crept into his head and he took a long drink. "Any night. Whatever."

She nodded, then trailed a finger over his forearm. "Travis, we've been seein' each other for almost three weeks now, and I don't know hardly nothin' about you."

"Mystery Man, that's me."

Two new frosty mugs appeared on the bar, and Tina's warm hand moved to his thigh. He took another swig of beer and savored the power of the erection straining against his tight jeans. *Yes, indeed. I'm gonna get* very *lucky.*

Her round eyes were intense. "C'mon, baby, tell me something about yourself. I'll bet you were the cutest little kid."

Oh yeah, I was real cute. His thoughts drifted briefly back to the childhood that haunted him. He glanced at his companion, wondering why she wanted to know. *What the hell.*

"I spent my teen years in Texas, moving from one ranch to the next. I worked my way up from cleaning barns to riding fence, then one of the wranglers broke his leg and the boss let me ride in one of the roundups."

"How come you were driftin' when you were just a kid? Don't you have no family?"

A band tightened around his chest and his gaze followed a rivulet of moisture drooling down the side of the mug. He thumbed it away, then downed his beer in one gulp.

"Trav?"

Her hand touched his shoulder and he jerked back to the present. His chest felt as though it would implode and his hand shook as he picked up a crumpled pack of cigarettes. Pulling out the last one, he motioned the barkeep for another round, then looked at Tina.

"My old man died when I was fifteen."

Her sympathetic expression bolstered the simmering rage in his chest. He'd never talked about it, just lived that day over and over in his own head. He drank some beer and wrapped his mind around the past.

"The bitch of the thing is, he didn't have to die." Travis stared at the glowing bud on the end of the cigarette, transported back to the rubble of his father's sorry life. "He should've been stronger, been a real man, stood up for himself."

Tina exhaled softly and laid her hand on his. The personal touch unleashed the anger caged inside for so many years. He stared at his reflection in the mirror behind the bar, seeing the hatred that empowered him.

"After the old man shattered both knees in a bull ride, his rodeo career and jock status were in the toilet. He started drinking and let the ranch go to hell."

"What about your mom?"

"She was a slut." His words came out as a snarl. "And my dad didn't do nothin' about it." The familiar rage grew. "She fucked everyone in town, then just ran off one night and never came back."

Tina slipped off the barstool and wrapped her arms around his shoulders, pressing her large breasts against him.

"C'mon, honey. Let's go home. I'll make it all better, I promise."

7

Kellie leaned against the back porch rail and soaked up the silence of dawn. A pale aura of peach stretched across the sky at the horizon and, while she watched, the dark fields crystallized into discernible features. The fence line, a clump of mesquite, the faint outline of a tractor waiting for the day's work to begin. Shadowy horse silhouettes ambled across the pasture. Something about mornings filled her with optimism. A new start, second chances for almost everything. Her gaze drifted to the main barn and uncertainty trod on her serenity. Tina's bold defiance wasn't the reaction she'd expected. Vehement denial, fear–anything but smug confidence.

Sara's voice came from the kitchen. "Mama, Sheriff Campbell's on the phone."

Kellie's pulse quickened as she took the receiver. Should she tell him about her visit to the city, or leave it alone?

His voice held no friendly overtones. "I understand you called Tina Brown's mother. Why?"

"To find out where Tina is."

"That's *our* job. I don't want you getting involved."

Someone rapped loudly on the back door, and Kellie turned as Frank stepped into the kitchen and tweaked Sara's ponytail. "Fine, Sheriff, I'll be there." She hung up, praying he wouldn't call back.

"They've located Tina. I'm going into town in a while to give a statement."

"You really think Tina's smart enough to pull off

something like this?"

Kellie snorted. "Dumb enough is more like it. They're going to question her after they talk to me."

"Where is she?"

"Oklahoma City. She's working as a vet assistant, if you can imagine."

Sara piped up. "I didn't like her. Neither did Dancer. One time she was in his stall and he wouldn't let her touch his feed bucket. He pinned his ears and pawed the ground, and she backed out the door." Sara laughed gleefully. "And she said the F-word. It was *so* funny."

Hyde's comments sprang to mind and Kellie glanced at Frank. This mess had to be Tina's doing. No way would Frank purposely harm the horses.

As she headed to the barn, she thought about her impending meeting with Ed. He was clearly annoyed, and she'd need to be careful not to antagonize him. His call had taken her by surprise, but now that she had time to think about it, she prickled with irritation. *I was only trying to help.* She stared at her boots as she walked, musing about how she should start the conversation. Maybe she'd begin by showing him the photographs. A ripple of anticipation cooled her ire, and she smiled. She could handle this–she'd always been able to get him to do what she wanted.

Her step slowed and she squinted at something hanging on the fence, then covered the short distance quickly. Another photograph was nailed to the post. She snatched it off and gaped at a picture of the new palomino foal, asleep in the straw. The full meaning of the mysterious snapshots hit her like a mule kick. The attacks on her horses were a warning–but, of what?

A silver truck and matching four-horse trailer turned into the lane, and she blew out a long breath. "Oh great."

Tucking the picture into her pocket, she hurried toward the road to direct the driver to the mare barn. She took a shortcut through the main barn, picked up a file folder, and reached the mare barn as a burly redheaded man stepped down from the duallie.

"Morning Darrell. You made good time."

"Yep, gotta pick up a load of grain in El Reno before headin' back. How's my girl this morning?"

Kellie grinned. "Barefoot and pregnant."

While Darrell haltered the mare, Kellie checked the breeding certificate and health sheets. "Final balance through yesterday is $3,000. That includes the second payment on the stud fee, the vet, and a week's board."

"Checkbook's in the cab." He led the mare out of the stall and stood her up, then walked all the way around her, stopping only to check a spot on her hock. "She looks good."

Kellie's smile felt wooden as she followed him to the trailer. *Lucky is more like it.*

He held out the lead rope. "Here, hold her a minute while I get the ramp down." He pulled the latch pins on the trailer doors. "How's the situation in your barn? Any leads?"

Caution moved into Kellie's head. *Don't offer any suppositions or opinions. Just facts.* "The investigation is in full swing."

Darrell reached for the lead rope and gave Kellie a wry grin. "That's your story and you're stickin' to it?"

She opened her mouth to reply, then frowned as another truck and horse trailer pulled into the drive. "Uh huh. Here's your invoice. Make the check out to Rocking S Ranch."

Five minutes later, Darrell's truck pulled away, and Kellie braced herself for an unpleasant conversation with another mare owner. The rats were jumping ship and she could offer no assurances that it was unnecessary.

A sharp-faced woman climbed out of the truck and glowered. "Why don't you return phone calls?"

Stay calm. "We've had our hands full and I'm behind in

a lot of things. I'm really sorry."

"I'm here to collect my mares."

~ ~

Forty minutes later, with close to ten thousand dollars in her pocket, but a huge dent in her business plan, Kellie walked toward Dancer's stall. The horrid odor grew stronger as she approached and fear clutched her heart. The nightmare she danced through seemed only to get deeper and darker with each passing day, and the strength she'd always drawn upon had evaporated somewhere along the rocky path at the edge of a cliff.

Then Hyde's phone call nudged her over.

"The x-rays show the coffin bone severely rotated...I wish I had better news."

A battering ram slammed into her chest and her throat closed, thickening her words.

"You said the corrective pads would prevent that."

"I'm afraid we were a little too late. I'll come out this afternoon to flush the abscess. We can make some decisions then..."

"What about the oxygen thing you were talking about? Wouldn't that help?"

"Kellie, I think we're out of time. The closest hyperbaric chamber is in Kentucky and I honestly don't think Dancer could survive the drive up there."

"I can fly him."

"Let's wait and see how he is later today."

Kellie held the phone for a long time after he hung up. She couldn't give up–she *wouldn't* give up. If a slim chance existed that the oxygen therapy would save Dancer, she'd do it. And she wasn't waiting until later to decide.

She scanned a list of telephone numbers, then dialed.

"Ferris Air Bus. Jeff here."

"It's Kellie Sutton. I need an emergency flight for three

horses to Lexington, Kentucky."

The sounds of shuffling papers and the charter pilot's mumbled calculating seemed to take an inordinate amount of time. Frank walked into the room and stood next to the desk, a frown creasing his forehead. A quiver of concern ran through Kellie's head–another argument in the offing if he'd overheard her.

The pilot came back on the line. "On short notice, it'll be twenty-eight hundred bucks each horse, one way. When do you want to go?"

She glanced at Frank again and cleared her throat. "As soon as possible, but I'll have to get back to you. Thanks a lot."

Frank crossed his arms and pinned her with a hard stare. "What do you think you're doing?"

A defensive retort sprang up, but she bit it back. "Hyde thinks some type of oxygen therapy will save Dancer, but the closest facility is in Lexington. We'll have to fly him up there."

"And you were planning to tell me about this *when*? I know he's your favorite horse, but at some point, we need to be realistic about how much money you spend on a lost cause."

Kellie leaped out of her chair, anger and adrenaline exploding through her body. "No! These are *my* horses and *my* life, and I'll spend as much goddamned money as I damned well please to protect them!" She pulled the crumpled checks from her pocket and threw them on the desk. "What's more, four mares went home early this morning, and we are still legally and financially responsible for the mare that was attacked yesterday. I'm *doing* this!"

Frank's features hardened and his eyes darkened. "Suit yourself, *Miss Sutton*."

He scooped up the checks, then turned on his heel and strode out of the room, leaving Kellie drained and confused.

Why was it so hard to communicate with him lately? What should have been a joint discussion about financial and management decisions had turned into a personal feud. And surprisingly, after all these years, Frank still resented that she'd kept her maiden name. She shook her head. He'd originally agreed that the Sutton name generated benefits and recognition that couldn't be bought. In a small town, heritage played an important role in business success.

A lot of good it did her now–all the prestige and money in the world might not save Dancer and Boots. Or the young chestnut mare.

Kellie slowly reached for the phone. She couldn't procrastinate any longer–she had to call the mare's owner.

An answering machine drawled the fact that they were away at a show, and relief surged through her head. She focused on a yellow sticky note with Hyde's scribbled handwriting, then dialed the Kentucky phone number.

"Bluegrass Equine Clinic. Mason speaking."

"This is Kellie Sutton in Oklahoma. I have some horses that are–"

"Hold on, let me transfer you."

Recorded Lexington weather information filled the brief void, then a friendly female voice came on the line.

"Ms. Sutton? This is Dr. Charles. What can I do for you?"

"I have three horses that were injected with something caustic, and–"

"Oh my, the ones in Oklahoma?"

"Yes. Can you help?"

Compassion rounded the woman's tone. "Do you know anything about hyberbaric oxygen therapy?"

"Only that it is relatively new."

"If you took physics in school, you'll remember that normal atmospheric pressure is about 14.7 pounds per square inch, and air is 79% nitrogen and 21% oxygen. Under normal atmospheric pressure, hemoglobin is saturated with approximately 97% oxygen, and those hemoglobin molecules are the primary delivery system to the tissues. Several other calculations and issues go into the process, but the end result of hyperbaric oxygen therapy is the ability to dramatically increase breathed oxygen, and that increases the amount of dissolved oxygen in the plasma...Still with me?"

"Hanging on for dear life."

Dr. Charles chuckled. "Sorry–this is such exciting stuff, I tend to get carried away. Anyway, all tissue damage injuries have swelling and some necrosis. Tissue swelling compromises oxygen delivery to the site, which inhibits the body's ability to repair and reconstruct. Hyperbaric oxygen therapy decreases the swelling and allows improved oxygen and nutrient delivery to the area, while stimulating the production of collagen."

Kellie shuddered at the reminder of how horrible Dancer's wound looked. "Even when the horse's foot is almost eaten away?"

"First, we clean out the dead tissue and flush the wound. The horse spends time in the chamber two to three times a day, then we utilize stem cell therapy to accelerate re-growth of the cartilage."

"Stem cells?"

"I know–this is a tremendous amount of new information I'm serving up. Veterinary medicine has come a long way in the past ten years. I'll send some literature to your vet, but to simplify the explanation, researchers have found that body fat contains large numbers of stem cells that will re-grow whatever substance we mix with them. Put them with bone, they make bone. Put them with nerve tissue, they grow nerve tissue. It's phenomenal–almost like magic–but it works."

"Isn't stem cell research illegal?"

"This is different from embryonic brain stem cell

research, where the embryo must be killed in order to acquire the cells. In this procedure, the collection of the fat doesn't even cause pain for the animal."

Kellie was silent for a moment, allowing a glimmer of hope to grow. "As long as it works."

~ ~

Travis groaned and rolled out of bed, fireworks going off in his head. His mouth tasted like crap, and his eyeballs felt as though they hung out of the sockets like gag eyeglasses. He squinted at the dim light coming through the window, listening to the voices outside–the crew was already up.

He pulled on his boots and shuffled across the rough wooden floor to the kitchenette. The light in the refrigerator sent a barb of pain blasting through his eyes and he closed them for a minute before reaching for a soda. He hesitated, tempted to grab a beer instead. *Hair of the dog...nah, I'd get my ass kicked for drinking on the job.* Another throb of pain slashed through his temple. *Fuck it–who cares?*

The beer fizz burned down his raw throat, and he leaned against the counter and grinned, thinking about his night of debauchery. Tina was some piece of work. Man, that girl knew tricks he'd only dreamed about. He downed the last of the beer, and wiped his mouth with his sleeve. Women were such suckers for a sob story. Then he frowned. What exactly had he said the night before? He shook his head slowly. *No clue.*

Putting Tina out of his mind, he opened a cupboard door and lifted out the jar of specimens. The curved glass distorted and magnified the creatures inside, making them look like the figment of a horror movie producer's imagination. They were lethargic now that they'd been captive for over two weeks. If he didn't hurry up, they'd start eating each other.

He arranged everything on the counter, then unscrewed the metal lid. His heartbeat accelerated and pain thumped through the base of his skull. Holding a spoon in one hand, he tipped the jar over a cereal bowl. Four of the small bodies tumbled into the dish and he immediately started crushing them.

Before he could react, another one jumped from the lip of the jar onto his right hand, and pain seared through his flesh.

"Shit!" He slammed the jar down on the counter, and shook his burning hand. "Goddammit! Fuck!"

A surge of adrenaline screamed through his body as he scrambled to twist the lid back onto the container. He searched the floor for the escapee, but the rogue had disappeared.

A minute later, he stared at a white blister rising in the center of a small red circle. *Calm down. This is not lethal.* He squeezed his eyes shut. *But it hurts like fucking hell.*

~ ~

Ed stepped out the front door of the county building and stopped to gaze at Kellie at the bottom of the steps. "I was just on my way out to your place. Come on up."

She looked hesitant, then mounted the stairs and silently followed him down the hall.

He kept his tone neutral. "You want coffee?"

She shook her head and he turned away from her wonderful green eyes, hardening his heart and preparing himself for the confrontation. Why was this happening? After all the years and distance between them, a brutal act of cruelty had brought them together again, as though no time had passed. Yet the wound still festered.

"Kellie, you cannot meddle in an official investigation."

Her eyes flashed with anger. "*What* investigation? I don't think you even believe these are anything other than freak injuries! It's been five days and you've done *what?* Sent some deputies to poke around the barn!"

"We've been working on it, but your actions could compromise our efforts to make an arrest." He tried to soften his tone a little. "*More* important is that these vicious acts were done by someone without a conscience, and you might get hurt."

Her expression relaxed a little. "Did your men find anything?"

"A syringe in one of the stalls–I don't know which one–but the lab can't identify the residue, only that it's organic. We'll send it up to OSU."

She fished three photographs from her pocket. "I think you should see these. I don't know who took them, or where they came from, but they all just appeared at the barn over the last three days." Her voice cracked. "I think someone's watching me."

He took them from her, his chest thumping with the struggle to restrain his anger and alarm. "Why didn't you show me these before?"

"I–don't know. They didn't seem important until now."

He slid the snapshots into an evidence bag. "I'll have them dusted for fingerprints, but I'd guess they'll come back clean. For now, let's concentrate on Tina Brown. I need to know everything you can remember about the girl. Don't worry about whether *you* think it's important or not–I'll decide what is and what isn't."

Kellie laid a business card on his desk. "She was defensive when I showed up. We only talked for a few minutes, but she said she has nothing to hide, that she's been spending all her time with a new boyfriend."

"Jesus! You *went* there?"

She recoiled at his outburst, and her confidence clearly faltered. "I'm only trying to help. You can't begin to imagine how I feel!"

He took a deep breath. "If you won't cooperate, I'll be forced to put you in protective custody."

Her stunned expression confirmed that she understood he meant business.

He stapled the card to a file folder and set it aside. "Why did you fire her?"

"She was unreliable, always late. With so many horses, I need–"

"Okay, late. Anything else?"

"One of the ranch hands caught her in my office one night, going through the file cabinet."

"Anything valuable in there?"

"No, just breeding records and pedigrees–Oh my God, that explains it! Only really good horses have been targeted."

Ed wrote that down, then looked up. "You have some high ticket animals on the property. She might have been planning to steal one."

Kellie snorted. "How would she do *that*? She's just a kid."

"A kid with access to important information. She could easily have been the insider for a theft ring. Stealing horses is big business–you should know that. Goes way back in history around here. Whether the horses end up at the killers or on a truck headed to some other state, it's a lucrative operation. Firing your little stall cleaner might have cost her a big chunk of money."

Kellie thought for a moment. "She wasn't very good with the horses. I had reservations about hiring her, but we were so short handed." She shook her head. "But why would she be taking pictures of me?"

"To get inside your head, make you nervous. I think she's a good suspect. She knows your barn, your routine, she has access to syringes, and she has motive."

The intercom hummed. "Oklahoma City on line one."

Ed picked up the phone and listened while Kellie fidgeted in his peripheral vision. He jotted a note on his desk mat. "Thanks, I'll see you then." He set the phone back in the base. "The polygrapher will be out to your place this afternoon. Let your staff know."

Her eyes reflected disbelief. "Do you really think one of my people is responsible?"

"Probably not, but in order to be thorough, we have to find ways to sort through the suspects using a process of elimination...Make sure Frank is available too."

Her skin paled. "Oh boy, thanks a lot."

Ed studied the woman he'd always thought would be by his side. Strength and determination had replaced her youthful eagerness for life. Where was the gentle girl who'd loved him so much? Were the two of them still meant for each other? Had they ever been?

~~

Around midmorning, Travis shifted in the saddle and took a long slow breath to quell the nausea coiling around his insides. The sensation faded, then his stomach bucked. He gathered the reins and turned to his partner.

"I feel like shit...tell Dusty I'm goin' in."

The ride back to the cabin was the longest mile he'd ever traveled. His eyes ached, each breath came with difficulty, and his guts threatened to explode. *I ain't never gettin' that plowed on a work night again.* He dismounted in front of his quarters, and loosely tied the horse. As he stepped through the door, his nausea returned with a vengeance. For ten minutes, he retched and gagged, then sank to the bathroom floor, tears streaming down his face, his nose dripping snot. Every muscle trembled from the violent episode.

Finally, he managed to get back on his feet and lurch into the bedroom. As he hit the bed, his cell phone rang. He fumbled it open and rolled over onto his back. Tina's shrill voice pierced his hammering headache.

~~

Kellie's conversation with Ed numbed her, making it

impossible to put one thought in front of another as she drove home. She parked in front of the barn, then pulled down the visor mirror. Why had she applied lipstick before going to town? The bright gash of color accentuated her pale skin, making her look gaunt. She swiped her mouth with a tissue, and self-admonition pressed in. How could she dwell on the past while her present was crumbling?

At Dancer's stall door, she froze. Her beautiful copper penny stallion stood motionless, not even the tiniest movement of breathing. His coat glistened, almost reflective. His heavy mane and long tail were brushed and free of straw. She blinked, then focused on the objects braided into his mane. Sprigs of something dark green, leaves of wild olive, a small bone. *Hyde has been here.* She stared at the horse's grotesquely swollen front legs, and her chest caved in with despair.

"I promise I will get whoever did this to you," she whispered.

Back in her office, she gazed at the paperwork scattered over the desk. Four of the eight outside mares were gone, and only two of them were checked in foal. She shook her head. The woman who'd picked up hers that morning had been adamant that she didn't care if two hadn't settled. She wanted them out of there before something happened to them. Kellie sank into her chair. *What a nightmare.* If they didn't catch whoever was responsible, her business was doomed. No one would ever take a chance with Rocking S again.

The answering machine blinked steadily and, with a heavy heart, Kellie pressed "play." Two more owners wanted answers.

They'd have to wait.

She dialed Ferris Air Bus and listened to the charter pilot's instructions for preparing the horses to travel.

"How much for one of my employees to ride along?"

"It's included in the price. Just be sure that person has

good control over the horses. You might want to sedate them a little before we load."

Kellie made a note, thanked him, and hung up, then rose and hurried out of the office. Roy was in the feed room, and she handed him the details of the transport.

"Just before you load, give them all a shot of Ace to calm them."

The dogs began barking and she stepped up to the small window. A plain white car rolled to a stop by the fence, and a thin man with a shiny bald pate climbed out. He wiped his forehead before donning a hat, then hiked up his trousers and retrieved two metal suitcases from the backseat. *The lie detector tests. Why now?*

The man smiled and stuck out his hand. "Miss Sutton? I'm from the Oklahoma City Police Department. Where can I set up?"

Kellie noted the dry warmth of his palm as they shook hands. Despite his less than attractive physical stature, he had amazing eyes. Intelligent-looking, dark blue, and fringed by long black eyelashes.

She nodded toward the barn. "You can use the office. I'll get everyone rounded up–you got here sooner than I expected."

After removing a few things from Frank's desktop, she headed toward the stalls to find Roy.

"We have some more police business to take care of. Would you ask the staff to gather in the tack room, please?"

Roy's eyes narrowed. "More questions?"

Kellie hesitated. "Actually, they're going to administer lie detector tests."

"Are you accusing one of *us*?"

"No, no, this is supposedly standard procedure in any criminal investigation. They want to rule out as many people as possible."

Roy turned and stalked off toward the barn doors. "Damned kid, comin' back to town with all his medals, thinkin' he's better'n the rest of us."

Though Kellie wanted to find and punish whoever had attacked her, she knew this situation would forever tarnish the confidence of her employees. That they would think she suspected them nearly broke her heart.

"Miss Sutton? I'm ready."

Kellie moved toward the office door. "My manager's gone to tell everyone you're here."

"We'll start with you, then."

She stopped in mid-stride. "The hell, you say! Why would you test me? *I'm* the victim!"

The man's calm demeanor only added insult to injury. "We need to test *everyone* who has any connection with this barn. Anyone who refuses puts themselves into a position of being suspect." He gestured toward a chair he'd placed beside the desk. "Please sit down and take a couple of deep breaths to calm down."

This is ludicrous! Why would I attack my own horses? Horror stories whirled through her thoughts–insurance fraud by the owners of racehorses and high ticket show horses. She grudgingly acknowledged the rationale behind the process.

"I'll be asking you a series of questions after we hook you up, but first, I'll read the questions."

She nodded, wondering why they'd let her know the questions ahead of time.

"These are in the order I'll ask them: Is your name Kellie Sutton? Is Paris the capital of France? Have you ever administered dangerous medications to any of your animals? Is a tangerine orange? Do you have any knowledge about the attacks on your horses? When questioned by the sheriff, did you answer any question falsely? Did you give something to your horses that harmed them?"

Kellie's nervous curiosity at the first two questions on the list changed abruptly to dismay when the man asked about medications. She listened to the remaining questions, telling herself she had nothing to worry about. She'd had nothing to do with the attacks, and the test would prove that.

"Okay, Miss Sutton, now I'll hook you up and ask the same questions. Just relax and breathe normally."

Moving briskly and without speaking again, he slipped a blood pressure cuff over her right arm and secured it, then attached small sticky circles with wires to two fingers on her left hand. Finally, he wrapped rubber tubes around her torso and abdomen, then attached another electronic lead. The assortment of wires made her feel like she was sitting in an execution chair.

"Okay, just about ready." He turned some dials and, on the far side of the machine, a printer hummed and a strip of graph paper began to move past the ink styluses. "Answer the questions only with yes or no, and look straight ahead."

"Is your name Kellie Sutton?"

"Yes."

"Is Paris the capital of France?"

"Yes."

"Have you ever administered dangerous medications to any of your animals?"

"No."

"Is a tangerine orange?"

"Yes."

"Do you have any knowledge about the attacks on your horses?"

Kellie's heart thumped. "No."

"When questioned by the sheriff, did you give false answers to any question?"

The deception about contacting Tina rolled through Kellie's mind, and she tried to remember if that had been during questioning. It all seemed so long ago.

"No." She glanced sideways to see if he reacted to the reading on the machine, but his face was stony.

"Eyes straight ahead, please. Did you give something to your horses that harmed them?

"NO!" Tears burned her eyes and she struggled to keep from leaping out of the chair and slapping the crap out of him.

The printer hummed for a few seconds more, then he turned it off and closed the lid. "That went well." He calmly began unhooking her.

"Does that mean I passed?"

"I don't read the tests." He picked up a sheet of paper. "Would you ask Franklin Frazier to come in, please?"

"He's not here."

"Then he'll need to make an appointment and come down to the offices." The man made a note on the list. "I'm ready for whoever's next."

Kellie's thoughts raced as she stepped into the aisle and walked toward the tack room, dreading the prospect of facing her employees and their judgments. But the closer she got, the more she calmed down and, within minutes, her confidence returned. She had vowed to do whatever it took to find Dancer's attacker, and it included this. A small price to pay.

After talking briefly with the staff, she headed for Dancer's stall. Hyde turned at the sound of her footsteps and, the moment she met his gaze, she knew. Jerking her eyes away from his, she looked down at Dancer's feet. The bandage had been removed, exposing a gaping wound that sent revulsion and disbelief surging through her head.

Hyde's tone was gentle. "Kellie, you need to look at this."

He picked up Dancer's hoof and the horse grunted with pain.

"This hole in the flesh goes straight to the bone. The cartilage, tendons, muscles, and nerves are gone. The necrosis seems to have stopped, but the foot is destroyed." Hyde gently placed the hoof back on the ground, then looked up at her with sad eyes. "There's nothing I can do. Even if the wound heals, he'll never be sound, and he'll always be in pain."

Desperation raged through her. "What about the hyperbarics? The charter plane is standing by, and Roy will prepare Boots and the mare–"

"I believe it's too late. I'm really sorry."

Her knees began to shake and her lungs stopped functioning. She shook her head, mouthing a protest, but no sound came out. Slumping against the stall wall, she fought the shroud of darkness threatening to engulf her.

Hyde slipped his arm around her waist, his face etched with sorrow.

"Come away. I'll get Roy to help me with Dancer."

She tore herself out of his grasp and lurched against the stallion's body, sobs gurgling through her breath. Burying her face in his mane, she bawled, her words jerking through her spasmodic gasps.

"I'm–so–sorry–"

Dancer's smooth coat felt like satin beneath her fingers, a sensation she wanted to preserve forever. A soft deep nicker rumbled through his chest and her world crumbled.

An hour later, drained and numb, she crouched in the shavings in Boots's stall, watching him nose through the hayrack. His fair appetite and alert eye gave her hope that whatever he'd been given wasn't a strong enough dose to inflict critical damage. His legs were wrapped with bandages to the knee, and the protective pad on his good foot seemed to have done its job. Every so often, he'd turn to look at her with curious interest, then return to eating, and another wave of sobs would consume her.

Somewhere in the distance, a heavy growl broke the still air. She closed her eyes, struggling to block out the sounds of a backhoe digging Dancer's grave.

8

Kellie entered the mare barn and absorbed the chorus of whinnies that echoed through the old building. She headed toward Belle's stall, feeling a bond of loss with the mare. At the door, she focused on the horse's beauty, building a baffle against the pain. The mare nickered eagerly, and Kellie smiled. Leo's Belle, one of the last granddaughters of the legendary Leo, was almost too pretty to be a Quarter Horse. Kellie had loved hearing her father's story about purchasing the yearling filly amid jocular speculation that an Arabian stallion had sneaked into the dam's stall. Though Leo's get were sought for their speed, Joshua Sutton had been more interested in Leo's reputation as one of the greatest broodmare sires in history, and Belle had joined the maternity wing when she matured. Wise breeding choices had positioned her to become one of the foundation mares for the Sutton herd.

Brushing the dark brown coat, Kellie's gaze followed the steady rhythmic motions, her mind centered on what she was doing, her subconscious barring any thoughts of Dancer. She smoothed a hand over Belle's back. The mare had maintained good tone through her recent pregnancy and, with Hyde's skilled care, had weathered the traumatic delivery of a stillborn colt. Kellie's eyes watered as she stroked the mare's neck, unable to imagine what it would be like to carry a baby for eleven months, only to lose it in the last hour of pregnancy.

A few minutes later, she settled into the saddle and turned the mare toward the field in front of the main barn.

Belle spotted a band of two-year-olds and neighed loudly. Kellie relaxed the reins and the mare picked up a brisk trot. Foaling and breeding season had jammed Kellie's schedule over the past two months, robbing time from her riding, and she sorely missed the communion with horse and nature. Why had she let this part of her life take a back seat to everything else? Was success that important? Had her drive for success caused her current circumstances?

Belle's muscles bunched and Kellie tightened the reins to pull the horse back to a walk, moving to the fence line where she'd have less chance of finding a gopher hole. Relaxing into the gentle gait, she watched the young horses move toward her. The horror of the day dimmed and she allowed numbness to claim her.

A flash of yellow caught her eye and reality returned. As Sara got off the school bus, Kellie steeled herself against the pain of what would come.

Sara ran to the fence and waved. "I'll go get Juicy and we can ride together!" She dashed toward the barn.

Kellie urged Belle into a fast trot and followed.

Dancer's stall door was ajar and, a second later, Sara stepped out, her face pale.

"Mommy, where's Dancer?"

~~

Travis guzzled the last of the beer and glowered out the window at the sun, sinking low in the sky. Tina flap-mouth was starting to piss him off.

"Goddammit!"

The brown longneck bounced off the wall and careened across the wooden floor, wheeling in a crazy spin-the-bottle frenzy. He yanked open the fridge door, then swore again. Out of beer. Jamming his hat down over his forehead, he headed into the bathroom. The angry mound on the back of his hand glowed in the light of a single naked bulb over the sink. The red circle had turned dark purple and grown to about two inches. The raw center of the bite stuck up a quarter of an inch, oozing pus. He doused the wound with alcohol, sucking in his breath and squeezing his eyes tightly.

The pain dulled and he leaned on the sink. The reflection in the cracked mirror bore no resemblance to the wimpy kid he'd left behind. His dark deep-set eyes, black goatee, and scraggly soul patch added the right amount of macho to his appearance. He grinned, cringing at his ugly teeth–a good reason to keep a scowl as his expression of choice. Years of working outdoors year-round had weathered his skin, almost erasing the acne pits. He adjusted his beat-up straw hat to a more rakish angle. Getting rid of that faggy curly hair had been a stroke of genius. When folks saw the shaved head, they gave him a wide berth.

He wrapped a gauze bandage loosely around his hand, then nodded at the man in the mirror. "Okay, cowboy. Head 'em up and move 'em out."

At the Perkins city limits, he slowed down. The town's claim to fame was a livestock auction, and one police officer in residence spent all his time handing out speeding tickets to the ranchers and farmers who rolled into town once a week. Travis spotted the front bumper of the patrol car protruding from behind a brick building on the corner. He crept past the policeman, tipping his hat and offering a nasty grin.

"Fuck you," he muttered.

The town's only liquor store looked closed. He squinted at the clock on the dashboard, then killed the engine and climbed out. The entrance was locked, but he could see someone moving around inside. He pounded on the door, but the shadow at the back of the room didn't come forward.

"Shit-hole town."

He strode back to his truck, and punched the gas as he pulled onto the road. Gravel rattled beneath the chassis and sprayed out behind the wheels. He flicked on the radio and relaxed a little, bobbing his head and belting it out with Toby Keith. *"How do you like me now?"*

He snorted. "Bitch."

Turning onto Highway 33, he settled back and glanced at the package on the seat beside him. His pulse thumped with anticipation, sending a slice of pain through his swollen hand. A billboard loomed ahead, and he squinted to make out the words. The annual 89er Celebration in Guthrie. He'd had some good times there as a kid, especially watching his dad ride in the rodeo.

Darkness crawled into Travis's heart again, and his fingers clenched the steering wheel.

~~

Ed yawned and took a sip of coffee as he started looking through the stack of lie detector test results. He read Kellie's first and shook his head, imagining her indignation at being questioned. A soft knock on the doorjamb intruded, and Danielle stepped into the room. Her demeanor was more subdued than usual, and Ed braced himself.

"Morning, Danielle. What's up?"

She settled into the chair across from him, a friendly smile crinkling the corners of her wide set eyes. "Not much. It was a quiet night." Her glance moved to the folder in front of him. "Those the polygraph tests on the Sutton case?"

Ed relaxed and nodded. "I was just starting to read through them. I understand Kellie was upset about being questioned."

"Can you blame her?"

"No, but since the circumstances at the crime scene shout "inside job," I'm sure she'll realize the validity of excluding everyone we can."

Danielle nodded, a flicker passing through her eyes that set off alarms in his head. She unfolded from the chair and smoothed the dark brown gabardine over her thighs.

"I don't suppose you want to go get some breakfast?"

He gazed at her for a moment. "Close the door, will you?"

When they had complete privacy, he pursed his lips. "Danielle, I simply cannot have a personal relationship with you, or anyone else on the force. It would be highly unprofessional–what's more, I'm only here until a new sheriff is elected."

Anger flashed in her eyes and venom curled through her words.

"In your dreams! Who do you think you're kidding? Everyone in town knows the *real* reason you're here."

Concern blipped across his radar screen, but he controlled his tone. "And what would that be?"

"Kellie Sutton, of course."

"Don't be ridic–"

The door snapped closed behind her, leaving a waft of spicy scent curling through the air. He exhaled sharply. *That went well.*

He picked up the polygraph tests and quickly read through each one. They all came up negative, providing him some small satisfaction. Kellie didn't deserve to have one of her trusted employees be the person who did this. Or worse, Frank or one of her brothers. Ed's gaze dimmed and thoughts of his love for the red-haired girl twisted their way into his work. Given a chance, could he shuffle the past into some dark corner and speak the words in his heart?

He flipped the folder closed and shoved it away. And what good would *that* do? Would she be by his side when he returned to Washington? Not likely.

He picked up the phone and punched in a number, then waited for Frank to answer. The man was up to something and it had damned well better not have anything to do with

Kellie's horses. Frank came on the line, his tone cautious, and Ed steadied his own voice.

"I want you to call Oklahoma PD right now and make an appointment for a lie detector test, since you weren't around yesterday."

"You're shittin' me! Is this Kellie's idea of a joke?"

"No joke. I'll expect a call from the polygrapher later today."

Frank's tone turned ugly. "You know, Campbell, you've got a lot of nerve comin' into town and throwin' your weight around, just 'cause you won a little tin star. You can't force me to take the test."

"Listen up! Mutilating livestock is a felony. Five grand in fines for starters, and up to seven years in jail. You want to argue any further?"

"I'm the *victim*, for Chrissake!"

"Goodbye, Frank."

Ed punched the disconnect button on the console, then slammed the phone back into its cradle, knocking a logbook off the desk. He reached for the radio on his shoulder, turned it on, then headed down the hall, stopping briefly at the dispatcher's office door.

"I'm going out for breakfast. Be back later."

Anger shifted into irritation as he pushed through the heavy glass door to the street. His role here in Guthrie was one of deep federal importance–what was he doing screwing around with a bunch of cowboys? He stood on the sidewalk for a moment, trying to decide whether to walk to the café or drive. A movement across the street caught his eye and he watched Jesus Hermano emerge from the title company. Ed ducked into the front seat of his unmarked car.

Staying a safe distance behind Hermano's silver Escalade, Ed wound through the downtown streets. Alerted by the man's erratic driving, Ed dropped back even farther. When the Escalade reached the library, it pulled into the parking lot and stopped, but Hermano didn't leave the car. Ed drove past, glancing sideways to see what the driver was doing. He didn't move, just seemed to be waiting for something. Ed drove on, wondering if he'd been spotted. At the next corner, he turned left and pulled into an alley. Creeping back toward the previous street, he could view the library parking lot and Hermano's car. He stopped and waited. In about five minutes, Hermano pulled out and headed north. Ed watched until the Escalade reached the intersection and turned west on Route 33.

Hermano turned in at the new subdivision at the old Red Creek Farm, and Ed continued down Route 33, an idea taking shape in his mind. At Sutton Corners Road, he spotted Frank's Hummer approaching the intersection. Ed accelerated and whizzed past before Frank reached the stop sign. In the rearview mirror, Ed watched the big black vehicle turn right, then he wheeled into a lay-by farther up the road. When Frank's car disappeared from view, Ed gunned it and went after him. It was no coincidence that Hermano and Frank were in the same vicinity at the same time.

To Ed's disappointment, Frank didn't even slow down at the construction site entrance, instead, heading straight into town. Disgusted with the wild goose chase, Ed followed him for a few blocks and, when Frank pulled into the bank parking lot, Ed headed off in the opposite direction to take care of his growling stomach.

The breakfast crowd at the Cowboy Café had long since departed and Ed had the place to himself, at least long enough to get a cup of coffee, order some eggs, and wonder why he was so determined to find Frank dirty. The cowbell on the door announced a customer, and Ed turned as Hyde Browning shuffled in and pulled off his hat.

"Hey, Doc, how's it going?"

The vet's expression sent a bolt of concern through Ed's

chest, but he remained silent.

Hyde sat down and dropped his head into his hands. "Jesus, Ed, I had to put Kellie's stallion down yesterday afternoon."

9

Kellie stepped out onto the front porch and gazed at the patrol car parked in the driveway. She'd spent a sleepless night grappling with images of Dancer evaporating into the darkness as she reached for him, and Sara's heart-wrenching grief. How long would this nightmare last?

Across the lane, Roy emerged from the barn leading Boots. The horse trailer ramp clanged shut, Roy secured it, and closed the doors. Kellie glanced at her watch as the old man started across the yard toward the house.

"Mornin' Miz Kellie. Horses are loaded and we're leaving. I'll be back tomorrow."

"Good, I feel much better knowing you'll be with them for the trip up there."

"They'll be fine."

Walking slowly down the hall toward her room, she thought about what else the day might bring. At the door, she stopped and gazed around, wondering how the room had become such a mess. A hackamore bridle lay in a jumbled heap on the floor. A pair of brown paddock boots stood near the bed and yesterday's jeans hung on the doorknob. A sequined show jacket in need of repair was a sharp reminder of the unexpected changes in her summer plans. Would she ever know any joy again? Why did happiness ebb away, stealthily and unhindered?

She moved to the oak dresser and picked up a wood-framed photograph–the last portrait of a now-disintegrated family. Her father's weather-beaten face scowled from the middle of his brood. Kellie stood in front, her impudent smile framed by flyaway red curls. Three lanky young men stared at the camera, each face almost a clone of the old man. The twins mirrored expressions of boredom, and solemn-faced, grown-up Randy held the hand of his young son, Jethrow.

Kellie's chest tightened as she drew her fingers lightly over the little boy's image–a sullen child who'd borne the fallout of a disastrous marriage. Her only nephew might be the last Sutton in the dynasty, but he was no longer a part of their lives. The familiar sadness surfaced and she drew a ragged breath.

The signs had been there, right in front of her, but she'd preferred to think she understood Jethrow's adolescent misbehavior. The suspensions from school, his surly attitude in the face of authority. Rebellion against a hellish home life? She shuddered. Everyone had given him space, sure that he'd outgrow the phase. Then he'd disappeared without a trace, the final act in a family tragedy.

Her throat ached. How long had they searched for him? Weeks? Months? Why had they all given up so quickly and returned to their own lives and problems?

The barrage of thoughts drained her, opening a chink to vulnerability and self-pity. All the years she'd spent single-handedly guarding the heritage that was hers and her brothers' had been for nothing. No one cared about anything but the money, and *she* had lost everything she'd ever loved, except Sara and the horses.

Who was trying to destroy the only thing she had left?

Small arms slipped around her waist from behind.

Sara's voice was almost a whisper. "Thank you for letting me ride tomorrow."

Kellie turned and stroked the child's velvety cheek, her heart shattering at the sadness in Sara's eyes.

"Hard to believe I waited this long to agree–I was riding in parades when I was seven."

Sara sat down on the edge of the bed. "What are you going to wear to the barbecue?" She wiggled her eyebrows, and the familiar mischievous grin brought out her dimples. "Something sparkly and sexy, I hope!"

"You are too interested in come-hither clothing, young lady. I'll wear something appropriate for my age."

"Mom! You were a rodeo queen, for heaven's sake! You should wear the tiara and everything!"

Kellie couldn't help laughing out loud. "That was a million years ago, and I don't even know where it is."

"*I* do!" Sara jumped up and headed toward the door, then turned back. "Will you wear it?"

Kellie sighed. "We'll see. Right now, get a move on or you'll miss the bus."

Sara's face became solemn. "I love you, Mama."

~~

At ten o'clock, a tour bus turned in at the ranch entrance. Donning her hat, Kellie stared at her reflection in the tack room mirror–her grief was ill concealed. *Think about Ed. Think about Sara. Think about* anything. *Just get through this.* She headed out to meet her visitors.

The bus hissed to a stop and twenty-two people emerged, most of them senior citizens. She preferred this age group for her tours–the younger generations seemed to care nothing for heritage or history.

She smiled woodenly and walked toward them. "Welcome to Rocking S Ranch Quarter Horses on the historic Sutton Estate. I'm Kellie Sutton, a direct descendant of one of the original 1889 Oklahoma Land Rush settlers."

The sea of faces smiled as one and white heads bobbed like dandelion seedpods in a breeze.

"First, we'll take a quick tour of the barns. We've been breeding champion Quarter Horses here since 1977." She moved her arm in a sweeping gesture to include a bank of stalls on her right. "We have five–"

Reality crashed in and she fought the burn behind her eyelids. Emotion shook her voice as she struggled to remain composed. "Four world champions live here, and ninety percent of our colts and fillies go on to win national and regional championships."

A man's voice piped up from the rear of the group. "You race 'em?"

"No, although some of our bloodlines come from strong racing backgrounds. Rocking S horses are bred for the Quarter Horse work ethic–cutting, reining, all-around stock horses." She moved down the aisle and the group followed. "We have forty horses here–correction, forty-one–we just had a new baby. If you'll follow me, we'll go to the mare barn and you can meet her."

Kellie led the way across the gravel to the small building, listening to the sighs of relief as her guests entered the cool interior.

"This is our newest addition, Dancer's Delight."

The name caught in her throat, a reminder of her loss, but the frisky palomino filly took center stage and Kellie pushed the pain back into its hiding place.

One woman put her hand over the stall door and crooned. "Oh, she's so cute."

"Ma'am, please step back. Mares are very protective of their babies. I don't want you to get hurt."

The woman's eyes widened and she jerked her hand back. The man beside her scowled at Kellie.

"If this is dangerous, you shouldn't be having the public in here."

Oh crap, here we go.

"Sir, the tour company passed out information on this facility, which included a disclosure about the possible dangers of being around farm animals." She smiled tightly to take the sting from her rebuke. "I'm sure this mare wouldn't hurt anyone, but I don't want to take chances."

The man huffed loudly and guided his wife to the back of the group.

Kellie headed toward the small office where refreshments had been set up. Why did she go through this every year? There never failed to be one hard-ass in each group, and she always promised herself it would be the last year. However, her determination to educate people on the importance of retaining history and protecting heritage and historic lands always overruled her irritation at human nature.

Fifteen minutes later, she led the group out of the barn and instructed them to line up along the fence.

"For as far as you can see–and farther–is Sutton land. Six hundred-and-forty acres, or one square mile. My great-grandfather, Philander Sutton, was appointed as a federal marshal in 1889. He was instrumental in the preparations for opening the land to settlement. At Noon on April 22, 1889, twenty thousand people dashed across the Kansas and Missouri borders to lay claim to land in the Territory."

A deep voice pierced the warm air. "*Indian* Territory. Land stolen by the government through the cunning Dawes Act."

Kellie exhaled slowly. *This is definitely the last time I'm doing this.*

An elderly gentleman stepped forward through the group. Well-dressed and neatly groomed, he looked like one of the many college professors who spent their holidays traveling.

"Yes sir," she said. "The land was originally inhabited by several Indian tribes, but–"

The man's gray eyebrows came together over piercing

blue eyes. "There are no 'buts'–Guthrie was built in a day at the expense of our Native Americans."

Kellie had only been challenged once before, and she now tried to figure out how to maneuver away from the sensitive subject. The heckler did it for her.

"Sorry. I'm a history professor at Kansas State." He smiled sheepishly. "I can't change history, but I sure can complain about it."

The group laughed nervously and Kellie nodded.

"I understand. Anyway..." She gestured toward the fields. "Philander Sutton was one of the smart settlers, in that he recognized that the poor soil would better support cattle than agriculture. By 1895, he'd purchased parcels from dozens of other settlers who'd given up and returned to their home states. At one point, Philander owned over six square miles of land. Eventually, he sold all but his original stake, here where we stand.

"When Philander died, my grandfather, Daniel Sutton, took over the ranch. In 1913, this red dirt spewed black gold and he became a millionaire overnight." She pointed at the old ranch house she called home. "He built what was then considered a mansion, and raised a daughter and son. My father, Joshua, took an interest in Quarter Horses in the late seventies, and inherited the land when Grandfather Daniel died. The Sutton family has lived and worked here for over a hundred years." She turned back to the group. "Heritage is a precious commodity, and urban sprawl is threatening historic lands such as this. In twenty years, you might not be able to roam this beautiful country or absorb the echoes of the past–"

"Kinda puts you in the Indians' moccasins, huh?"

Kellie gazed at the professor, knowing she had no appropriate response.

She broke eye contact with him and continued. "As you spend the weekend in town, be sure to look at the wonderful architecture. Guthrie is the largest contiguous historic district in the United States, containing over two thousand buildings, many of them meticulously restored.

"Thank you for visiting the historic Sutton Ranch. If you have any questions, I'll be happy to answer them."

The sun had taken its toll on the visitors and most of them mumbled their thanks as they moved quickly toward the air-conditioned bus. Kellie's heart sank as the college professor approached her.

"Ms. Sutton, I'd like to learn a little more about your great-grandfather."

"What would you like to know?"

The man's features hardened a little. "I'm sure you're aware that most of the federal marshals illegally grabbed all the best land before the opening gunshot...How do you feel about that?"

Stay calm. Kellie composed her features into what she hoped was a condescending look.

"Sir, for all the speculation about who jumped the gun, the majority of claims were accepted as fair. With thousands of people swarming over the area, who could possibly have proven otherwise?"

The professor smiled. "And at this point, who cares–right?"

~~

By mid-afternoon, Kellie was losing the battle to keep her anguish at bay. For a while, work details had consumed her brain, filling every moment with ordinary thoughts and activities. Organizing the next ranch tour. Finalizing her speech for the opening ceremonies. Getting Belle shod for parade duty. Then the workday ended and the steel jaws of grief snapped at her again. This was only a bad dream–she'd wake up and find Dancer nosing through the hay. Sorrow and loneliness pressed into her, the memories almost more than she could bear. What would her dad have done in all this? Right up until the end, he'd always had the right answers.

Suddenly, she felt as though she had to get out of there or she'd explode. She hurried out to her truck and, moments later, took a deep breath as she turned onto the highway. Letting her brain absorb the soft browns and yellows of the fields falling away on both sides of the road, she funneled her thoughts to happier times. There *had* been happier times, though they were buried behind the sharper edges of tragedy. She'd dig them out and let them temper her sadness.

Farther up the road, her optimism faltered. The new construction site was no longer a mass of shifting mounds of red dirt. Foundation blocks in geometric designs mapped out a series of structures that would soon have walls and roofs. The speed at which the development was progressing was hard to believe. How soon would the newly sold farm next to her own be transformed?

Twenty minutes later, she drove between the stone pillars marking the entrance to Summit View Cemetery. She stopped, letting the peaceful quiet of the setting wash over her, stilling all the prickles of irritation and disappointment. Lush green grass wandered between elaborate headstones, their polished marble surfaces reflecting the light. Mature trees shaded the road and cast silhouettes against the bright sky. Kellie eased the truck forward and wound slowly along the lane toward the back of the cemetery, admiring the contrast of salmon pink quince and bright yellow forsythia against the myriad shades of green. She pulled over and parked, then sat for a moment, gazing at the Sutton family plot. She hadn't been there in a long time, and apology crept into her thoughts. She'd neglected many things in her quest to be the biggest and the best, and now someone had knocked her down to size and brought her back to her senses. So many things needed reconsideration. She left the truck and stepped through the iron gate surrounding the

Sutton graves.

She stopped to gaze at a large red marble headstone with a bucking bronco and cowboy carved into the polished surface. "Randy Sutton. Always a Champ." She ran her fingers lightly over the stone, thinking back to the day of the funeral and wondering if she'd ever know what happened to Jethrow. Shaking off the unhappy thoughts, she moved toward the rear center of the plot where a simple granite obelisk towered over the other headstones. Kellie had read the inscription many times during her life, and could recite it from memory. "Philander Sutton. A Man With a Vision. Born 1859 - Died 1909". What would he think of Guthrie now? He'd been a forward thinking man who relished growth and prosperity, but would he have welcomed the big-city folk with open arms?

Philander's only son, Daniel, lay buried at the base of his father's monument, and Daniel's son, Joshua, rested beside the obelisk. Kellie dropped to one knee and brushed some dry grass clippings from the base of her father's marble headstone. The family plot was well cared for and she wondered briefly if Roy still made the weekly trip to trim the grass around the grave markers and fence. Shame crept into the thought–it should be her. She cared so much about preserving the land, but couldn't seem to make time in her busy schedule to care for her departed loved ones.

Without warning, her brain flashed an image of a backhoe and Dancer's lifeless body tumbling into a huge hole. Pain slammed her back into reality and she sank to the ground in a fresh torrent of tears.

"Kellie?"

The familiar soft drawl whispered through the stillness.

She scrambled to her feet, swiping the tears from her face and chin, a barrage of emotions rolling over her at the sight of the one person she needed most right then.

Her voice squeaked. "What are *you* doing out here?"

"Came by to visit Dad's grave..." Ed touched her arm, sympathy clouding his beautiful eyes. "I saw Doctor Browning earlier...I'm so sorry."

The full impact of what she'd given up so many years ago hit her hard. She began to sob again, her grief spanning a lifetime.

Ed pulled her into his arms, crushing her against him. His badge bit through her blouse, but the emotional intensity of the embrace dulled the pinch. She sank against him, her body aching for a long lost passion, her mind closed to everything but the man she'd always loved.

"I'll get whoever did this, Kellie. I promise."

She choked back a sob and pressed her face into the smooth fabric of his shirt, inhaling the heady scent of safety. His heart thumped steadily against her ear, and more memories rose to claim her as he stroked her hair and kissed the top of her head.

Her turbulent emotions rose to a boil and she lifted her chin to gaze at him, examine the intricate mosaic shading in his gray eyes, the small white z-shaped scar on his chin, the lips that had always driven her crazy with their softness. The face was familiar, but now mature and bearing signs of a life she knew nothing about.

Her voice broke. "Eddie, we never even had a chance. What happened?"

Pain hovered behind his words. "More than I could have imagined."

"I wrote to you every week. You never answered."

"But I read your letters 'til they disintegrated."

She caressed his cheek, absorbing the warmth and texture, waiting to hear what his eyes were saying.

He broke eye contact and his voice grew husky as he released her. "I can't talk about this right now, but I promise we will."

A million questions whirled through her brain as she watched him walk down the cemetery lane toward his car. Would all the answers fall into place for them? Could she help fit the pieces together, or would her inborn resistance to change trip her up again? She rubbed her shoulders where his arms had been, the sensation of the embrace still singing through her body. For the first time in years, she felt a ripple of joy and optimism in her heart. It was up to her to change the course of her destiny.

10

Ed unlocked the door to his apartment and stepped into the small living room, a whitewater surge of emotions and memories rushing through his head. Kellie in his arms had sent his world-weary brain into teenage overdrive. The scent of her hair, her body pressed against his, trembling with grief, seeking his protection, if only for the moment. The years melted and she was his again–his alone, with an entire lifetime to savor every moment of their love. He sat on the side of the bed and stared at the carpet. He had less than two months to find out if she'd disappoint him again.

The small white phone vibrated against his chest and he tucked Kellie into a private part of his brain.

"Hello Chief, I was about to call you. I spotted Hermano in town again this morning. He was at the title office, then I tailed him out to a big new development west of town. He seemed pretty cozy with a couple of the workers."

"Let me know if you see him around there again. I might need to send in one of our Hispanic agents to get near him." Some papers rustled on the other end of the line. "We have a new twist in Okee City. Seems Columbian drug lord Estevan Rodriguez has set up headquarters at Remington Park. Perfect cover–the place is teeming with Mexicans and money. I'll have the agent in charge down there bring you up to speed. I think we're getting close."

Ed nodded thoughtfully, trying to piece together the connections between Frank's race activities and his apparent association with Hermano. How would racing tie in with real estate? Ed squinted at a spot on the carpet. Had Frank received part of the Sutton land in the divorce settlement? Maybe land with a lot of strings attached? Land worth a lot of money to the developers? Enough money to destroy Kellie's business so she'd sell out?

"Ed? Commissioner McBee tells me you have a high visibility crisis going on down there. Anything I need to know?"

"Nope. I can handle it."

Tossing the phone onto the bed, he exhaled sharply. "Crap. How did this get so complicated?"

He shook his head and toed out of his black trooper boots. "I should have busted Frazier in the chops."

No, that would have taken the situation to personal. Can't let anything jeopardize shutting down these scumbags.

He donned faded jeans and a dark blue polo shirt, then pulled on a pair of scuffed brown western boots. He looked around at the unassuming quarters he'd called home for the past four months. A vivid contrast to his upscale condo in DC's Germantown.

He picked up the bedroom phone. "Campbell here. Did Frank Frazier's polygraph come in this afternoon?"

"Yeah, but the guy said he wanted to talk to you about it. I told him you'd be in tomorrow."

"Okay. Tell Deputy Stearns to go out to the Rocking S and stick close to Kellie Sutton. She's being stalked and I promised her some protection."

An hour later, Ed cruised through the mass of cars at Remington Park race track. Every imaginable make, color, and style of vehicle produced a sparkling art deco pattern in the early evening sun. The array covered the gamut from faded broken down pick-up trucks to tenderly cherished vehicles costing many thousands of dollars. Horse racing–everyman's game. Eventually, he spotted the black HumVee parked inside a gated area marked "Owners Only".

~ ~

Frank leaned both elbows on the table, and ran his finger through the condensation on the beer bottle in front of him. Loud voices, laughter, and the clamor of televised races filled the dim smoky bar, and he retreated into his thoughts. He needed some time to figure out what to do about the situation at the ranch. The newspaper editor was a loose cannon, and Frank could do nothing to keep the details of Dancer's death off the front page. Kellie's devastated face crowded into his thoughts and a small trickle of remorse found its way into his head. Under normal circumstances, he should have comforted her, shared her grief. But nothing had been normal for them, not even in the beginning. And though he'd never admit it to anyone, he had no one to blame but himself.

He rubbed his arm where the blood pressure cuff had squeezed. *Fuckin' sheriff, all full of himself, struttin' around town like he owned the place, making a big splash to impress Kellie.* How could Campbell think he, Frank, would destroy perfectly good horses? And for what reason? Dancer had been the biggest moneymaker on the ranch. Frank thought hard, trying to remember how much semen they'd collected and frozen over the winter. The gravy train would come to an end eventually, but now that the stallion was gone, Frank could raise the stud fees for the horse's valuable genes.

Another surge of anger bristled over his skin. Kellie had no business treating him like the hired help. He'd kept the ranch finances in the black for years. She could at least show some gr–

A short dark skinned man slid into the opposite seat. "Frazier, there's a problem. Boss wants to see you."

"What problem? The horse is jacked up real good. He'll win."

"I wouldn't keep the man waiting, if I were you."

Son-of-a-bitch. I know exactly where this is headed. Frank rose, threw a dollar on the table, and followed the groom. The afternoon races were in full swing, and throngs of bettors crowded up to the windows and filled the passageways to the grandstands. The concrete floor was sticky with spilled soda and beer, and littered with popcorn and discarded tickets. He usually enjoyed the ambience, but now it seemed depressing, shadowed by the prospect of a conversation with the man in charge of his financial future.

Frank followed the groom through a door at the end of the public area and descended a flight of iron stairs. At the bottom, the messenger turned left and they passed a dark red fire door guarded by a thuggish looking man with a rifle. At the end of the hall, Frank rapped twice on another fire door, then entered a small dim office.

He stepped up to a gray metal desk, face to face with Estevan Rodriguez. The Colombian scowled, accentuating the deep acne scars that peppered his cheeks.

"Why are you all over the newspapers?"

"I didn't know that was going to happen. My ex-wife went off the deep end and the story got out before I could stop it."

"My people say your property is crawling with cops. Is this so?"

Frank nodded numbly, and Rodriguez rose from behind the desk, malice thickening his accent.

"You fix it. Understand?"

"I don't know what I can do–"

"Figure it out. Every day we are out of operation costs hundreds of thousands of dollars."

Frank swallowed hard. He was a mere pawn in something so big and so sinister that he had no control over his fate.

The Colombian's smile was little more than a grimace.

"I see that your beautiful daughter and her pinto pony will be part of the celebration this weekend. What a shame if it would be spoiled by an unfortunate accident."

~ ~

Ed pulled his baseball cap down over his forehead and slipped on a pair of dark glasses as he strode toward the entrance to the wagering area. The temperature was still warm, and the gun in his waistband stuck to the skin at the small of his back. Inside, he stopped and pulled the glasses down to let his eyes adjust. Signs indicated the direction of the barns, the clubhouse, the bar, the restrooms, and the restaurant. He pondered for a moment whether to try to locate Frank at the barns. Too risky. He'd stay here where the crowds would provide good cover.

Just then, Frank and a short Hispanic man with a limp emerged from the bar, and Ed shrank back against a pillar. The two men walked toward the end of the concourse and Ed followed, moving with groups of people who milled about, waiting for the next race to begin. Frank's companion opened an unmarked door and the two of them disappeared. Ed waited a few moments, then followed. The door led to a flight of stairs, and he heard footsteps echoing somewhere ahead of him, then a door closed with a thud. At the bottom of the stairs, he rounded the corner and came up short, face-to-face with an armed guard who looked like something out of a 30's mob movie.

"You don't belong down here."

Ed affected a silly grin. "I'm lookin' for the crapper."

The man's stony expression didn't change, but his fingers tightened visibly around the barrel of the rifle. "Upstairs."

Ed kept his eyes on the guard and backed toward the stairs. "Uh, sorry. Thanks."

In his peripheral vision, a door opened at the end of the long hallway, and Frank emerged alone. Ed hurried up the steps and strode down the concourse toward the safety of the crowds. If he had to bet on anything, it would be that Frank and Estevan Rodriguez were doing business.

~ ~

The heavy fire door closed with a thump behind Frank and he strode down the passageway toward the stairs, his footsteps echoing against the concrete walls. Bile rose in his throat. *Goddamned Spic! I oughta break his ugly neck!* Grabbing the handrail, he took the stairs two at a time, and pushed through the door to the main level. The odor of stale popcorn and cigarette smoke hit him in the face, and he exhaled sharply. He looked up at the large clock over the entrance to the track, then glanced around and caught sight of Celeste. She walked toward him in sexy open toed high heels, her curves moving seductively under the soft folds of a peach colored dress. Her blonde curls were caught back in a chiffon scarf, and her dazzling smile immediately took the edge off his anger. She made him feel good because she always cared about what was going on in *his* life. Kellie had never made that effort–the specter of Ed Campbell had always been between them.

Celeste's perfume caressed Frank's senses and he pushed away all thoughts of his ex-wife.

He slipped an arm around her waist and squeezed. "Ready to watch Dawg win?"

Her eyes sparkled as she waved several pink stubs. "I already put all my money on him."

"My kind of girl!"

He took her elbow and guided her through the crowd toward the entrance to the owner skyboxes. Just touching her soft skin sent his internal temperature soaring. They wouldn't dally long after the race.

When they were seated, he focused on the horses warming up in the paddock. Sleek, nervous Thoroughbreds frothed at the mouth and tossed their heads, while grooms and jockeys kept light control on the energy that would be the controlling factor in a race.

Celeste's tone was animated. "He looks real good, Frankie."

"Yeah, I have a good feeling about today. We gave him something for that pulled tendon, and he was pretty frisky at the stall a while ago."

Her eyes widened. "You gave him *pain killers*? Isn't that a little dangerous?

He chuckled and whispered into her hair. "There are ways, my dear, of getting around the authorities."

"When are you running that new horse you got?"

"The one Kellie was so pissed about?"

Celeste shook her head. "I can't see why she got mad, since you paid for him."

"She doesn't approve of racing. Her precious Quarter Horses are too good for *that*."

"Well, for crying out loud! Isn't that how they got their name? Quarter Horses–quarter mile? *Duh!*"

"She thinks Boondoggle would have made a better cutting horse, but I'm here to tell you, his pedigree is pure race, all the way back to Three Bars. The ranch is a goldmine of racing talent, but I'll never get a chance at 'em as long as she has any say."

He settled back into the seat, wondering if he dared confide his secret to Celeste. She made him feel so secure and confident–surely nothing would change that.

~ ~

Ed rolled down the windows in the car and turned up the fan. The temperatures had been unusually warm for April, especially for an Easterner who kept a winter coat on through the end of May. He gazed out the windshield, thinking about the upcoming weekend festivities. It had been a long time since he'd been part of the 89er Days, his favorite time of year as a kid. Tomorrow, he'd see what kind of nag the department had lined up for him to ride in the parade.

The temperature inside the car equalized, and he opened his record book to make notes on Frank. The blonde woman must be Celeste Harding. A real dish, enough to make any man's head swim, but her coy manner and clingy body language turned Ed off. He preferred strong, intelligent women–outdoorsy, exuberant women. Like Kellie. He stopped writing and frowned. What had she ever seen in Frank? What an unlikely match.

Frank Frazier. Town hoodlum turned jock. His stellar high school football record had attracted the attention of the scouts, and he'd gleefully thumbed his nose at Guthrie and headed off to training camp. Ed snorted and started the car. While dodging gunfire and breathing sand, he'd laughed like hell when he read the news clipping from his dad. Frank had washed out and come skulking back to Guthrie with his tail between his legs. Ed slammed the gearshift into drive. Why the fuck would Kellie marry someone like that?

His own reaction startled him, an emotion still as strong as when he'd first heard the news. Frank was an all-around loser and, right now, he was on the road to proving it big time.

Ed squinted at Tina Brown's address in his record book, then headed south toward the city.

~~

Grunting, Travis tried to straighten one leg over the seat back, but the steering wheel hindered the effort. He struggled to sit up, then gazed through the windshield at the small plain house surrounded by brown fields, hazy in the early morning mist. *Home. Big fuckin' deal.* His neck and back muscles twanged with the attempt to change position, and his head thumped with the aftermath of a six-pack at midnight. He bumped his hand against the door handle and a searing pain ran up his arm.

"Shit! Shit!" He closed his eyes and waited for the agony to subside.

His cell phone rang and, a second later, he snatched it away from his ear and swore. "Jeezus, Tina, calm down! I can't understand a fuckin' word you're saying."

The girl's voice shrilled with panic. "I've been trying to call you all night! Where were you? That sheriff from Guthrie was at my apartment when I got home from work. He thinks I was casing the Sutton ranch to steal some horses!"

Travis swallowed a chuckle. *Oh yeah, right.* This broad couldn't organize a feed schedule, let alone a theft.

"They want me to take a lie detector test–what am I gonna do?" She started to cry.

Anger slammed through his gut. He hated goddamned tears.

"Knock it off, Tina. If you're innocent, the test will prove it."

"What do you mean, *if* I'm innocent? I've been with you for weeks. You told me I needed an alibi. Will you talk to them?"

A slab of concern moved through his brain. *Shit. How could getting laid have fucked me up so bad?*

"Yeah, okay. Quit yer fussin'. I got stuff to do, I'll call you later."

He closed the phone and punched the truck into gear. Tina was history.

On the drive into town, his thoughts returned to his careless comment. She'd continued to press, asking why he thought she needed an alibi. He'd finally convinced her the comment was a throwaway, that she had nothing to worry about if she could prove her whereabouts when questioned. Still, the issue of timing had hung in the air. He'd have to tread carefully around her. Better yet, ditch her. *Too bad. I was kinda starting to like her.*

11

Guthrie hadn't changed much–it still looked like the movie set for a western shoot 'em up. But Travis had to admit the place looked pretty good all duded up for the celebration. He cruised slowly down Second Street, then turned onto Oklahoma. The town hadn't wakened yet, and he allowed himself the luxury of thinking about happier memories on those streets–recollections of a small boy and his hero father. The drugstore windows were dark, but Travis visualized sitting on the red vinyl stool at the soda fountain, spinning 'round and 'round 'til his dad told him to knock it off or go sit in the truck. Damn, those milkshakes were good! He'd have to get him one before he left town. He squinted again at the sign on the window.

"Shit. Drugstore Museum? Who the hell cares about a bunch of dusty old crap?"

As he approached Division, he looked up at the sparkling white dome of the Gray Brothers Building and grinned.

"God damn! Got my butt whipped for that disaster!"

It had been a cinch to jimmy the lock on the stairwell and, from his aerie at the top of the tower, the sky had been so brilliant and blue. The dusty old room had been the perfect place to hide–no screaming fights, no slamming doors, no one bellerin' at him to go to his room.

Anger surged through his head. All he'd wanted was to be left alone. But no, his wimpo father had made a big deal, called the police, reported him missing...

Someone honked behind him and he punched the gas, sending the memories back into the dark.

For as long as he could remember, The Cowboy Café had been a local haunt, and he found some comfort in seeing that it hadn't been gobbled up by the tourist-driven community and turned into some damned side show.

He sat down at the counter and a robust young woman beamed. "Howdy. Beautiful morning, huh?"

He nodded and reached for the newspaper on the seat beside him. "Just coffee. Black."

"You from around here?"

He looked up and glared. "Nope. Can I have that coffee sometime this morning?"

She huffed indignantly and moved toward the coffeemaker at the end of the counter as he unfolded the paper.

*"**Tragedy Strikes Rocking S Ranch**. World Champion Cutting Horse Docs Dirty Dancing was destroyed yesterday after a battle with infected wounds caused by vandalism. In what can only be described as something from a thriller, someone apparently slipped into the barn about two weeks ago and injected the Quarter Horse stallion and two other horses with an unidentified substance that ate away the flesh and bone of their left front feet. Veterinarian Hyde Browning was reluctant to give details, but did say that the infection itself was not life threatening, but the resulting acute laminitis, also known as founder, had crippled the stallion beyond saving. Docs Dirty Dancing was the foundation stud of one of the most prestigious Quarter Horse breeding operations in the country.*

Owner Kellie Sutton was unavailable for comment, but sources say that the other horses have been transported to Kentucky for hyperbaric oxygen therapy–a new frontier in equine medicine.

No suspects have been identified, according to Sheriff Ed Campbell, but Rocking S has offered a $50,000 reward for information leading to the arrest and conviction of the person or persons responsible."

Travis laid the paper aside. A mug of coffee sat in front of him and he took a swallow, listening to the sounds of other people in the café. He glanced down the row of stools along the counter. A couple of faces were familiar and, for a moment, he wondered if coming into town had been too bold. The café door swung open and a hard-faced man stepped inside. *I'll be damned, that's the old guy from the newspaper–he hasn't changed a bit.*

The man stepped up to the counter next to Travis and motioned to the waitress. "I need some of those fancy doughnuts and a large pop." He turned and lowered his voice. "Women in the office all look like hippos–you'd think they'd stay away from this crap."

Travis grinned. The guy didn't have a clue who he was talking to. "You'd think."

"You in town for the big doings?"

"Yep. Just got in from Tulsa. Is there a schedule posted somewhere?"

The editor picked up the newspaper, turned to an inside page, and folded it back. "Everything you need to know. This is the 89er special edition. I'm the editor." His gaze dropped to Travis's bandage. "What'd you do to your hand?"

"Got it caught in a dishwasher. She beat the crap outta me."

The newsman threw his head back and roared with laughter, then grabbed the paper sack of doughnuts off the counter and tossed down a couple of bills.

"Enjoy your visit."

"You can count on it."

~~

Frank wheeled the Hummer into a parking spot in front of the Logan County Sheriff's Department. The sexy evening with Celeste had cleared his brain and, on the drive home from Edmond, he'd given more detailed thought to the scene with

Rodriguez. The man was a cockroach, but a dangerous one. He held the reins on Frank's fortune and had the capability to destroy Frank's life with a single word. *Time to get involved.*

Inside the old fashioned building, Frank approached the heavy glass window of the dispatch office.

A deputy looked up. "Oh man, Frank, I saw the paper. How's Kellie holding up?"

"Fine. I need to see Ed Campbell."

The deputy seemed taken aback for a second. "He's out on a call. Want to leave a message?"

"Will he be back soon?"

The young man shook his head. "I don't think so. He and Jimmy–oh, there they are now."

The old animosity rose in Frank's chest as he stepped forward to meet Campbell. "I need to talk to you privately."

"Be with you in a minute." Campbell reached across the counter for a clipboard and signed in. "Hold my calls."

Frank followed him down the hall, irritation mushrooming into anger. The asshole was being damned close to rude. He seemed to think the badge gave him a lot of leeway.

The sheriff closed the door, motioned Frank toward a chair, then sat down at the desk. "What's up?"

Frank ignored the gesture to sit down. "I need to be in the loop on this mess. Christ, the ranch is crawling with deputies, the local news is focusing on the situation and disrupting business, and Kellie's a wreck."

A sharp glint flashed through the steely gaze, the only ripple in Campbell's cool demeanor. "And you're surprised?...I understand your concern about the horses, but our responsibility for keeping anyone in the loop extends only to the owner."

A vein throbbed in Frank's temple. He was getting damned tired of sucking hind tit. "I *am* an owner. Now give."

Campbell pushed three photographs across the desk. "I think you should see these. Kellie's being stalked."

Frank glanced at the snapshots and a knife drove through his insides. Kellie had gone straight to her old flame–another chance to be with him, maybe even hook up. Were they already screwing?

He snorted. "Her imagination is in overdrive. Those are just old snapshots she doesn't remember."

Campbell's tone hardened. "Look a little closer, *friend*–these were taken through a long range lens."

Frank picked them up and stared at the grainy pictures, seeing them clearly for the first time. Fear replaced derision. The organization was sending a message–not to Kellie, but to *him*. He laid the photos back on the desk and swallowed, taking a moment to put some confidence in his voice.

"You have a good suspect and you haven't arrested her yet. What's the holdup?"

"We're checking out her alibi."

"Which is?"

Campbell exhaled in exasperation. "Frank, this is police business."

Frank shook his head and grinned, softening his tone. "C'mon, Ed–I might be able to help. I get around, I hear things."

Campbell studied him for a moment. "She claims to have been with some local cowboy every night for the past two weeks. We just have to find him."

"What's his name?"

"Nice try, Frank, but that's all I can tell you. We're working on this full time. Just let us do our job."

He stood up and Frank glared at the lawman's tense features. "When was the last time you worked full time on *anything*? You come waltzing back to town, taking a job that should have gone to a local. It seems to me you have a personal stake in this mess."

The sheriff's jaw hardened and a muscle in his right

cheek twitched once. Frank almost smiled. He'd hit a nerve.

Campbell's tone was terse. "I think it's called loyalty to a friend. What's *your* excuse?" He took two long strides and opened the office door.

Frank brushed past him, anger surging through his head as he moved quickly down the hall. Campbell's footsteps echoed close behind him.

As they passed the desk, the duty officer spoke.

"Sheriff, Tulsa PD has a line on Travis Mack. And Kellie Sutton called."

~~

Ed watched Frank slam through the front door and descend the stairs to the sidewalk. Something about the urgency in his step said trouble was afoot.

Ed started toward the door, calling over his shoulder. "I'm going out for a bit. My radio will be on if you need me. If the polygrapher calls, get a number and I'll be right back to him."

He hurried down the steps, catching a glimpse of Frank's vehicle turning toward the railroad tracks. Jumping into the unmarked car, he did a U-turn and cruised to the corner just in time to see Frank pull into the parking lot of the old depot building. Ed removed his hat and eased along the street until he could see the Hummer parked behind the train station. Through the camera, he watched while Frank made a phone call.

Ed's gut reaction was right: though Frank's lie detector test had come back negative, he was up to no good.

~~

Frank dialed, then slouched in the front seat and scowled. *Even a blind man could see Campbell still has the hots for Kellie.* A long slow breath took the edge off the annoyance. Kellie had never really loved him–he knew that. She'd needed a ranch manager, and he'd happened along. At the time, it had seemed like a good idea, and the Sutton fortune hadn't been easy to ignore, either. Still, the rumors around town about her broken engagement had made him uncomfortable, but he'd eventually managed to put it out of his mind and stumble through their pretend marriage.

Who'd have thought the local hero would come home? Frank squinted at the railroad tracks ribboning off into the distance. Question was–who had enough influence to get Campbell that county appointment on such short notice?

A gruff voice came on the phone and Frank straightened up in the seat. "I have to find someone. Can you help?"

"Depends. How much you pay?"

"Two grand for an address."

"You clear this with the boss?"

"Hey, you want the money or not?"

"Don't want my ass shot off."

Frank closed his eyes and steadied his voice. "Rodriquez told me to take care of something, and I need some information. I'll take full responsibility."

"What's the name?"

"Travis Mack. He hangs around with a girl named Tina Brown. She lives at 6 South Hanes there in the city."

~~

Pete Dayton telephoned as Kellie was organizing the staff for another ranch tour.

"Last night at a breeder's banquet, I saw that exhibitor you filed the complaint against, and in the course of conversation, I found out she just returned from four weeks in Europe, so I guess she couldn't be responsible for the attacks on your horses."

"Yeah, I'd already eliminated her–she'd be a fool to jeopardize her career. But thanks for letting me know what you found out."

"Any new developments?"

Tears sprang to Kellie's eyes. "Dancer died yesterday," she squeaked.

Her words echoed through the silence on the other end of the phone, and she prayed that Pete's sympathy wouldn't unravel her. Finally, he spoke and the message was there.

"Yes, I know–I'll be up there for the weekend. Please let me know if there's anything I can do for you."

She sat quietly for a few moments after he hung up. How long would it take for the intense pain to fade? She pushed idly through a stack of mail, pulling out two small white envelopes hand addressed to "Kellie Sutton and Family." She slid her finger under the flap and removed a card with a drawing of a horse head on the front. Her throat ached as she read. *"My heart goes out to you in your loss. Your pain is felt by all horse owners, and I only wish I could do something to help you. My prayers are with you and your family."* Tears blurred the signature of someone she didn't know in California.

She picked up the other envelope and struggled through another statement of sympathy from Iowa. *"Of all the things I have experienced in twenty years with Quarter Horses, nothing saddens me like this whole nightmare. Please know that there are a lot of us out here you may not know, but we care very deeply. My heart goes out to the whole Sutton family."*

Others had felt her personal pain, and the thought was somehow comforting. With such support, she'd get through this, but she'd never know peace until Dancer's killer was brought to justice.

At noon, a tour bus rumbled away from the barn and Kellie released a long sigh of relief. Twenty-nine fifth graders–more exuberant energy than she'd been up to, but they'd seemed to enjoy meeting the foals. She flipped the light switch in the office, instantly irritated by the sight of Frank's deserted desk. So far, he'd done a disappearing act for both ranch tours.

Her annoyance faded. *Maybe he's as tired of this charade as I am.*

She moved toward her own desk, then focused on an object lying there. She sank into the chair and picked up a stick decorated with beads and feathers. One end of the wood had been carved into a horse's head, complete with fine leather halter and beads for eyes. She touched the fine, dark red horsehair knotted at the poll to form a forelock. More strands ran the length of the neck and another long hank made up the tail. Pressure grew in her chest. The wood had been painted and burnished to a deep copper. She pressed the effigy of Dancer against her chest and struggled again with her loss, absorbing yet another offer of sympathy.

12

Kellie glanced in the rearview mirror to check on the trailer, then looked over at Sara. "Ready to bring home the trophy?"

"Of course! Sonny Black will be the only other good rider there, and he's been grounded a week for skipping school."

"Meaning?"

"He isn't allowed to ride when he's in trouble, so he'll be out of practice."

Sara's smug expression didn't sit well with Kellie. "Don't gloat over someone else's misfortune, my dear. Bad chickens always come home to roost."

"Where do they go before they come home?"

"It's just an expression meaning–"

"I know what it means, Mother. I'm not *stu*pid."

Sara's pre-show jitters were obviously getting the best of her. Kellie changed the subject.

"What do you want for your birthday?"

"A roping saddle."

Kellie threw her a sharp look. "You are *not* going to rodeo. Period."

"Why? Because I'm a girl? *You* did it!"

"I know, and Grandpa nearly went crazy every time I competed." *Not to mention my boyfriend.* "It's too dangerous, honey. I want you to grow up with all your parts intact."

Sara's jaw jutted out in defiance. "You are *so* mean.

When I'm older, I can do anything I want."

Kellie pushed away the painful jab and concentrated on the road ahead. *God help me when she enters puberty.*

Two hours later, Kellie dropped onto a bench in the fourth row of the bleachers and watched the ground crew set up for the next event. Melancholy swept over her. Sara was growing up, seeming to need less and less of her mother's support, gravitating more toward her circle of friends at school and in the horse club. Getting ready for a horse show had always been an enjoyable mother-daughter event, but today Sara had made it clear that she wanted to hang out with her friends and prepare Juicy all by herself. Quelling her disappointment, Kellie scanned the audience, hoping for a familiar face.

~~

Travis scuffed through the dusty parking area behind the 4-H building, pulling a last drag on his cigarette before he entered. He'd spent the afternoon in a tavern on the east side, and the heavy warm air was making him sleepy. Nature pressed him to find the men's room and, as he entered, he glanced at a young boy standing at the urinal. The kid's gaze dropped immediately to the bandage, and Travis stepped into one of the stalls and latched the door behind him. A second later, he heard the urinal flush and the restroom door bump closed. His bandaged hand was attracting too much attention. He gingerly unwound the gauze and dropped it into the toilet, grimacing at the nasty looking colors and textures covering most of the back of his hand. The center of the wound had tunneled into the flesh, spreading to the size of a dime.

He glowered at the soggy gauze floating in the toilet. *Shit, maybe that wasn't such a hot idea.* He savagely kicked the flush handle. Not a helluva lot he could do about it now.

Minutes later, he sat down on a hard metal bench and scanned the grandstand. She'd be there–he'd already checked the show office. As he finished the thought, she climbed up to a good vantage point in the bleachers. Even from a distance, he could see the strain on her face.

~ ~

A tall man in a brown county uniform stepped through one entrance, and a jerk of excitement raced through Kellie's chest. Everywhere she went now, she anticipated seeing Ed. The officer removed his hat, and disappointment drained away the brief rush. She looked over the spectators in the next section, seeing some familiar faces, but mostly tourists. At the top of that section, a man sat with his elbows on his knees, staring intently at the arena. She focused on the unfriendly features and dark eyes staring from beneath a battered straw hat. He looked out of place in this country setting.

The public address system boomed the opening of the pole bending class, and she sat back to watch. The first three competitors did poorly. One of them knocked over two poles, and the other two riders either had slow horses or were too cautious. Outside the gate, Sara walked Juicy in circles to keep him supple. Another rider entered the ring, and Kellie watched with little interest.

"Hey Sis!"

Frick and Frack. Kellie jumped up from her seat. "You were going to call, remember?"

Cliff wrapped his arms around her and squeezed hard. "I forgot." He stepped away, and Kellie smiled at her other brother.

"Clarke, what a wonderful surprise!"

Her discerning eye didn't miss the pallor and thin body. She hugged him hard, feeling the edges of his bones through the soft chambray shirt.

His voice was strong and deep. "Haven't been to a celebration in years, so when Cliff said he was coming up, I hitched a ride." He stepped back. "Where's Sara?"

Kellie pointed to the in-gate where Sara waited for the

signal to enter the ring.

"Wow, she's really grown!"

Kellie grimaced. "You don't know the half of it."

The starter bell clanged and Sara shot through the gate, light in the saddle, letting Juicy do the work. They wove in and out between the poles, clearing each one by only inches. At the end of the course, Juicy wheeled on his hind legs and raced toward the out-gate, Sara leaning forward until she was almost flat. The audience shouted approval, and the announcer gave the results. Sara's time was the best by a full 7 seconds.

"Damn, she's really good! Looks like you might get your crown taken away."

Kellie glowered good-naturedly at Cliff. "No chance. She'd have to beat me in everything else, and that won't happen 'cause I'm not letting her do anything but poles and barrels."

Cliff shook his head. "I seem to remember you having the same argument with Dad, and look how *that* ended up." His expression sobered. "What's going on at the ranch? We saw something on the national news last week about attacks on the horses."

Kellie steeled herself, then began to describe the horror of the past week.

Clark whistled. "Holy crap. I'm sure sorry. What are you going to do?"

"We've installed security cameras and offered a reward. Other than that, we just have to wait while the sheriff's department investigates."

An uncomfortable silence ensued, then Cliff cleared his throat. "Listen, we need to talk about some things."

~~

Travis straightened on the bench and watched the two men approach Kellie. *Damn! I couldn't have done this better if I'd planned it!* He waited until the three of them sat down, then moved down the bleachers to a seat four rows behind them.

A fat woman in a bright red shirt and stained cowboy hat grinned. "Great show, huh?"

Travis gritted his teeth, suppressing a snarl. "Yep."

She leaned over, lowering her voice to a conspiratorial tone. "Those are the Suttons down there in front of us. They're real important here...founding fathers and all. Got good horses, too."

He nodded. "So I hear."

"Yeah, and someone–"

Travis stood up and moved down two rows, then stared at a distant point across the arena, listening carefully to the conversation about Kellie's rodeo days.

A small girl on a brilliant pinto flashed into the arena and raced skillfully through the poles. Travis followed her progress and grinned. *So that's the brat, huh? She's pretty good, a real Sutton.* When the applause died down, he tuned in again to the conversation taking place below him.

"Cliff, I can't believe you're bringing this up! I am *not*–repeat–*not* going to sell! What part of this don't you understand?"

"Kellie, we all stand to make a lot of money on the deal. This area is exploding and absorbing the overflow from Oklahoma City. Edmond is saturated, and this is the obvious direction of the expansion."

"I don't care about the money. I want to die right here on the land where I grew up."

"*You* may not care about the money, but the rest of us do. Hell, I could–"

"Cliff, you're forgetting one thing. Part of the estate belongs to Jethrow. Without his agreement, we couldn't sell it anyway."

Cliff snorted. "Like we even know if he's still alive. That argument won't work. With the amount of time that's passed, we could have him declared legally dead."

Kellie jumped up from her seat. "This conversation is over. I need to go help Sara load her horse onto the trailer."

The two men rose and followed her to the aisle. "We can talk about this again tomorrow at the ranch."

Kellie walked away, and the men looked at each other knowingly.

Travis sat back on the bench, consumed by an awesome idea.

~ ~

"Sheriff Campbell here." Ed cradled the phone against his shoulder, listening to the lieutenant in Oklahoma City.

"Did you have a chance to look at Frank Frazier's polygraph?"

Ed frowned and slipped a sheaf of reports into a folder. "Yeah, he seems to have passed with flying colors."

"Only insofar as the questions relating directly to the crime at the horse ranch. If you look at the report, you'll see very erratic reactions to a couple of questions. His readings were all over the map when I asked him if he'd ever been involved in anything illegal, but when asked directly about attacking the horses, he was unruffled. He's lying about *something*, but I don't think it pertains to this particular crime."

"Thanks a lot, Lieutenant. Ms. Sutton will be relieved to hear that. What about Cliff and Clarke Sutton?"

"No answer. I left a message for them to call."

Ed hung up and stared thoughtfully into space. Frankie Boy was beginning to look like somebody's pawn. Noise in the hall broke the chain of thought, and Ed glanced at his watch. Change of shift. He rose and closed the door, then pulled out the small white phone.

"Chief? I'm starting to connect the dots here. I'm certain the Columbians have recruited one of the locals, and he just happens to be a principal in the horse vandalism crime. Can you get me a profile on Franklin Frazier?"

"You'll have it within the hour. Latest update is that Jesus Hermano is the go-between for the racetrack drug cartel and some land developers. We're thinking money laundering."

Ed thought for a moment. "Makes sense. This area has exploded with condos and fancy homes." He snorted. "If you've never been to Guthrie, you wouldn't know what I mean. This town has aggressively preserved its heritage from the Land Rush days, and I suspect all this shiny new construction is driving the locals crazy. Every week, another old farm is plowed under."

"I'll get the info on Frazier. Any chance he's part of the land scheme?"

"Don't know, but I intend to find out."

Ed gazed at the fading screen and thought about his sudden involvement in Kellie's life. It certainly wasn't how he'd envisioned the reconnection. He shook his head. Too much going on to spend much time pondering. He picked up the desk phone and dialed.

An old man's voice answered on the fourth ring. "Rockin' S, this is Roy."

"Is Ms. Sutton there? This is Sheriff Campbell."

"Nope, she and Sara went to a horse show."

"How about Mr. Frazier?"

The old man snorted. "Not here. Never here. Just left, said he was going to check fences, but he's probably goin' to the ponies."

Ed hung up, grabbed his hat, and hurried down the hall. Danielle stepped out of the break room and they collided. Ed grabbed her arms to steady her, but she pulled away and gave him a haughty look, then stalked down the hall, her round butt undulating beneath the close fitting trousers.

How the hell am I going to put out that *fire?* He shook his head, then continued out of the building. *Frank Frazier is the key to this mess and, by God, I'm going to get to the bottom of it.*

Ten minutes later, he turned onto Sutton Corners Road. Up ahead, a rental van was just pulling onto the road, and he slowed down. An elderly couple stood in the front yard, talking to Jesus Hermano. Ed pulled off his hat and slouched into the seat, pulling onto the shoulder to let the van pass. Hermano was smiling and shaking hands with the old man, and the exchange appeared to be pleasant. As soon as the van cleared the driveway, Ed drove on, reaching for the radio.

"Guthrie One, calling for backup at Sutton Corners Road."

"Unit 3, Chief. We're at the entrance to the Sutton place."

"There's a silver Escalade, license Rambo-seven-four-Peter-Mary-eight, parked at the Borden farm. Follow him, tell me every place he goes. I'll be on channel four."

~ ~

Frank gritted his teeth and drove down the back section road toward the winter hay barn. Fuckin' Campbell was becoming a problem. Rodriguez had suspended operations for three days now, and Frank needed to make his plan work or he would find himself at the bottom of the East Oak Landfill. The last thing he needed was playing dodge ball with the sheriff.

Celeste's tender tone curled through the phone. "I miss you, Frankie."

He leaned back in the driver seat, staring across the vast hay fields. Why didn't he just walk away from the damned ranch? Kellie would probably be glad to see him go.

"Baby, you know how 89er weekend is, and the thing with the horses–I can't get away until tomorrow."

"I wish you'd let go. We could be so happy together."

Instead of his usual irritated reaction to her plea, he felt gratitude. She was right, but he'd dug himself in so deep now with the Columbians that he feared he'd never be able to extricate himself. How could he tell her about *that*? And what about Sara?

He squeezed his eyes against the pain in his chest. "I know."

"I love you."

"Me too."

He closed the phone and leaned his head back against the seat. Until the mess at the ranch was sorted out, he couldn't think about walking away from anything.

A cloud of red dust appeared ahead and his gut clenched. Sometimes these guys made him really nervous. He glanced at the gun on the passenger seat, then reached over and released the safety. A minute later, a dented green pickup with one red fender and no front bumper pulled up beside the pole barn. A thick-necked man stepped out into the tall grass, and hitched up pants that sagged below a large belly. He turned and stared at Frank's Jeep, then pulled out a pack of cigarettes.

~ ~

Ed continued past Kellie's place, automatically glancing toward the main barn. Frank's Hummer was parked at the side, and Ed slowed down. Why was Frank's vehicle there if he'd gone somewhere else? Across the fields, a cloud of red dust rose, unbroken by any breeze. He accelerated, then turned down the next section road and proceeded slowly, keeping his eye on the dust cloud. Through the brush at the side of the road, he spotted the roof of an immense pole barn. A barely-used track led into that field, and he caught a glimpse of an old Jeep parked in the tall grass. He drove past the entrance and, farther down the road, found a tractor path that ended behind a stand of trees. He parked the car and jogged across the road and into the tall weeds. A loud engine rumbled past his hiding place and he parted the brush to watch a dilapidated pickup truck turn into the lane leading to the pole barn.

Loosening his collar against the heat, he crept through the cover until he could see Frank and a dark skinned man approaching each other. He pulled out a small camera and hit the burst button.

~~

"Shit!" Frank leaped out of the Jeep and ran through the grass. "Hey! Don't do that out here, you idiot! Jeezus, you ever seen a wildfire?"

The man scowled. "Señor Frayjur?"

Frank nodded curtly, eyeing the unlit cigarette. "You have something for me?"

"Money first, *por favor*."

Frank pulled a packet of bills from his pocket and held it out. The man grasped it and pulled, but Frank held on.

"Mutual trade."

Confusion darkened the man's eyes, and Frank snorted. "Hand over the address at the same time, dumb shit."

A deep red flush spread over the man's neck, illuminating a jagged white scar that ran from beneath his collar to below his left jaw.

Frank wished he'd picked up the gun.

The man reached into his shirt pocket, pulled out a small folded piece of paper, and held it out, never breaking eye contact. Frank released the money and stepped back. Without another word, the man climbed into his truck. dirt spewed behind the tailgate as he wheeled around and roared off. Frank willed his heart to stop thumping. Breaking the connection with the Columbians was beginning to look better and better. Once he'd located this Mack asshole and put him out of his misery, he and Celeste could disappear and live quite well on his stash.

~~

Sara's blue ribbon had restored her youthful charm, but

Kellie only half listened to the excited chatter.

"That girl from Stillwater really thought she was hot stuff! She kept looking at Juicy and me like we were hicks! I guess I showed *her*!"

"Yes, you did, but there's always a next time. She's local and you'll compete with her many times, so don't do anything you'll regret."

And what have I done to bring on all my *trouble?* The heated conversation with Cliff had only strengthened her suspicion that they'd have their way about the land, whatever it took. Her thoughts snapped back to the conversation with Pete. Had the sheriff's office even questioned the obnoxious horse show exhibitor? Even though she supposedly was out of town, she could have paid someone to take them. Or maybe they weren't even related to the attacks.

"Mama, is Uncle Clarke coming to the barbecue tonight?"

"I think so."

"He doesn't look like he used to. Is he sick?"

"Yes, he is, honey, but I think he's getting better."

Sara's voice took on a dreamy tone. "I hope so. He's *so* handsome."

Kellie didn't respond. Once upon a time, Clarke Sutton's good looks bordering on beautiful had been the focus of every girl in town. By graduation, it was common knowledge that the boys liked him too. Rural Guthrie hadn't taken to the modern ideas of alternative lifestyles, and Clarke took off for the big city, where he'd made a small fortune as a cover model. He was clearly losing his battle with the consequences of his lifestyle choices. And because of it, what could have been a large happy family had splintered into a loosely held together group of related individuals with no common loyalty for the group, or each other. Cliff's hard determination to press the land issue proved that.

"Oh, goody! Daddy's here!" Sara jumped out of the truck and started toward the barn.

"Hey, get back here and put your horse up!"

Sara's happy expression changed to a sullen scowl and she stomped back toward the trailer.

Frank was in the office, looking at the mail when Kellie walked in. She removed her hat and hung it on the coat rack, her arm brushing against Frank's jacket. The scent of expensive perfume wafted from the garment, and anger snapped to attention.

"You missed your daughter's big win today."

He didn't look up. "I had business in Oklahoma City."

"I'll just bet you did." She brushed past him and headed toward her desk. "Are you planning to join us tonight? Or are you otherwise involved?"

"What, exactly, is your problem?"

She whirled to face him, seeing only a stranger who didn't know her at all.

"I've done *both* ranch tours by myself, my brothers showed up to start pressing me again about selling out, and our daughter needs *your* support as much as mine. Does *that* answer your question?"

Sara's hysterical cries ricocheted into the moment. "Mommy, Mommy! Juicy's hurt!" Her frightened face appeared in the doorway. "Come quick! He's limping really bad!"

A sickening jolt surged through Kellie's chest and she turned to Frank, but he was already hurrying out the door.

Sara started to cry again. "What if he has the same thing as Dancer?"

Kellie grabbed her and hugged tight, stroking her hair. "Honey, calm down. Let's go have a look."

Heart thumping, she took Sara's hand and hurried down the aisle.

In Juice's stall, Frank kneeled beside the horse's front feet and squinted. "I don't see a wound. Maybe he knocked his ankle against the trailer door, or he might just be sore from competing."

Kellie stepped in. "Let me look–I've seen what the injection site looks like in the beginning stages."

Running her hand down the horse's leg, she grasped the ankle and he lifted his foot. The white hair on the fetlock had been clipped for the event, and the pink skin showed through. She rubbed a thumb over the same area where the other horses had been injected. He jerked his foot away and Kellie closed her eyes. This couldn't be happening again. She picked up the foot and held it firmly while she examined the area. One small spot was reddened, but she could see no obvious puncture site. She released the foot and straightened up, a flood of perspiration prickling over her neck and chest.

"I don't see anything obvious, but I'll ask Roy to keep an eye on him this evening while we're out. If he gets worse, we'll call Doc Browning."

~~

The digital photographs came up on Ed's computer screen and he squinted at the images–a little blurry, but still discernible. The first four frames clearly showed money in Frank's hand, but Ed couldn't tell how much. He moved through the series to the shot showing what the man held. Zooming in, Ed swore under his breath–unrecognizable, whatever it was. He downloaded the images to a folder and forwarded them to the communications room, then pressed the intercom.

"I just sent you some photos. See if you can blow them up enough to see what's being handed off. I need it ASAP."

He sat back and pursed his lips. Wouldn't it be something if Frank were dealing drugs. Or buying them, for that matter. Again, the foremost question became what Frank's possible involvement could be in the horse attacks. Ed considered what he knew about the Suttons. *Not much.*

A quick glance at the clock told him it was quitting time all over town, but he reached for the phone anyway. Commissioner McBee picked up on the first ring.

"Ed Campbell here. I need some information, but I don't want anyone to know about it."

"I'll help if I can."

"Land records on the Sutton estate, including any restrictions on its disposition."

A long silence made Ed nervous.

McBee cleared his throat, doubt coloring his voice. "Does this have anything to do with your, uh, mission here?"

"Unfortunately, it might. I don't want to discuss it on the phone, but when I have more information, I'll bring you up to speed."

"I'll see what I can find in the morning. I'll do it myself, otherwise, it'll be all over town in an hour."

Ed narrowed his eyes. Small town ways might work in his favor.

"I don't suppose I could find out what was in Joshua Sutton's will."

McBee laughed. "*Nothing's* private in this town. Ol' Josh didn't take kindly to Clarke's life choices, and I know for sure that the boy was cut out of the will. And Kellie's been right up front about her father's deathbed demand that the land never be split up or sold to anyone outside the family. You haven't been here long enough to see her in action, but she's a holy terror when it comes to heritage and historic preservation. Far as I know, those are the only two things in the will that were ever a topic of gossip."

Ed nodded, his brain piecing together the puzzle pieces. "That's a big help, Commissioner. I appreciate it."

He hung up the phone as the communications technician stepped into the office.

"Sheriff, I blew up those photos and enhanced the resolution...Did you know that one of the subjects is Frank Frazier?"

Ed stared hard at the young man, causing him to take a step back from the desk.

"Uh, anyway, Sir–the bills in Frazier's hand are hundreds, the stack is thick–I'd guess it's a couple grand. The item in the other guy's hand is a piece of paper, but I can't make out what it says."

Ed opened the Rocking R case file and jotted a note inside the file folder. "Make me a set of prints, delete the digital file from your computer, and don't discuss this with anyone."

"Understood, Sir."

The technician disappeared down the hall and the phone rang.

"Chief, that guy you had me follow dragged me all the way down to the track in Oklahoma City. What do you want me to do now?"

"You see him with anybody?"

"Nope, just a bunch of Mexicans. Smokin' and laughin'."

A deep feeling of satisfaction grew like a mushroom. Things were beginning to click into place.

"Okay, you can head on back, relieve Unit 5 at the Sutton place."

The phone rang again and Ed's disappointment grew as he listened to the crime lab technician. "The three snapshots were clean for fingerprints, except for one smudge. Couldn't get enough to run it through AFIS. Sorry."

Ed hung up, then leaned back in the chair and closed his eyes. "God, what I'd give for a beer right now."

The white cell phone vibrated and *that* idea evaporated.

"Frazier's clean. Not even a DUI. I'm afraid you're on your own with this one."

"It was a long shot anyway, but I'm uploading a file as we speak. I photographed him trading a lot of money for a piece of paper. Might be racing information, or something to do with Hermano or Rodriguez. Maybe you can identify the other guy in the photographs. The hell of it is, I'm too high profile to tail Frank myself–this town is like a sieve when it comes to rumors."

"So I understand."

His boss's tone sent caution spiraling through Ed's head, but he forged on. "Any more thoughts on the money laundering angle?"

"The Conklin-Anderson Development Group appears to be a shell company for a group of California investors. At least one of those principals has some questionable history. We have a couple of agents undercover with CAD Group down around Edmond."

"They're up here too. Just broke ground west of town for a multimillion dollar gated community. Town's in an uproar." Ed snorted. "And Frazier has a girlfriend in Edmond. How coincidental is *that*?"

"I'll get an agent from Oklahoma City to come up and take over surveillance on Frazier. You concentrate on Hermano. We're running out of time real fast–those good ol' boys in the county commission aren't likely to take kindly to keeping you on for another four years."

Ed nodded, pondering the feasibility of staying in Guthrie. *Never happen.*

"Ed, do you have anything *else* you'd like to share?"

A wiggle of concern moved through his head. "Did you have something specific in mind?"

"How about your long time relationship with Kellie Sutton? Is that the reason you were so eager to take this assignment?"

"Ancient history, boss. You can never go home."

13

Kellie shifted in the hard wooden chair on the raised platform, scanning the sea of faces in front of the courthouse and blocking out the mayor's drone about Guthrie's long history. His delivery made the subject about as interesting as watching manure decompose. She stifled a sigh. At least she could stop worrying about Sara's horse. Hyde had called from the ranch to report that Juice wasn't even limping. A simple bruise, nothing sinister. Kellie threw a glance at the deputy contingent at the rear of the crowd, disappointed that Ed wasn't there. She'd like to think they were on the same thought wavelength, but he'd given no indication that he'd ever forgiven her. On the other hand, if he'd loved her enough, wouldn't he have returned home after his overseas tour, wanting to sort things out? She looked down at her hands, touching the finger where the tiny diamond ring had been for such a short time. If she could do it over again, would she be willing to walk away from the ranch?

She suddenly became aware of an expectant silence around her. The mayor was looking at her with raised eyebrows.

"Kellie? Don't you have something to say?"

Leaping to her feet, she laughed nervously as she stepped behind the podium. Composing her expression, she launched into her speech.

"Land hunger...An obsession that conquered the West and changed the face of America's civilization. For those hopeful souls who braved the unknown for the chance at a piece of the promised land, these rolling grassy uplands and wooded river bottoms seemed to give close reality to the distant charm of green and purple forest growth rising to meet the brighter hues in the sky. Imagine their joy at seeing the swelling redbud trees silhouetted against the April new growth, the promise of fertile meadows and apple orchards."

Warming to her subject, Kellie let her gaze sweep over the audience. At the front of the crowd, the Kansas State professor smiled. One row back, Pete's ruddy face beamed and he touched the brim of his hat. Kellie's confidence grew, fed by the conviction that history should be protected at any price. Toward the rear of the crowd, the unsettling cowboy from the horse show stared back at her with bottomless black eyes, and a twitch of distraction blipped through her pulse.

She looked down at her notes and cleared her throat. "The Indians named Oklahoma the 'beautiful land,' and the landless and home-hungry men and women who arrived at the Kansas-Oklahoma border on April 22, 1889 saw only the prospect of a bright future. Very soon, they learned the exact character of the land–dry red sand, worthless for farming. Hundreds of these people soon returned to their home states, carrying with them all they had left: disappointment."

Kellie stepped from behind the podium. "If you think land hunger is only a thing of history, you are wrong. Today, every smidgeon of land that can support building is being gobbled up at an incredible rate. Land developers are scooping up the outlying farmlands where elderly farmers and ranchers can no longer make a living in today's import-oriented markets. Developers are virtually *stealing* this land, and banking on the future population explosion and outward spread of urban areas." She put her hands on her hips and nodded to a man in the front row. "You think you're out in the sticks? Well, think again."

Then she looked directly at the professor. "Some folks believe that this is no different than what the Indians experienced, so long ago. In some ways, yes–we are walking in their moccasins." She paused for effect. "But if our children and grandchildren are to have anything other than steel and concrete as a heritage, we *must* fight for the land.

"As president of the Historic Ranches Association of Oklahoma, I'm actively working to protect this pivotal part of America. When you return to your homes, think about the impact your own area has made on history, then get involved to ensure that it's not buried under urban expansion. Thank you."

The crowd applauded with enthusiasm, and Kellie stepped back. The mayor ended the ceremony by inviting everyone to the Chuck Wagon Barbeque at the fairgrounds.

He turned and grinned. "Haven't seen you this fired up in a long time."

~~

Travis smoothed a hand over his shiny skull, then adjusted the aging straw cowboy hat and grinned at his reflection. *Hell, me and Toby been wearin' these hats long before they got to be high fashion!* Pulling the brim down in front, he scowled. *Damn but you're a mean lookin' fucker!* His tan skin broke a sharp contrast against the crisp white shirt tucked neatly into the new jeans. His fingers moved slowly over the four-inch-wide belt buckle, caressing the deeply engraved design. He knew every curve and depression, had memorized the words on the sterling silver face. Light glinted off the edges of the raised cowboy and horse in hot pursuit of a calf, and pain moved through Travis's chest. He turned away from the specter of the past and stepped up to a urinal.

A stout man pushed through the door and nodded, then shuffled across the floor. Travis eyed the man's gimpy leg, wondering briefly how he'd injured it. The man stopped at the next urinal, then glanced over.

"That's a mighty fancy buckle you're wearing. Must have done some real good riding to earn it."

Travis stared at the man for a minute, then grinned. "Hell, no. You can buy these things at any western outfitter."

The man turned back to his business, and Travis left the restroom. The high raftered grange building echoed with laughter and talk, kids squealing, and folks milling around with plates of food. He made his way to the bar and ordered a beer, then checked the far corner of the room where Kellie Sutton sat at a table talking to a dark haired man.

~ ~

After a quick stop at the apartment to change out of his uniform, Ed drove back toward town. His thoughts raged, blurring from one idea to the next–almost the same sensation as being in combat. Too many things going on at once, and no cover. Right now, he needed to figure out what information could be worth thousands of dollars to Frank.

On impulse, he turned south on Pine and headed for home–a place he hadn't seen since his father's funeral.

The old neighborhood had deteriorated and Ed's brain started sending signals to turn back. Better to leave the memories the way they'd been. But human nature won out and he slowed in front of the old house. His heart fell. Two scruffy dogs were chained in the front yard and had long ago killed the grass with their digging and running. A bicycle with one wheel missing leaned against the old pine tree, weeds growing up to the handlebars. Cheap plastic toys littered the driveway. One of the living room windows had plywood over it, and towers of cardboard boxes and plastic bins filled the front porch.

He punched the gas and drove to the next corner, bile rising in his throat. He and his dad had kept their home neat and tidy, the grass mowed, the paint fresh. How could people live like that?

He turned on Grant, then pulled over. If he continued this direction, he'd pass by his dad's old hardware store. Did he really want to do that? Surely, the new owners would have kept the place up. When the estate had finally closed, Ed thought the offer from a big chain would preserve some of Guthrie's history. Did he want to find out?

He pulled away from the curb and continued down the street, wondering why he'd ever thought he could come home. At the corner of Division, he stopped and a smile filled his heart. The hardware store had been expanded, was nicely kept up, had a new big window in the front, and the parking lot was filled with cars.

At least he'd made one good decision in the past fifteen years.

He headed south toward the fairgrounds and parked outside a small Mexican restaurant across the road. His business brain took over again. The boss's comment about Kellie disturbed him. Did it appear that he wasn't doing the job he'd been sent to do? McBee had a direct line to DEA–perhaps he'd been the one to send up a warning flag. Better watch what he said to the old guy.

Ed walked toward the restaurant entrance, the enticing aroma of spicy food sending an instant message to his stomach. He started toward a booth at the back, then stopped abruptly. Danielle White sat alone, staring straight at him with angry eyes. *Shit, now what?* He couldn't very well walk past her and sit by himself, but he sure didn't want to be trapped with her. Could he just turn around and leave?

The animosity faded from her gaze and she smiled that glorious smile.

"Come sit. I just ordered." She chuckled. "I won't bite, I promise."

A waitress appeared and relief curled through Ed's chest.

Danielle leaned forward, casually resting her arms on the table. "How's the Sutton case coming along? I haven't been involved much."

He made note of the veiled comment, but put on an easy smile. "You will be, I promise. I'm still thinking the Brown girl is involved, but until we find her boyfriend, my hands are tied."

Danielle cocked her head. "It must be difficult to be here and see your old girlfriend after all these years."

Ed's jaw stiffened. "My personal life is not up for discussion."

"Then why don't we talk about work–about how after ten years on the force paying my dues, working my way up to Under Sheriff, when the top job opens up, I'm bumped by an outsider."

Ed quickly looked around at the other diners. "Not here, Danielle. This is inappropriate." He rose and laid a twenty on the table. "I'm late. Dinner's on me."

He strode out the door and jammed his hat down over his forehead. Women were the bane of his life.

Ten minutes later, he stepped into the grange building at the fairgrounds and scanned the crowd. The atmosphere was festive, lightening his mood somewhat. Then he spotted Kellie in the corner talking to Doc Browning. A jerk kicked through his gut and his sour mood faded. He stepped up to the bar and ordered a soda, glancing briefly at the dark eyed man next to him. A sinister looking guy in cowboy garb, a person who alerted Ed's nose for troublemakers. In a town swelling with thousands of visitors, this one stood out too much.

Picking up his soda, he turned to face the stranger. "Good party, huh?" He drank long and deep, then turned to look out over the crowd. "That beer looks mighty good."

The man chuckled. "Yeah, but this one's for me."

Ed laughed. "Don't think I've ever seen you around here.

You come in from out of town?"

"Oklahoma City. Just passin' through, saw the billboard about the big doin's, thought I'd check it out."

Ed's gaze dropped to the man's belt, and a memory stirred. "Nice buckle." He squinted at the inscription. "You don't look old enough to have been a High School Rodeo champ in 1985."

"Nah, found this in a pawn shop."

"What do you do in Okee City?"

The man hesitated, a familiar glimmer of wariness darkened his gaze. "Oil company. I manage the vehicle garage."

"Seems like hazardous duty, from the looks of your hand."

The guy snatched his hand off the bar, accidentally smacking it against the edge of the counter.

"God *damn!*" He set his beer on the counter, shaking the injured hand. "Yeah, I burned it on an exhaust manifold."

Ed nodded and looked back over the crowd. "That would do it." He pushed away from the bar. "Well, nice talkin' to you. I'd better get along to the missus."

The stranger raised his beer bottle and grinned. "Here's to the old ball-and-chain." His cell phone rang and he pulled it out to glower at the display. His sharp features hardened, and Ed was struck by how menacing he looked. After gulping the last of the beer, the cowboy headed for the door. Ed reached over and grabbed the bottle off the counter.

~~

"Nice speech, Kellie." Hyde dug into a plate heaped with beans, ribs, and potato salad.

"Guess I got a little wound up."

"That's why you're so effective...Nice touch about the moccasins. The horses make it to Kentucky okay?"

"Yes and I had a long conversation with the vet in charge.

These new techniques are mind-boggling. She says they've had a 90% success rate so far." An ugly thought slipped into Kellie's mind. If Hyde had been more on top of current veterinary medicine, Dancer might still be alive.

Her friend's eyes clouded briefly, and she blanched, wondering if he'd read her thoughts. Shame washed over her. Blaming him wouldn't bring back her horse.

She lowered her voice. "Did you leave something on my desk yesterday?"

He nodded. "It's a horse stick. Our people make them to honor a favorite horse, either for courage in battle or when it dies...I want you to know how sorry I am that I couldn't save him. He was a proud and noble animal."

The gesture of love and friendship softened the circumstances of the gift.

"Thank you. I'll treasure it." She picked up her napkin, anxious to move away from the emotional subject. "Have you heard anything more from the labs?"

"No, but I did have a long conversation with that friend of mine I was telling you about. He considers himself kind of an amateur sleuth, so he's real interested in what's going on. Maybe you know that racetracks use cobra venom to block pain in injured runners so they can compete. The venom is refined, so it's not lethal, but he says if a contaminant gets into it or it's not processed right, the stuff could cause exactly what we've seen here."

"Is there any way to test for it?"

"Not yet, but the Kentucky Equine Drug Council has organized a research project to do just that. Could be a real threat to the racing industry, I understand."

Kellie lost her appetite and pushed her plate away, horrified at the obvious connection to Frank. "Do you think that's what we're dealing with?"

"Could be, but according to my buddy, some other similar

toxins cause tissue necrosis and systemic shock, but leave no identity markers. Simple formalin, for one–and, it's easy to buy. Other possibilities include some rather exotic toxins from poisonous toads, snails, and spiders. Bottom line is, they all cause the immediate reaction, followed by tissue destruction and nervous system damage."

Kellie sat in stunned silence, digesting the new information, but unable to ignore the fact that one of the poisons pointed a finger directly at Frank. She shook her head. How could she even think that Frank would do such a horrible thing? And for what? Just to make her miserable? Why did he stay on at the ranch? He could get a good job anywhere in this part of the country. *And why do I keep him on? I could certainly find someone just as capable...For Sara–we do this for her.*

"Kellie, you okay?"

She focused on Hyde's concerned expression. "It's a lot to think about. If we have no way of identifying the toxin, how can we treat the horses?"

"I think the hyperbaric oxygen therapy is the best bet." He set aside his empty plate. "Right now, it's more important to concentrate on catching this lunatic before he or she hurts any more horses."

"The sheriff's department is work–" Kellie spotted Ed at the door. Maybe she could talk to him for a minute, find out if he had any new information.

She saw Hyde's mischievous smile and a blush warmed her cheeks. "Don't you dare say a word!"

His cell phone rang and he checked the display, then stood up. "Gotta go. I'm on maternity call."

Kellie nodded, then turned her attention back to the bar. A new wave of uneasiness settled in. Ed was talking to the dark eyed cowboy in the rumpled straw hat. This was the third time she'd seen him. Why did his presence bother her so much? She examined his face, the hard expression, the sharp angles. He looked like any other cowboy around this area, but different.

Ed turned away and the stranger pulled out a phone, a nasty scowl furrowing his forehead as he headed for the door. Kellie scrambled to her feet, determined to catch Ed before he left the party.

"Hold up, Sis." Cliff's voice was so close she jumped.

She glanced at Clarke's heaped plate and chuckled. "Miss down home cooking, do you?"

"I'm tired of living on arugula and tofu."

Cliff eased his bulk into a chair, then cleared his throat. "Let's talk about the disposition of the land. I know you don't want to leave, but Clarke and I want our share so we can do the things *we* want. We shouldn't have to be tied to *your* hundred-and-sixty acres."

Kellie started to reply, but he held up a hand. "I'm not finished. We met with a lawyer, and he's confident that we don't need your signature to sell our parcels."

Disbelief roared through her brain. Her own flesh and blood would abandon her. How could they come to the place where they'd grown up and tell her of their plans to destroy the family heritage? A painful thought pierced her heart. Were they determined enough to try to destroy *her*?

She dismissed the traitorous thoughts and rose from her chair. "Don't be too confident–I have lawyers too."

She swept across the room, seething with inner turmoil, blocking out the celebratory noise.

Ed's throaty voice arrested her anger. "Hey, where you headed in such a hurry?" His quirky smile faded when he saw her face. "What's the matter?"

She glanced back at the twins and sighed. "My brothers are at it again. They've hired a lawyer to find a way to break Dad's will." She bit her lip. "They absolutely do not care about this land, or what it means, or what it cost." She gazed at the empathy in Ed's eyes. "I can't bear the thought of being surrounded by housing developments."

He touched her arm. "I might have some information on that. But more important, we just got a line on Tina Brown's boyfriend–a guy named Travis Mack. He works at a ranch outside Perkins, been there about eight months. He's off this weekend, but I have a deputy in place to question him when he comes back."

~ ~

Travis rose up on one elbow and grinned down at Tina's flushed face. Perspiration sparkled over her forehead and upper lip, and her eyes had a dreamy glaze. Hell, if he squinted a little, she wasn't half bad looking. Especially if he avoided her little pig nose. But she was a damned good poke.

"Feel any better now, baby?"

A smile curled the corners her full mouth. "What do *you* think?"

He reached for the dark triangle between her legs. "I think I could go for seconds, that's what."

She groaned and closed her eyes, arching against his touch.

Tina, Tina, Tina. What am I gonna do about you?

At dawn, he slipped out of bed, throwing only a cursory glance at Tina's bulk beneath the sheet. In the tiny kitchen, he lit a cigarette, then put water on to boil. While he waited, he peered at his hand under the weak light bulb over the sink.

The sucker hurt like hell, and didn't seem to be getting any better. The gaping hole in his skin had expanded to the size of a quarter. Fatty tissue and stringy muscle had become mushy and black. His stomach bucked. He'd better find a doctor today.

He turned his thoughts to his predicament. After hearing Tina's tale of interrogation, he knew the end was near. The law was closing in. Her goddamned big mouth had ramped up his timeline, but that *could* work in his favor. One final step and he could disappear again. Then, when the time was right, he'd own the Sutton empire.

A singsong voice drifted from the bedroom. "Traa-vis, come and ge-et me."

The invitation stirred through his loins and he grinned. *Why not? I always did like breakfast in bed.*

Tina sprawled herself over the bed in a lecherous pose, and licked her lips as he approached. "Ooh, is that for *me*?"

Ten minutes later, he flopped onto his back. "Jeezus, woman! You're gonna kill me!"

She licked his ear. "But what a way to go."

He pulled away. "Listen, I have to work today, but I thought we'd get some breakfast, then I have a little surprise for you."

She squealed like a schoolgirl, and he controlled the urge to smack her. *Two hours. That's all I need.*

The Northside Diner wasn't busy at that hour on a Saturday morning, and he guided Tina to a booth in the back. She walked ahead of him, her big butt wiggling under Capri pants better suited to a teenager. He put the image of her naked body out of his mind. When they were seated, he leaned back in the soft cushioned seat and took a long drag on his cigarette.

"Tell me again what all the sheriff asked you about."

Tina took center stage, embellishing her earlier story with comments about how the whole thing made her feel.

"And boy, I wish you could have seen the look on Kellie Sutton's face when I told her I had a permanent boyfriend. I'm so glad you're gonna back me up when they come to talk to you."

She reached across the yellow Formica tabletop to touch his hand, and he jerked it away.

A frown spread across her chubby features. "You

should really get that wound looked at. What'd you do to it, anyway?"

A hard knot formed in his stomach. "Burned it. Did you tell them where I work?"

She sat back in the booth. "Looks more like a bite to me."

"Goddammit, answer me! What did you tell the cops?"

She jerked with surprise. "Just that you work someplace outside Perkins–come to think of it, you never told me the name of the ranch."

Shit, lady. You only just realized that? "Not important. I'll call the sheriff later this morning." He gave her a sheepish grin. "Sorry I snapped at you."

She leaned forward, her eyes sparkling with anticipation. "What's my surprise?"

"Something I've never shown to anyone. Eat your breakfast so we can get going."

14

Frank jerked his arm from the deputy's grasp. "God dammit, Jimmy, lighten up. I'm not going anywhere!"

His former high school varsity teammate shook his head. "Jeezus, Frank. What were you thinking? Campbell's so pissed I didn't need the phone to hear him yellin'."

Frank crossed his arms, resisting the urge to confide in his old friend. "I told you, I'm here on business. Thinking about buying some beef cattle to upgrade my herd."

The deputy snorted and pointed at Frank's revolver, lying on the front seat of the jeep. "And what were you going to do with that? Shoot the guy if the price wasn't right? Shit, you must think I was born yesterday."

Frank settled his features into a buddy grin. "Come on, you know we've had some intruders at the ranch. I'm just keeping it handy in case I need it...and, anyway, what are *you* doing out here at the crack of dawn?"

The deputy's features sobered. "Can't say...all I know is I'm gonna miss watchin' my kid in the parade." His face brightened. "Hey, you see Veronica at the barbecue last night?"

Frank's gut clenched. "I didn't go."

His friend leered. "Whoo-ee, I don't know when she got back to town, but those boobs still set my Johnson to jigglin'!" He shook his head. "Never could figure out why you broke up after all those years–especially to marry the Queen of the Range."

A hollow feeling crept into Frank's chest, opening up a part of his mind that he'd closed twelve years ago. Veronica Stepp had been the love of his life, and he'd blown it. How could he have known she'd dump him when he was no longer a celebrity? And what the hell was the matter with him now? Celeste could make the rest of his life worth living. His gaze drifted down the road toward the entrance to the cattle ranch. Travis Mack was somewhere on that property, the only remaining loose end. There had to be a way to ditch the deputy.

Frank leaned casually against the car door. "I don't suppose you have any inside information about the shit that's going on out at my place, do you?"

A grin. "Now you know I can't talk about that. Campbell would have my job." The grin faded and the deputy shook his head. "Him droppin' in from nowhere to take over has everyone in a tailspin–not that he ain't good, mind you, but Dani White has been first deputy for five years. It shoulda been her the commissioners appointed. I don't care if the guy does have a medal for bravery–it ain't right, givin' employment to outsiders."

Frank scowled, but wisely kept his knee-jerk response to himself. *The Golden Boy returns and the town falls all over itself.*

The deputy's phone rang, and his face contorted into a puzzled frown as he listened.

"Okay, Chief." He closed the phone and met Frank's gaze. "Speak of the Devil...We're going back to the station."

"Okay, let me get my wallet and lock the car."

He reached into the Jeep and picked up the gun.

~ ~

Wrapped in a towel, Kellie padded across her bedroom to the dresser, the long night weighing on every muscle. The disturbing conversation with Hyde had kicked her imagination into fast forward, and she'd wrestled until daybreak with the possibility of Frank's involvement. She stared at her drawn face in the mirror. Perhaps she could simply wear a mask for the day's festivities.

Rummaging through the bras and panties in the underwear drawer, her fingers bumped against something hard in the back corner. A murmur ran through her pulse and she closed her fingers around the hidden box. Withdrawing it slowly, her thoughts jumped back to the first time she'd laid eyes on the small velvet case. A time when she'd thought the world was hers, when love was all that mattered. When her perfect world had crumbled.

She gazed long and hard at the box. Did she want to open the past any more than she already had? The pull of memories was stronger than her reticence. The hinge squeaked, and she caught her breath as light glinted on the tiny solitaire diamond. Tears burned her eyelids, pain and longing surfacing, overpowering any vestige of control she might have.

"God, Eddie, how could I have been so stupid?" she whispered.

Removing the ring from the case, she hesitated, then slipped it over the tip of her finger. The small circle resisted at the knuckle, then slid home. The delicate ring looked foreign on her work-hardened hands, but memories of the first time she'd worn it took precedence. That night had been magical, her ticket to the secure future Ed promised. She smiled, wiggling her finger and watching the glitter move through the gem. He'd looked so handsome in his uniform, his body fit and ready for duty, his eyes filled with love and hope. Her shoulders sagged and she felt the smile fade. She wouldn't ask herself why again.

She grasped the ring and pulled, but it wouldn't budge. She exhaled sharply. "Oh, crap." Wiggling the small circle toward her knuckle, she pulled and seesawed, but the ring stuck. She raced into the bathroom and soaped her hands, working the ring painfully against the now swollen joint. She stopped the futile effort and leaned her hands on the counter. She'd either have to wait until the swelling subsided, or have the ring cut off. But right now, she had a parade to attend.

Thirty minutes later, she checked her appearance in the mirror. Her cheeks were flushed and a light film of perspiration crawled beneath her heavy turquoise and gold shirt. She adjusted the old-fashioned cowboy hat, heavy with the elaborate sparkling tiara. Suddenly she felt like a fool.

"I don't know why I let Sara talk me into this," she muttered. Light flashed through the diamond on her finger and she groaned. "What the hell am I going to do?"

She pulled at the ring one more time, but it was there to stay.

From down the hall, Sara called out. "Mom! Sheriff Campbell's on the phone, but hurry, we're gonna be late!"

Kellie twisted the ring upside down, then slipped her hands into a pair of soft buckskin riding gloves. With one last glance at the woman in the mirror, she hurried down the hall.

Anger rumbled through Ed's voice. "Did you tell Frank where Travis Mack works?"

"No, I haven't seen him since yesterday after the horse show."

"Well, he showed up this morning at the ranch in Perkins, carrying a gun."

"Ed, I honestly don't know anything about it."

His tone softened. "Okay–sorry."

She gazed at her left hand, feeling the circle of love against her skin beneath the leather glove. "See you at the parade?"

"Probably not. I have to take care of this mess right now."

~~

On the drive to Guthrie, Travis tuned out Tina's mindless chatter and focused on the latest change in plan. Going back to work today was out of the question. By now, the sheriff would have been to the ranch and his anonymity was blown. Good thing he'd picked up his few personal belongings before he left for the shindig in Guthrie. He probably should have dumped the specimen jar, but the ones that were left would be dead in a day or two. He glanced at his throbbing hand. *Good enough for 'em.*

A billboard appeared ahead and Tina squealed. "Are we going to Guthrie? It's 89er Days, and I *love* parades!"

He glanced over at her. "I grew up there."

Her jaw dropped and she blinked. "No shit? Why didn't you ever say so?"

He focused on the highway. "Bad blood, bad memories."

She reached over and stroked his arm. "I'm so glad you want to show *me*..." Her voice dropped to a whisper. "I love you, Travis."

Ice slithered through his veins. Such a declaration had seldom been made during his life, mostly when he was a kid, only by his dad. Never a woman.

Tina withdrew her hand and looked out the truck window, obviously waiting for his response. For a moment, he wondered if he was acting prematurely, if he should wait and see how things progressed. The idea passed. He couldn't afford to get close to *anyone*.

Turning off the highway, he drove the pickup down one of the section roads, and Tina's tone returned to conversational.

"Hey, this is the way to Rockin' S."

"Really? You'll have to show me where it is."

Tina laughed. "I oughta know...I drove this road at the crack of dawn every morning for months."

"Why'd you get fired?"

"For being late. Big deal, huh? Kellie Sutton's a friggin' control freak–oh, there's the gate to the ranch."

Travis looked in the direction she pointed, a surge of hatred boiling through his head. "Big place."

A mile and a half down the road, he turned right onto a numbered gravel road, then slowed down. Childhood memories swirled through his head, early mornings and the sweet scent of freshly mown hay. The mockingbirds calling to one another, and cattle bawling in the distance as the day opened up–a low chorus of comfort sounds. Another world, a lifetime ago.

"Boy, talk about being in the middle of nowhere–what's out here?"

"Home. Haven't been back in a long time."

Another right turn put them on a rough red dirt road and the house came into view.

Tina exhaled softly. "It looks empty."

"Yeah, I've been savin' it for a rainy day."

~~

People jammed the staging area at the old train station, excited chatter and laughter resounding through the cool morning air. Several workers were putting the finishing touches on a huge float decorated with thousands of red, yellow, and white blossoms. The 89er Royal Court in their beautiful satin gowns waited nearby to take their places on the elaborate rig. Farther down the block, a flatbed truck was stacked with bales of hay and decorated with crepe paper streamers. The Little League baseball players chased each other around the truck while their coach tried to maintain order. The Guthrie High School marching band stood in formation, their smart royal blue and black uniforms neat and crisp. A soft breeze ruffled the black feather on each hat, and the sunlight reflected off brass instruments.

Sara was fairly bouncing on springs while she brushed Juicy's flashy coat.

Kellie laughed. "Careful, honey, you'll wear away his color."

The child's giggles sent a surge of love through Kellie's heart and, for the first time in days, her problems and anxiety faded.

"Mommy, Belle has dust on her ankles. Aren't you gonna clean her up?"

Kellie smiled and took the offered brush. "My, aren't *you* the fussy one all of a sudden."

"Well, *everyone* in town will be here and see us. Shouldn't we look real good?"

A light brush of pink dusted Sara's cheeks and a hint of rose bloomed on her lips.

Kellie narrowed her eyes. "Young lady, have you been into my makeup?"

Sara's face fell. "Just a little. I wanted to look pretty for my first parade." Her gaze flitted toward a group of youngsters nearby, and more color rose to her cheeks.

Kellie followed her gaze to the young riders and immediately spotted a boy with dark red hair staring at them. *Aha! First love.*

"Okay, but you ask next time."

A brown truck pulling an eight-horse trailer eased into a spot at the corner of the parking lot. The gleaming rigs were emblazoned in gold with the Logan County Sheriff insignia. The sheriff's posse in full regalia had been Kellie's favorite part of the parade for as long as she could remember. Sadness crept into her thoughts. As kids, she and Ed had always ridden side by side in the horse club contingent and, in those days, Ed had been adamant that one day he'd be part of the posse and have a silver-studded saddle and wear a beautiful white Stetson. And she'd always thought she would be part of those future plans.

She had been riding in the parade for years, but today would have been Ed's first time.

Half an hour later, the mounted segment of the parade began moving up Oklahoma Avenue toward the center of town, with Kellie as Grand Marshall leading the contingent. She turned in the saddle to check on Sara, and a twinge ran through her heart. The red-haired boy rode next to her beaming daughter, the two of them deep in conversation. Seeing Sara so poised and grown up brought the realization that time was passing too quickly. Kellie couldn't afford to miss a minute of it. Time to put her priorities in order and make sure that enjoying life with Sara was at the top of the list.

Heavy iron horseshoes rang against pavement and she turned toward the sound. delight filled her heart as Ed trotted across the intersection and joined the posse behind her. He threw her a quick self-conscious smile, and she settled back into the ride, warmed by the past.

Belle responded to the excitement, snorting and arching her neck, sashaying almost seductively beneath the saddle. Kellie leaned forward and patted the mare's neck, delighted by the horse's response to the outing. As the parade approached Second Street, more people crowded the sidewalks and she eased into the festive mood, waving and tossing wrapped candies to the children sitting along the curb. The town's senior citizens smiled from their folding chairs in the shade, and a clown pestered a group of teenaged girls, making them squeal. Somewhere toward the back of the parade, the fire trucks cranked up their sirens, then the band began to play. Kellie gazed at the wonderful old buildings that fronted the street of this most historic town. The arched windows, fancy facades, and elegant brickwork made testament to the dreams of her ancestors. Her speech at the opening ceremonies had grown from a new slant on that history, and her right to preserve it.

At the corner of Division, someone shouted her name. Scanning the crowd, she spotted her twin brothers, grinning and waving. She waved back, but the joy of the moment dimmed.

~~

Travis drove the truck around behind the house and parked.

Tina tilted her head, puzzlement creasing her forehead. "Is this part of the Sutton property?"

"Uh huh. A hundred and sixty acres, to be exact."

"And you lived here? You bought it?"

Travis grinned and opened the truck door. "Not exactly. C'mon, I'll show you around."

For as dense as she'd seemed earlier, Tina's sudden wariness put him on alert. He'd have to tread carefully. She walked slowly around the front of the truck, doubt shadowing her face.

He slipped an arm around her shoulders and nuzzled her ear, his voice husky. "I've never had sex here...no one was good enough. But now I have you."

She immediately relaxed and giggled. "Ooh, that tickles!"

He ran his hand over her butt and squeezed, savoring his growing erection. "Right this way, milady."

On the previous day, he'd jimmied the lock on the back door. It opened easily, and they stepped into the dim kitchen.

Tina wrinkled her nose. "Smells musty. Why haven't you been living here?"

Anger tightened his throat. "I already *told* you! Bad memories. Jeezus, pay more attention!"

Her anxious expression returned and he shook his head. "Sorry. I just need me some time to get used to being here again."

Moving out of the kitchen, they entered a small living room filled with furniture draped in white sheets. The memories swirled around him, nibbling at the periphery of his brain, taking big bites out of his breathing. This room, this house, this property...his, but untouchable. All because of that bitch and her brothers. Anger raced through his chest like a freight train.

Tina stepped up close and brushed her fingers over his stubbly cheek. "Baby, I know you're hurtin'–let me help." Her eyes reflected sincerity. "I *do* love you. I could make you happy again."

Again? Had he ever been happy? He leaned his face against her hand, relishing the warmth of the caress for a moment, then pulled her tight against his rigid yearning.

"You can start right now. Let's inaugurate this place."

She slid her arms up around his neck, pressing her breasts against his chest and offering her full, wet mouth, her tongue teasing the inside of his upper lip. Lust obliterated all sense of caution and he pushed her down the hall toward the bedroom while he grappled with her tight pants. She moaned and pushed his hands away, then swiftly skinned out of the garment. He stared at her fleshy body while he opened his fly and released his friendly weapon.

Her eyes were feverish with desire. "God, Travis, you make me so damned hot!"

She lay back on the bed and he pushed between her thighs, lifting her up, and pounding away the past in a deadly whirlpool of abandon.

~~

The big palomino gelding shifted, pawing the pavement, and Ed leaned forward to pat the horse's neck. From his vantage point in the shade beneath a spreading pecan tree, he watched Kellie swing down from the saddle and loop the reins over her mare's neck. The temperature had risen quickly, and her face glowed beneath the brim of the sparkling red hat. She pulled a stirrup up and draped it over the seat of the saddle, and Ed urged his horse forward.

"You look great, Kellie. Been a long time since I saw that crown."

She whirled around to gaze up at him, unveiled delight sparkling in her green eyes. "You made it!"

Her reaction sent happiness racing through his head and he nodded. She was beautiful, more so than he remembered, bringing back the recent sensation of their brief embrace. How good she smelled, how right the intimacy seemed. There were so many things he wanted to say, but would the opportunity ever come? He couldn't wait for Fate to intervene–he'd have to make it happen. And soon.

Kellie's smile turned self-conscious. "I think I'm a little old for rhinestones. Sara dug it out and insisted I wear it."

They should be diamonds. "Beauty never ages."

He dismounted and fiddled with some fittings on the ornate Spanish saddle, avoiding her gaze.

"I'll call you later. We need to talk about some things."

~~

Travis led Tina across the back yard, glancing sideways at her. "Now I'll show you something *really* cool."

She giggled. "Better'n what we just did?"

He lifted an eyebrow. "Nothin's better'n *that!*"

They walked through the long grass and, as they neared the barn, another wave of fury assaulted him. For one second, he wanted to go inside, drawn by the past to confirm his existence. He cast a sidelong glance at Tina's flushed face. Her puppy-like adoration was a new experience for him, and he kind of liked the attention. When his plans were complete and he had what was rightfully his, it might be nice to have her willing body around for the taking, anytime he wanted.

He stopped in the shadow of the barn, staring at a large gap between the boards. Through that opening lay his past, a history he could never share with Tina. He knew absolutely nothing about her. He couldn't take the chance that her adoration would fail him.

Her soft voice intruded. "What's in there, Trav?"

"A lotta blood and bad memories."

She gasped. "Oh, babe, I'm sorry–I forgot this was where you found your dad." She stepped up close and slipped her arm around his waist. "You can talk about it to me, if it'll make you feel better."

And just where would that conversation end up? Travis steeled himself against the urge to push her away.

He pointed toward the middle of the field. "See the windmill? I used to climb clear to the top. Caught hell for it too." He guided her toward a large pile of boulders flanked by two small scrubby trees. "Ninety-one tornadoes came through here when I was five years old. The next year, my old man built this shelter."

Tina looked around. "What shelter? I don't see anything."

"Under the boulders." He pointed, then grabbed the edge of a piece of rusty corrugated metal.

Pulling it up, he motioned Tina forward. The morning sun illuminated a flight of concrete steps descending into the hole. "Come on...I'll show you my secret hideaway. I spent a lot of time here when I was a kid."

At the bottom of the stairwell, the air was cool and smelled of earth, triggering a memory. Travis lifted the latch on a heavy wooden door, then reached inside. A moment later, he switched on a flashlight and ushered Tina into the room.

"Wow! I've never been in one of these. We always went to the public shelter in town."

"No time to get to town from way out here!" He gazed

around at the cinderblock walls and low concrete ceiling. Folding chairs, camp cots, jugs of water, packs of paper plates and cups. "This place is big enough for eight people. We kept enough supplies to stay down here for a week."

Tina approached a stack of boxes. "Looks like it still does. This stuff must be ancient!"

Travis leaned over and peered at the side of one carton. "Twenty-four cans chili. Whew, *that* could be a problem in such a small space!"

She laughed out loud, then twirled in a circle. "What a great hideaway. I'll bet you loved being down here."

A memory moved through Travis's head and a band crushed his chest, making it hard to breathe. Tina moved toward a wooden crate in the corner, and his heart thumped as she lifted the lid.

"Aw, look at all your toys." She reached into the box and withdrew a naked doll, then chuckled. "Looks like you had some secrets down here." She looked closely at the doll, and the smile faded. "Crap, what'd you do to her? What are all these slashes and nails?"

He took a quick step forward, and snatched the doll out of her hands and tossing it back into the crate in one motion. "I went through a phase where I believed in voodoo, thought I could torment my teacher."

Wariness flickered across Tina's expression and he took charge again.

He wiggled his eyebrows and reached for her. "Maybe we should inaugurate this place too."

Her eyes sparkled with relief, and she sighed. "I can see I'm gonna need to take my vitamins every day!"

He reached down and unzipped his jeans. "Hold that thought, and I'll be back in a minute. Gotta pee."

He winked and walked out the door, closing it behind him. He stood outside, listening to the silence, then slipped a padlock through the latch and snapped it shut.

15

Kellie patted Belle's rump. The horse had been the model of obedience all morning, no small accomplishment for a broodmare who'd spent her adult life in pampered pregnancy, un-beholden to bit or spur. She eagerly snatched a mouthful of hay and dropped her head to chew, and Kellie's thoughts turned to images of Ed at the parade. His uniform shirt smooth across his chest, the sleeves sharply creased, the collar straight and crisp. The sun glinting off the badge over his heart reminded her of the ring, sending a whirlwind of thoughts spinning through her head. He was the only man she'd ever wanted, but she hadn't followed her heart. Given a second chance, would she make the same mistake? Her avowed priority list shuffled in her head and, in that moment, she knew things could be different if she wanted them to be. And she did.

She headed into the tack room and pulled off her gloves. Sun streamed through the window and exploded into a rainbow off the facets of the diamond. Warmth spread through her chest. More than anything, she wanted to leave the ring in place. She glanced out the window at the fields filled with horses. Had it been a fair trade?

Sara popped into the room. "Mommy, can I play with the new filly for a while?"

Kellie jammed her left hand into her jeans pocket, a shot of adrenaline dashing through the pit of her stomach. "Sure, just remember that she's only a few days old. Don't stay with her too long."

Sara skipped back out into the barn, and Kellie sank onto a tack trunk to still her thumping heart. She gazed at the glittering symbol of everything that had been so right. Perhaps when the nightmare ended, she could resurrect the past. With a long sigh, she reached for a bottle of saddle oil and set about removing her only connection with Ed.

A few minutes later, Hyde stepped into the room. "The hyperbaric clinic sent me some information on the facility. It looks very nice. They have a whirlpool, exercise pool, three hyperbaric chambers, and a full lab. Someone has spent a lot of money on that place. They even offered me a job."

"Hyde! You wouldn't leave us, would you?"

"No, Oklahoma is where I belong. Here with my people."

"Thank God. I don't know what I'd do without you, and I mean that."

He grinned self-consciously. "Guess I'd better go earn my keep."

Kellie's phone vibrated gently against her hip, and Ed's voice sounded far away.

"I have some bad news–Frank shot one of my deputies, then took off. We have an APB out for his arrest."

Has everyone gone mad?

"Did he kill–?"

"No. Do *you* have any idea why he was trying to get to Travis Mack?"

She shook her head. "I can't imagine. Frank never really believed the horses were attacked on purpose."

Ed cleared his throat. "My men are questioning Celeste Harding right now."

Kellie swallowed hard. She hadn't heard the woman's name in a long time. "Yes, I guess she'd know more about him than I would." Anger overrode the sting of humiliation. "Anything else I should know?"

"Yes, we–"

A dead silence ensued.

"Ed? Hello?" She snatched the phone from her ear and stared at the display. The battery icon flashed an exclamation point. "Damn!" She put the phone back to her ear.

Ed's voice came back, breaking up. "Kellie? You there?"

"I'll call you back. My battery's gone."

Five minutes later, she leaned back in her desk chair and balanced the portable phone on her shoulder. "Okay, let's start over."

Listening to Ed, she picked through the mail. Bills. Catalogs. An invitation to an open barn.

Optimism rounded Ed's tone. "Fingerprints showed up on that bottle cap. Mack had a DUI in Tulsa earlier this year, so he turned up in the system. I'm waiting on that report, but it looks like he's our man."

From the bottom of the stack of mail, Kellie picked up a small white envelope addressed to her, typewritten, with no return address. *Another sympathy card.* She slid her finger under the flap, then pulled out the contents.

She gaped at the snapshot and horror oozed into her chest, emotion so thick she could barely breathe.

"Oh my god! He sent me another picture!"

"I'll be right there."

The line went dead and Kellie laid the phone on the desk, staring at an image of Sara standing in the round pen, lunging Juicy. Kellie herself stood at the rail. The picture had the same grainy, long-range quality as the others, but something else caught her eye. Bringing the picture closer, she almost threw up. The distinct outline of crosshairs intersected Sara's head.

Kellie raced into the barn aisle, every muscle and nerve vibrating with adrenaline. "Sara! Where are you?"

The question rattled unanswered through the quiet barn.

The photographic image danced in her head, bringing on another deluge of fear. The office phone rang and she tried to calm herself. Sara had been right there with her only a short time ago. She was probably still out in the mare barn.

The male voice was strong, with a nasal twang.

"Aunt Kellie?"

Confusion muddled her thoughts as she walked quickly toward the back doors. "Who is this?" She spotted Sara riding Juicy in a large circle inside the round pen.

The man's voice penetrated her relief.

"Your flesh and blood, Auntie."

She stopped in mid-stride. "Jethrow? Is that really *you*?"

"Yes, Ma'am! How ya doin'?"

"Where are you? Oh my God, I didn't think I'd ever see you again!"

"Been busy growin' up. I'm thinkin' about comin' back home."

Joy overwhelmed her. "Your uncles are in town right now. It would be wonderful if–wait a minute, where are you?"

"Okee City. How about I come by tomorrow? We can all catch up on old times. I wanna see Dad's house too–I think I can deal with it now."

"Oh honey, anything you need, I'll see you get it."

"Yeah, I know you will. Always knew I could count on you. See you later."

He disconnected before Kellie could respond. Her joy paled a little at his parting comment and she pulled her lower lip between her teeth. If she'd ever let someone down when they were vulnerable, it had been Jethrow. She squared her shoulders. The past was over. Jethrow was giving her a second chance to keep the Sutton family together and, this time, she wouldn't blow it.

Roy came around the corner of the building. "You lookin'

for Sara? She went riding out the south gate." He frowned and stepped closer. "Is somethin' wrong, Miz Kellie?

"Someone's been taking photographs of us from right here on the property."

A flicker moved across his expression and he bobbed his head. "That explains it. The last few times I rode fences, I noticed the hay beaten down in a kinda strange pattern–not like a deer trail."

She frowned. "Why didn't you say something?"

His weathered old face crinkled with disbelief, underscoring his response. "Like what? The grass is bent in the south forty?"

Kellie blanched. She'd never heard a sarcastic word from this man who'd cared for all the horses for so many years. She'd obviously stepped over the line.

"I'm sorry–you're right. I'm just so rattled I can't think straight."

The old man grinned, gesturing toward the road. "Maybe your friendly local sheriff can help."

Ed climbed out of the patrol car, and she smiled. *Ol' Roy hasn't lost his powers of sharp observation.* A blanket of calm settled over her thoughts, smothering the terrifying scenarios that vied for her attention.

A few minutes later, Ed looked up from the snapshot, his eyes dark with concern. "This is state of the art–whoever owns this rifle-mounted camera paid big bucks for it. Someone is obviously trying to scare you."

"And doing a damned fine job!"

The strain of the past week crashed over her and she dissolved into tears.

Ed stepped up close and pulled her against him, cradling her body and stroking her hair. The refuge of his arms stilled her frantic thoughts and she rested her head against his chest, relinquishing her fear.

His voice rumbled through his chest, vibrating softly against her cheek. "I owe you an apology."

She focused on the weave of the shirt fabric, following the perfect tiny lines of fragile thread that meshed together to form one strong piece. Her own strength had been woven from similar single weak elements, but always, the missing thread had been Ed's love. She ran her fingers lightly over his shoulder, gathering the courage to finally have this conversation.

~ ~

Ed's heart ached at the sorrow in Kellie's voice, a whisper of the past. "What happened? I was sure you'd eventually come back and we'd get on with our life together."

Regret crushed him. "And I was sure you'd change your mind about leaving the ranch. I didn't want to believe you could choose the land instead of me."

Chagrin clouded her face and her voice tightened. "It wasn't a conscious choice. So many things happened after you left here the last time. Dad had a heart attack and, suddenly, *I* was in charge. Then Randy's rodeo accident devastated all of us. Dad survived the heart attack, but didn't ever return to work–he was too frail. So I became a care-giver in addition to everything else." She attempted to step back, but Ed held her firmly. "I couldn't even *think* about leaving. Sounds like a soap opera, doesn't it?"

He caressed her cheek, and then looked away, cringing at the flint in his voice. "No one can be prepared for how a war will affect him or her. I headed into the Middle East with my company, cocky and ready to be a hero, pumped up with my own self-importance." He shook his head and looked back down at her. "It only took about two months on the frontlines, watching human beings get blown up, and wondering why the hell we were over there. I memorized your letters, your face, relived all the memories. But suddenly I couldn't function, didn't know what I wanted. I wondered if we were too young to be so sure of our future. My ultimatum to you seemed so rash.

"When the war ended, I wanted to come back here, but didn't know what I would say to you. So I stayed in South Carolina and reenlisted for another tour, and let Uncle Sam put me through college."

Kellie's eyes widened and she slipped out of his grasp. "You made the choice to end it without ever consulting me."

His hands tingled with the sensation of touching her, and the familiar defense mechanism kicked in, distancing him from anything painful. "I realized I'd made a royal mess of my life and lost the only thing I'd ever wanted. I started carousing and drank myself silly. Guess I thought it would help get you out of my system. Then my dad sent me the newspaper clipping about your marriage and I knew it was really over. That piece of news was like a punch in the jaw, but I don't know why I was surprised. I'd basically abandoned you. A month later, I married a preacher's daughter from Virginia, but my wild lifestyle didn't sit too well with her and she left me after six months."

Kellie stared silently at him, her face a frozen mask, chilling his blood.

All the things he'd said were true, but he'd dodged the real point of confrontation. *Might as well get it out in the open.*

"When dad died, I vowed that while I was here, you and I would talk, see if anything could be salvaged." Anger began to grow in his chest and he could barely control the tremor in his voice. "But you couldn't be bothered to attend the funeral."

Her face softened and tears welled in her eyes, sparkling with the quivering movements of her chin. "Eddie, you can't imagine how many times I've regretted that. But it was too soon after my own dad died, and I just couldn't face you..." A tear trickled down her cheek. "...and my own mistakes."

He resisted the urge to brush the tear away, scowling instead. "After all our years together, you couldn't pay respects to the old man. That really pissed me off." He took a deep breath. "After the service at the cemetery, I drove out here to tell you exactly what I thought of you and your selfishness. Got as far as the entrance to Sutton Corners and decided you weren't worth even that effort." He shook his head, mentally kicking himself for the impetuous youthful bravado. "I drove on down to Oklahoma City and reenlisted with the MP division in Washington, D.C."

Kellie's face was ashen and tears rolled down her cheeks, making him feel like a heel. But the confession loosened something deep inside, and suddenly he wanted to tell her everything–what he'd done, how he'd always felt, what he wanted now.

She finally found her voice. "Why did you come back here now?"

Wariness stepped in. He hadn't really considered the possibility of this question. "I guess in deference to my dad, Barney McBee contacted me when the sheriff died. Said they wanted a hometown boy to be in charge." A deep breath calmed his quivering insides. "I took it 'cause I had to see if we might have a second chance."

Joy and understanding flashed across her face and glowed in her eyes, giving him a sudden glimpse of all the things she wanted to say, the thoughts swirling just below the surface. She didn't speak, but stepped up close to look into his eyes, sending one distinct message. He cradled her face in his hands, slipping his fingers through her tousled curls and closing his eyes for a moment. Then he leaned down and tenderly captured her mouth, an explosion of memories raging through his head. She slid her arms around his neck and kissed him back, releasing the past and giving her heart back to him without fear.

~~

Travis cracked a beer and lounged back on the sofa. He guzzled a long drink, then belched. Gazing around the small room, he attached a memory to each piece of furniture, each dusty bit of brick-a-brac, each picture on the yellowed wallpaper. The house looked exactly like the day he'd left it. Why? What had Aunt Kellie thought would happen–that he'd run away for a few days, then come home licking his wounds and let her coddle him?

He snorted. The stupid bitch had fallen all over herself when she heard his voice. Too bad she couldn't have saved herself all this trouble. His jaw muscle began to twitch and he pressed hard against it, trying to make it stop. A headache started behind his right eye and he took another gulp of beer.

Someone should have helped the old man. But, no–they were all too fuckin' busy to take care of family. He stared at his grotesquely swollen hand and took several deep, calming breaths. He'd find some peace soon.

He gazed at the expensive rifle beside him on the couch, a reminder of where he was headed. He picked it up and ran his fingers over the polished barrel, feeling the brutal chill of the metal, relishing the powerful capabilities the gun represented. He cocked his head and closed one eye, focusing through the lens of the fancy camera mount. The viewfinder framed an old oil painting of a bison, the crosshairs perfectly dissecting the animal's skull. A chill raced through Travis's chest. Too quick. Too humane.

He lowered the rifle and stared through the dusty picture window. The late afternoon sun changed the landscape into a charcoal sketch of shadows and brilliant slashes. A memory sneaked into the unguarded moment, and he turned his thoughts inward to the pain. Indecision rattled through his head, then he set the gun aside and rose to his feet. One last time–for confirmation.

He moved slowly down the hall, the old wood floor creaking under his weight. The room he'd inhabited for almost fifteen years was void of any of the normal things a child accumulates. His chest tightened with the memory of eons spent as an outsider at school, the fat kid with no skills, no personality, and no future. He sat down on the edge of the bed and let his thoughts wander, unhindered. The scent of sex still lingered in the air, and he glanced at the bedspread where he'd taken Tina in a rage. His thumping pulse sent hammers of pain through the oozing hole on the back of his hand. His fingers followed the design on the old chenille bedspread, then he lay down. Pulling the snapshot from his shirt pocket, he studied Tina's chubby face, taunting him. A stir moved through his groin and he tossed the picture aside. Sleep came quickly, filled with dreams he couldn't face awake.

A sob boiled up from the depths of his soul as a kaleidoscope of images rolled through his head. He awoke with a start, struggling with the misery. Festering anger replaced his agony. They would pay.

A sound outside sent him leaping off the bed to look out the window.

"Fuck! What's *she* doing here?"

16

Kellie watched Ed slide the new photograph into an evidence bag. Her body still hummed with the aftershocks of the kiss, warmth curling beneath her shirt. The heady sensation of having him in her kitchen, in her personal space, sent all manner of outlandish ideas tumbling through her thoughts. There he was, right where he should have been all these years. Did he feel it too?

He looked up and smiled, sending her heartbeat on another roller coaster ride.

"You had something to tell me?"

"My nephew Jethrow is back."

"Where's he been all this time?"

"He didn't say, but he called from Oklahoma City. He's coming out here tomorrow."

"That's great. It's about time something good happened."

Kellie's glow faded. "Hyde told me about some toxins that cause the exact kind of damage we've seen in the horses. He says it could be venom from snakes or spiders." She bit her lip. "But why would someone go to so much trouble to terrorize me?"

Ed looked thoughtful. "Would one bite cause the destruction of a whole foot?"

"Hyde says no, but in large doses, the venoms would be toxic enough to do irreparable damage."

"What did your horse's wound look like in the early stages?"

"A large dark red lump with a black center."

Ed's eyes widened. "Shit!" He whipped out his cell phone and punched a button. "Danielle, did that report from Tulsa come in yet?...okay, describe the guy."

A parade of expressions marched across Ed's face, then he snapped the phone shut and stood up. "I was standing next to Travis Mack last night at the barbeque. He had an ugly wound on the back of his hand. He said it was a burn, but you've just described it exactly."

The dark cowboy.

Kellie shivered. "I've seen him a couple of times this weekend. He gave me the creeps."

Ed's serious eyes sent another thump through her chest. "There's more–he was wearing a rodeo trophy buckle from 1985. Said he found it in a pawnshop, but Pete Dayton called me this morning. Said he got a close look at it last night and he's positive it's Randy's. We need to talk to your nephew as soon as he gets to town–see if he knows anything about this guy."

"I'll call you when he shows up...But why would this Mack person be after *me*?"

Ed's phone rang and he turned away to answer, and she stared at the floor, trying to push aside the thought nibbling at the back of her mind.

Ed hung up, his tone gruff. "I have to go. Let me know the minute Jethrow shows up."

Kellie watched the cruiser roar down the lane, the red and blue lights coming on when it reached the road. A chill crept over her bare arms and her head whirled with too many conflicting thoughts. One kept rising to the surface–a feeling she couldn't pin down, an idea she didn't want to believe. She hurried down the hall to her bedroom. Peering at the chubby little boy in the faded photograph, Kellie tried to imagine what he'd look like as an adult. But try as she might, she could not superimpose Travis Mack's sharp, angry features over Jethrow's soft, sad little face. She set the picture frame back on the dresser. What could possibly make him want to hurt her? His voice on the phone had sounded pleasant and mature. She replayed the conversation in her mind, searching for clues, listening for a trigger word or phrase, then shook her head. Jethrow's reappearance was coincidence, nothing more.

And what the hell was Frank doing? His interest in Travis Mack made his involvement in this mess seem more credible, but what was his motive? Pain knifed through her heart, followed by almost debilitating anger. If Frank had *anything* to do with destroying Dancer, she'd kill him herself.

The kitchen screen door banged and the twins marched in, all smiles.

"Where've you guys been? The parade ended hours ago."

Clarke laughed. "Been sight-seeing. Buying souvenirs. Had a killer burger at the Cowboy Café. Guthrie hasn't changed one bit!"

"And I intend to keep it that way."

Cliff looked around the spacious kitchen, then raised an eyebrow and grinned. "For someone who doesn't like change, you sure put a new face on this old place."

Kellie ignored the needling. "Day-to-day life in a 1930's kitchen isn't my idea of efficiency...I did leave the original cabinets, though."

Clarke ran his fingers along the edge of a cupboard door. "This is where I crashed on my skates, remember?"

Kellie chuckled, filled with memories of a childhood filled with rowdy brothers and constant turmoil. "See? I didn't change the good stuff."

"Where's Sara?"

"She was working her horse a little while ago. She's around here somewhere."

"We had a helluva time getting through the patrol cars at the gate."

"Yeah, but it's kinda like closing the barn door a little late."

The photograph with the crosshairs flashed on her mental widescreen and momentary panic seized her. She held her breath, trying to calm her jangled nerves. If this person had wanted to kill Sara, he or she would have already done so. The terror of the idea was far more effective.

Clarke touched her shoulder, his features chiseled with concern. "Kell, what's wrong? You're white as a sheet."

The burst of adrenaline faded. "Nothing. Sara's just been trying to grow up too fast."

He leaned against the counter. "Any leads in the case?"

"Ed Campbell thinks he's found who did it. Some drifter cowhand in Perkins. I think they're questioning him right now."

Clarke's voice reverberated with conviction. "If anyone can catch the bastard, it's Ed Campbell. Your ex-lover boy was one of the top Special Forces agents in Desert Storm."

Kellie leaned against the counter, briefly swept into the past. So much she didn't know.

She gazed at her brothers. "Jethrow called this morning."

Cliff scowled. "Just like that–from out of nowhere? What'd he have to say for himself?"

Kellie's protective instincts flared. "He's been growing up, just needed some time on his own. He's coming up from the city tomorrow to meet with us."

Cliff's words erupted on a snarl. "And have you brainwashed *him* about the land too?"

Her restraint disappeared. "I can't believe you guys. Dad's will is very clear–the land stays in the family."

Clarke's features hardened like she'd never seen before.

"Right. The family *he* approved of. Where the hell does that leave me?"

Cliff touched his twin's arm in a protective gesture. "I speak for both of us. The lawyer says a direct heir cannot be left out of a will. Dad screwed up, and we're going after what rightfully belongs to Clarke."

Kellie walked across the kitchen, struggling to keep her composure. "I have to go to the barn–we'll talk about this later. Make yourselves at *home*."

The afternoon air had thickened, and she looked up at the sky as she strode angrily across the grass toward the barn. A band of heavy black clouds filled the horizon to the south, with larger ones billowing up like mutant mushrooms. Maybe some rain, but probably not. A blip ran through her pulse. More likely a tornado.

She glanced back at the house, thinking about her brothers' treachery, and anger snapped at her pulse. Regardless of how persecuted Clarke might feel, Joshua Sutton had been adamant that no queer son of his would inherit. And now she was in the middle of it.

The barn phone rang and she sprinted toward the office.

~~

Frank moved through the brush, fending off the scratchy branches that tore at his face. Not a wisp of air stirred and the heat pressed into him. He shrugged out of the heavy denim jacket, and unbuttoned his shirt to the waist, but sweat still poured into his eyes and dripped off his chin. He sank to the ground and leaned against a dead oak. How the hell had he fucked this up? All he wanted was to take the heat off the ranch so he could get on with his life.

He tipped his head back and closed his eyes, imagining life with Celeste in faraway exotic places. No worries, plenty of money...

Something rustled in the brush, and he reached for the pistol tucked into his waistband. More rustling sent a thrust of adrenaline coursing through his system. Releasing the safety on the gun, he leveled it at the moving underbrush. A small brown head with a long nose and beady eyes poked through the grass. Frank exhaled sharply, and the armadillo scuttled back into the tall weeds.

His cell phone rang and he started, then stared at the "unknown caller" message. Nausea crawled through his gut.

Rodriguez kept his voice low. "You are a dead man. And so is your brat."

"Estevan, I can fix this. I've found the source of our problem and put him in the ground."

"I need proof. Carlos will come, you show him the body."

"But–" The phone screen went blank.

A gust of air whirled through the branches, cooling his feverish skin. He rose and headed along the tree line toward the section road, stopping every so often to listen for signs of traffic. A hawk screeched overhead and a train whistle moaned in the distance. Taking a deep breath, he made a line drive for the far side of the road and the relative safety of a wheat field.

A few moments later, sweaty, dusty, and itching with chigger bites, he emerged into the open and stood still briefly, gazing across the next open field toward safety. His phone rang and he hesitated, expecting it to be Rodriguez again. His discomfort faded at the sight of Celeste's number.

Her voice didn't have its usual musical lilt. "Frankie, are you all right?"

"Hot and dusty, wishing I was with you instead."

"The police were here this morning. What's going on?"

"Got into a little scrape, but it'll blow over."

"Honey, I'm right here–all you have to do is come over. We'll just disappear."

His heart lurched. It sounded so simple.

"Won't be long, baby. I got a couple things to finish up and then I'm all yours." *Forever.*

Somewhere behind him, a car engine roared and he ducked back into the tall wheat.

"Gotta go...I love you, Celeste. Don't ever forget that."

Her soft voice echoing in his head, Frank sprinted toward the winter hay barn.

~ ~

Ed gripped the phone, waiting for Kellie to pick up. God, he didn't want to make this call. An hour ago, he'd held her in his arms again, struggling to keep the promise of what might be. His chest ached with the emotions, but his mind opened to the calm knowledge that he had a chance to make it right with her, and start over. The sound of her voice sent a knife through the beautiful thought.

He swallowed, trying to level his tone. "Kellie, I'm afraid you're not going to like this–your nephew is Travis Mack."

Her disbelief snapped through the phone. "*No!* It's a mistake!"

"I wish it were, but fingerprints never lie."

"Why would you even have that checked?"

"Something in your eyes when I mentioned the rodeo buckle...you knew right then, didn't you? After Pete unequivocally identified the buckle, I ran the prints from Mack's beer bottle against the cap you found and the prints the state took when Jethrow disappeared. It's a match...I'm really sorry."

"That doesn't mean that he *did* it!"

"I know, but it does mean that he was on your property, and he never let you know he was back until today. Doesn't look good, Kellie. I'll be out there in about half-an-hour."

Kellie hung up on him, and he stared at the report on his desk. Maybe his dreams wouldn't come true after all. Her fierce loyalty to family and heritage could tip the scales. Again.

He shook his head and pressed the intercom. "Danielle, would you come in here, please?"

He took out the white cell phone and changed the ring to vibrate, then rose as Danielle stepped into his office.

"We got a break in the Sutton case. I want you to go with me, I'll fill you in on the way."

"I'll get my hat."

He watched her ramrod posture as she strode down the hall, and wondered briefly what she was really like beneath that brittle exterior. He half smiled to himself. He'd had every opportunity to find out...she'd been more than welcoming when he'd arrived in town.

A deputy stepped out of the next office and glanced down the hall after her, then grinned. "Some piece of work, huh?"

Ed kept his voice low. "You know anything about her?"

"Yeah, she's a hard-ass, ex-Marine, and the word around town is she's a lesbo."

Ed turned slowly and pinned the man with a hard look. "And why is that?"

The deputy blanched and stepped back. "Uh, well, she hasn't ever been seen with a man, and–" He nodded. "Just nasty rumors, that's all."

Ed didn't respond and the deputy ducked back into his office. Danielle reappeared at the end of the hall, and Ed's curiosity faded. A career in the Corps said it all.

They stopped at the dispatch office and he leaned his head in the window.

"We're headed out to the Sutton place. Have an available unit meet us there."

Inside the cruiser, Danielle's spicy personal scent tickled Ed's nose. Perfume on a cop didn't seem right. He cleared his throat, keeping his tone gruff.

"Do we have anything on Frazier?"

She snorted. “He won’t get far. That monster ride of his is easy to spot.”

“Don’t be too sure. He isn’t stupid. My guess is he’s driving something else.”

She didn’t respond, but the air grew thick with animosity.

He cleared his throat. “Listen, Danielle, I want to make this right. A lot of things went into my taking this job, but it’s only temporary. I’m *not* planning to seek re-election. You’re the one for the job, and I’ll support you a hundred percent.”

Her dark eyes considered him for a moment. “So, you’re going to just go off and leave her again?”

Surprise jolted through his gut, but he kept his expression neutral. “What I do after this job is nobody’s business.” He turned onto the highway and glanced over at her, hoping he’d made his point.

A wry smile curled her full lips. “Men. They never get it.”

~ ~

Kellie slowly replaced the phone into the base. This couldn’t be happening. Jethrow would never do anything to hurt his own family. Maybe he’d been afraid to show himself because he thought she’d be angry with him for running away.

Voices echoed in the barn, then Roy stuck his head in. “I’m goin’ down to the pond pasture to repair that gate.”

“Okay. Did you tell Sara her uncles are here?”

“She hasn’t come back yet.”

Kellie’s gaze snapped to the clock on the wall. “Oh God!”

She raced out into the aisle and ran smack into Hyde.

He chuckled and helped her regain her balance. “Where’s the fire?”

"Sara's been gone for too long. Something's wrong–I have to go look for her."

"I'll come too." He headed down the row of stalls toward the workhorses.

Kellie snatched open a stall door, talking softly to the nervous gelding inside. Five minutes later, she left the barn through the rear door.

Hyde sat bareback on a pinto with one blue eye. "We should split up. I'll head west toward the winter hay barn."

"I'll check the south forty. If you find her, call my cell."

They both moved through the gate, then set off at a brisk trot. Kellie glanced at Hyde, so light on the horse's back, leaning to the side to scan the ground for tracks and gopher holes, guiding his mount with a single rein and a hackamore.

Kellie's horse snorted and danced nervously, unused to being out in the open fields. Tightening the reins a little, Kellie scanned the horizon, seeing only a vast sea of long grass. The boiling clouds had broken up into brown-gray patches against the pale blue sky, and the mugginess had lessened.

She turned and headed toward the area where Roy had seen the grass beaten down. As she rode, everything began to come together. If Jethrow were back in the area, he'd have gone home. Despair writhed through her mind. She didn't want to believe it, but from the small house, he'd easily be able to walk unseen through the fields. The photographs had been taken through a long-range lens. If she examined them closely, the angle would be from this direction. Sadness moved through her heart. The fingerprint match put Jethrow right in her back yard.

Her horse neighed loudly, and a movement up ahead jerked her out of the awful thoughts. She squinted against the late afternoon glare, then a slither of fear moved through her chest, wrapping around her breastbone like a boa constrictor.

Juicy trotted toward her. Riderless.

17

Travis moved quickly and silently down the hall toward the kitchen. Standing to one side of the window, he watched Sara dismount and drop the reins onto the ground, then walk over to his truck and peer in. She turned and looked at the house.

He clenched his jaw so hard the muscles in his neck ached. The little brat was the spitting image of her mother. Frizzy red hair, ski jump nose, skinny legs. What the fuck was she doing nosing around out here? This was *his* place–weren't almost five hundred acres enough for them? He stepped back from the window and waited for her to leave, taking deep breaths to calm the surging pulse that sent shocks of pain into his hand.

The door latch jiggled and he shrank back into the dark pantry. The door opened slowly and Sara's head appeared.

"Hello? Anybody here?"

She hesitated, then stepped into the kitchen, closing the door softly behind her. Travis stopped breathing. What the hell was he going to do? She could fuck up everything! Then he almost laughed out loud. What difference did it make? In a couple of hours, they'd all be history.

He stepped out of the pantry. "Looking for something?"

She jerked and wheeled around, her eyes almost popping out of her head. "Holy shit, who are *you*?"

"Tsk, tsk. Does your mother know you talk like a cowpoke?"

Her small features hardened into a scowl, and the green eyes glinted. "What are you doing here? This is private property. My mommy owns it."

He chuckled. "Feisty little bitch, ain'tcha?" He took a step forward, taking pleasure in seeing her back away. "Let me introduce myself, Sara. I'm Cousin Jethrow."

Surprise widened her eyes and lifted her eyebrows into peaks that wrinkled her freckled forehead. Then suspicion crept across her face.

"No you're not. Jethrow's dead–I heard my uncles talking about it."

Anger rushed in, but Travis quelled it. Nothing mattered at this point.

He grinned. "Let's play twenty questions and I'll prove who I am." He walked across the kitchen and reached into a cooler. "Wanna beer?"

She giggled. "I'm not allowed."

"Hell, I was drinkin' whiskey when I was three."

"Did your parents know?"

He handed her a soda, then cracked a beer. "They gave it to me."

"Are you *really* my cousin?"

He headed toward the living room. "*You* decide."

Sara perched on the ottoman and gazed around the room. "I've never been in here before. Mom said it was filled with sad memories."

"She got *that* right." He swigged some beer and wiped his mouth with his sleeve. "You're a helluva good pole bender."

Delight widened her eyes and a smile opened up dimples in her cheeks. "How do you know?"

"Watched you yesterday. That's some fancy pinto you got. What's his name?"

"Dancer's Juice, Juicy for short." Suddenly she leaped off the footstool. "Oh my god, I didn't tie him!" She ran into the kitchen and out the back door.

Seconds later, her wail drifted on the afternoon air, and Travis watched her through the kitchen window. She scanned the empty fields, calling the horse's name, moving farther away from the house, skirting the barn, then heading across the open field toward the windmill. He snatched open the door and shouted her name, then took off after her, catching up to her fifty feet from the tornado shelter.

She turned to face him, tears pouring down her cheeks. "Mom will kill me!"

"Come on, I'll take you home. Horses always head for the barn when they're loose. He's probably already in his stall, munching hay."

She gulped back a sob and nodded. A hollow thud hummed through the quiet, followed by another, and she jerked around to look behind her. "What was that?"

"Nothin'. The windmill needs adjusting."

She gazed up at the blades, which barely moved in the soft breeze. The thumping echoed again and she hesitated, then followed him back toward the house. When they reached the yard, she started toward the truck, but Travis took her shoulders and steered her toward the kitchen door.

"I wanna finish my beer. Besides, we haven't played our game yet."

She slumped down on the ottoman and sniffled, her expression sullen. Irritation prickled across his neck. Maybe he should lock her up with Tina–they could bawl on each other's shoulder.

He gulped some beer, then grinned at his guest.

"Hey, you ever seen someone with their brains blown out?"

~ ~

Kellie reined in and dismounted, keeping her eye on Juicy as he approached. The pinto neighed and Kellie's horse answered. Moving swiftly through the long grass, Kellie lifted a hand and called the horse's name. He trotted up to her and blew the dust from his nostrils, then dropped his head to snatch a mouthful of grass.

Her heart thumped as she gathered the reins. One had broken off where he'd stepped on it–at least, that's what she hoped. Fighting images of Sara sprawled on the ground somewhere with a broken neck, Kellie led Juicy back to her own horse, then remounted. She nudged the horse into a brisk trot, turning in the direction from which Juicy had appeared. The southern section, and Randy's house.

Her thoughts raced as she searched, terrified she'd find her daughter's small body. The past fifteen minutes had lengthened into what seemed like hours. The house came into view and the worst scenarios faded, quickly replaced by new ones. Was Jethrow in there? Was Sara with him? Would he hurt her, as he'd hurt the horses? Kellie slowed her horse to a walk and circled toward the west to get a view of the back of the building. What would she do if there were trouble? She stopped to unbuckle the small saddlebag behind the cantle. If someone hadn't been too efficient, her coyote gun would be there. Her fingers closed on cold metal and her fear subsided a bit.

Urging the horse on, she kept her eyes on the house, watching for signs of life. A pickup truck with Texas plates sat parked outside the back door. She hesitated, then trotted the horses into the shade of the barn and stopped. Nearby, the hum of bumblebees working through a clump of fleabane was the only sound in the heavy afternoon air.

"Sara! Where are you?"

Nothing stirred and Kellie's fear grew. She called out again, the screen door flew open, and a small streak of blue denim dashed out.

"Mommy!"

Kellie jumped down and met Sara just behind the truck. Curling her arms around the small trembling body, she buried her face in the flyaway red curls.

"Oh my god, baby, you scared me half to death!" She hugged harder, and Sara began to squirm.

"Mom, you're choking me!"

A soft male voice resonated from close by. "Howdy, Aunt Kellie. Come on up."

She released Sara and stared at the angular face, the hard eyes, the thin lips curling into a smile that more resembled a sneer. This couldn't be the adult version of the somber teen who'd run away so long ago.

Travis stepped closer and removed his hat. "Ma'am, good to see you again."

Kellie tried to absorb what she was seeing and hearing. Campbell was wrong–this wasn't her nephew. Jethrow had masses of curly hair, the Sutton trademark.

She glowered. "Who *are* you, and what are you doing on my property?"

"*Your* property? Why, Auntie! I'm wounded to the core–surely you haven't forgotten your favorite brother's only child." The sneer opened into a nasty smile, revealing familiar crooked teeth. "But then, maybe you have. After all, if he doesn't exist, you can keep all this oil rich land for yourself."

Kellie took a deep breath and turned to Sara. "You get back home, right now. I'll deal with you later."

The child's eyes widened and she opened her mouth to protest, but Kellie was firm.

"*Now!* And don't tell your uncles about this, you understand?"

Sara started to go, but Travis snaked an arm out and grabbed her wrist. "Hold up now. We're just getting acquainted."

Sara's eyes glistened with tears. "You're hurting me!"

Kellie stepped forward, but Travis pinned her with a look that set her blood to running cold.

"We have some catching up to do, don't we, Auntie?"

~~

Ed's chest tightened as he related the chain of events and his suspicions to Danielle. She listened intently, making only one comment.

"If the nephew is our man, why would he reveal himself?"

"The kind of person who could do something like this wants closure, proof that he has accomplished whatever goal he's set. Something in the Sutton family history will be the key. I'm sure of it."

Danielle was silent for a moment and, when she spoke, her tone was cautious. "You probably know the family better than anyone. Anything come to mind?"

"On the surface, the Suttons were very clannish, but the truth of the inner relationships is ugly. The kid was a strange one, I remember that much."

"Seems kind of stupid to chance getting arrested."

Ed shook his head slowly. "A sociopath doesn't believe it could ever happen."

They turned into the lane leading to the ranch, and pulled up beside another patrol car parked in the grass. Ed rolled down the window.

"Anything going on out here?"

The deputy assigned to protect Kellie shook his head. "Nope, just watchin' the grass grow." He grinned. "Pretty good duty."

"Nap time's over–stay put until we call you."

He drove on up the lane and turned into the gravel parking area in front of the house, a painful knot forming in his stomach. He glanced over at Danielle.

"You wait here. Call dispatch and tell them where we are."

He stepped out into the muggy warm air and positioned his hat, staring at the heavy oak door to his past. His boots thumped on the wood planks, matching his heartbeat. He rapped loudly, his muscles twitching with tension.

The door opened and Clarke Sutton's handsome face broke into a wide grin.

"Eddie Campbell! You old son-of-a-gun!"

Ed's tension faded and he grasped the outstretched hand and laughed. "I sure didn't expect to see you here."

"Hey, we have to keep up with our family heritage, and 89er Days is as good an excuse as any." He yelled over his shoulder. "Cliff! Come look who's here!"

Ed stepped back as the two men came out onto the porch. "Is Kellie here?"

"No, she went over the barn for something. She'll be back in a few minutes. Tell us how the investigation is going."

Ed pursed his lips. "Slowly. I take it you two didn't get a message from Oklahoma City PD."

Cliff's eyebrows shot up. "What do they want with *us*?

Ed glanced at Danielle watching them from the car. "Just routine. We're trying to eliminate as many suspects as possible."

Clarke's face darkened, all vestiges of friendliness disappearing. "And *we're* on your list? Who the fuck do you think you are?"

Ed stared back. "I'm the sheriff of Logan County, and I'm doing my job."

Cliff stepped up close, his voice filled with threat. "Listen, *Eddie*–you just take your hero ass back to town. This is our property and we aim to protect it, not destroy it."

Ed didn't budge. "Is that a fact? So why are you working so hard to force Kellie to sell out? Would destroying her livelihood help your cause?"

Cliff's arm snapped back, and a loud click nearby froze the action in mid-air.

"I wouldn't do that, if I were you." Danielle's dark eyes were hard, and her revolver held steady.

~~

A quick stab of nostalgia pierced Kellie's fear as she stepped into the familiar kitchen and looked around. Images swirled through her head. All the times she and Randy had sat at the table, sifting ideas and solving problems, making plans, strengthening the deep loving bond between them. She ran her fingers lightly over the back of the old oak chair, wondering how to start with her nephew.

The unmistakable slide of the deadbolt made her pulse jump, then Travis's soft voice wrapped around her growing fear.

"The old place brings back memories, huh?" He pulled a beer out of the cooler. "You oughta swing through the barn while you're here. Now *there's* a memory!"

His jerky movements made his gestures look as though marionette strings controlled his hands and arms. A muscle in his jaw twitched incessantly, and his small dark eyes focused on something in his head. Kellie's skin prickled. She felt like she was caged with a lion. Was he on drugs? Mentally unstable? Panic rose in her chest. She knew nothing about this man–where he'd been or the life he'd led.

Sara scuttled over and clung to her waist. "Mommy, I want to go home."

Kellie stroked the soft curls, garnering all the confidence she could muster. "In a few minutes, honey. You go in the living room while I talk to your cousin."

She met Travis's amused gaze, silently defying him to challenge her. He nodded, and Sara walked toward the front room, stopping once to look back, her features pinched with fear.

Travis raised the beer bottle in a mock toast, and Kellie's fear turned to nausea. A gaping wound on the back of his hand was identical to the gory hole in Dancer's foot.

He leaned against the kitchen counter and crossed one boot over the other. "I'm lookin' forward to the big barbeque tonight."

She took a shallow breath to level her voice. "Everyone's excited to see you again." She refocused on the chameleon change in his demeanor and, with the transition, a hint of the familiar returned. This man really was her nephew–surely that meant something to him. She took a step forward, softening her tone. "How long have you been out here, Jethrow?"

"Don't call me that! My name's Travis!"

His eyes bugged out with the intensity of his words.

"Jethrow was your great-great-grandfather."

"I don't fuckin' care if he was the fuckin' president! You got any idea what it's like to have a fuckin' sissy name?"

He pushed away from the counter and Kellie fought the reflex to step back.

His expression changed to a wide grin. "Anyway, I've been here long enough to know I want what's mine."

She avoided looking at his hand, resisting the urge to ask him about the pictures, the horses, all of it. *Don't play detective. Just get the hell out of here.*

"While we have some time alone, would you tell me why you ran away?"

His eyebrows came together. "Figure it out, lady. Being your little puppet wasn't what I had in mind." He pushed away from the counter. "You never had the time of day for any of us when Dad was alive, then all of a sudden, you're Earth Mother, fawning all over me like some precious posy you grew yourself."

The tic returned to his jaw and his agitation grew.

A plan formed in Kellie's head. "I made some mistakes, Jeth–Travis. I can see that now, and I'm so sorry. When your dad died, something inside me died too–I couldn't focus on anything but the pain. I let you down, but I'll make it up to you, I promise." She gestured around the room. "We'll get the place cleaned and painted. I'll help you get started with whatever you want to do out here–cattle, alfalfa, anything you want."

His voice came out a growl. "You just don't get it, do you? If any one of you had really cared about Dad, he'd still be alive."

A cold chill raced over her skin. "What do you mean?"

His agitation escalated, the twitch taking on a life of its own. "A shambling moron could see his desperation, but no–you fuckers were too busy with your fancy lives!"

Sickening reality oozed into Kellie's thoughts. The boy wouldn't have known about her efforts to help Randy pull himself back together. The mortgage payments she'd forked over to keep the land from being seized while her brother wallowed in self-pity. The offers to pay for professional counseling.

Jethrow had embraced his hatred with a vengeance, and now the concept of an eye-for-an-eye had cost *her*.

She assumed a soothing tone. "You're right, and I'm so sorry. Please let me help you now."

His words were thick with malice. "Oh, I plan on it."

She struggled to maintain a neutral expression as she stepped over to the living room door and looked in. "You okay, honey?"

Sara sat on the couch, her gaze glued to something on the cushion beside her–a gleaming rifle with a mounted camera scope.

Pain and anger fought for first place in Kellie's head.

18

Cool air washed over Frank's sweaty skin and he blew out a long breath of relief. Locking the door behind him, he turned to the crude shelves lining three walls. If he could outwait the law and get out of here with even a fraction of this stuff, he'd be set forever. His heart warmed with thoughts of spending the rest of his life with Celeste. The visions faded and his throat tightened. He'd never see Sara again. He leaned on the worktable and closed his eyes, remembering her wide-eyed curiosity about his life outside the ranch. Why had he made so many bad choices?

His phone rang and he stared again at "unknown caller" on the screen.

Rodriguez kept his message short. "Carlos will be there any minute. You give me proof, I let your family live."

Frank shook his head. The man's word was about as reliable as a smoke ring. "You'll have it."

He disconnected, then set the phone to vibrate mode. *Carlos is in for a big surprise.*

Roaming around the room, he took stock. On the floor beneath the shelving were several cardboard boxes with black marker writing on the sides. He squatted down and pulled one out. It contained several gallon jugs of water. He dragged out another box and opened the flaps. Canned beans, tuna, evaporated milk, and a box of crackers the mice had discovered. The third box held an assortment of paper plates, plastic utensils, cups, paper napkins, and toilet paper.

He rocked back on his heels and chuckled. He could hide for a long time with these provisions.

A sound outside the door brought him to his feet. He pulled the revolver from his waistband and released the safety. A sharp rap. A gruff accent, muffled by the thick wood.

Frank stepped up close. "Who's there?"

"Carlos."

"I'll be out in a minute. Go wait in your truck."

He stepped back from the door, thinking over his plan one more time. Carlos was slow-witted, so it wouldn't be hard to lure him to the back side of the barn. Frank smiled grimly. A year's worth of hay could hide a body for a long time.

Suddenly, a gun retort echoed in the stairwell and the doorjamb splintered. Frank leaped back and aimed his own weapon. It looked as though he'd have no need for a cover story.

The door swung open and Estevan Rodriguez stepped over the threshold.

~ ~

Kellie's insides recoiled at Travis's tone. Sara had risen from the couch, but Kellie shook her head, warning her to stay put.

The child turned to Travis. "Are you coming to the barbecue tonight?"

"Hell, yes! I been planning this reunion for a long time."

Sara relaxed visibly, her curiosity taking over. "Do you ride?"

The tension in the room lessened and he guffawed. "Missy, I got calluses on my ass from spendin' my days in the saddle, wrangling cattle."

"Bet I can out-ride you on the poles."

"Yeah, you probably could."

"May I go to the bathroom?"

He nodded, then turned to Kellie. "Want a beer? We've got some catchin' up to do."

She watched Sara disappear down the dark hallway, then followed Travis into the kitchen, scrutinizing the man who bore no resemblance to her memories. He was hard and lean and tall, with a confident swagger that mirrored his expression. His mood swings might afford an opportunity for them to escape. She'd play along.

The brew fizzed down her parched throat. "What do you want to talk about?"

He moved to the kitchen window. "That barn. I think it needs to come down, build something better."

"We can do that. The guys at the ranch built an equipment garage in a weekend. I can–"

Travis turned his head slowly and stared at her from fathoms of darkness. "You think I need *you*?" He snorted and returned his attention to the landscape.

He'd retreated into his own head again, and Kellie wondered if the front door was unlocked. With him right there in the kitchen, she wouldn't be able to use the back door.

She let her gaze drift to his swollen hand. It was a clue to what happened to her horses–she was sure of it.

"What happened to your hand? Looks like you could use a doctor."

He glanced at the wound, then shook his head. "Nah, it's just a spider bite. I've had worse." He set his beer bottle on the counter with a bang. "Where's that kid?" He moved to the living room door and hollered, "Hey, get back in here. You've had enough time to have a baby in there!"

Sara didn't respond and Kellie started toward the hall, but Travis grabbed her arm hard, sending pain deep into the flesh.

"I'll get 'er."

He pushed Kellie back into the kitchen, and headed down the hall. She followed, her heart thundering in her ears.

Sara screamed and Travis's voice echoed in the bathroom. "You little bitch!"

Sara screamed again, then began to cry. Kellie charged into the bathroom and stopped short.

Travis had reverted to the personality that empowered him, his eyes smoldering with hate. "Your little brat was on her way out the window."

He shoved Sara toward the door, then stepped up close to Kellie's face. His breath smelled of stale alcohol and cigarettes. But worse, at that intimate distance, she saw the depth of his intent.

His eyes glittered. "Go out in the living room."

Kellie bit back the knee-jerk reaction to say something nasty, instead taking hold of Sara's shoulders and guiding her into the hall.

"It's okay, honey. Just do what he says."

Sara whimpered. "I was only trying to help."

Travis snarled, "Shut up! Get over on the couch!"

Kellie approached the worn sofa and eyed the gleaming rifle, wondering if she could grab it and hold him off long enough to escape.

He picked up the rifle and laughed. "Nice try. Now don't move unless I tell you to."

She would have to talk her way out of this. Maybe she could think of something to say that would put her nephew back into his other personality. She scanned the room and spotted the empty shadowbox where Randy's treasured rodeo buckle had been displayed for so many years.

She gestured toward a framed photograph of Randy roping a steer. "I remember how proud you were of your dad. We all were–he was a true champion."

Travis's expression softened a little. "Yeah, and he

could've been even greater..." The softness disappeared. "If that bitch hadn't dragged him down."

Kellie struggled to keep her tone level. "After you disappeared, she came around and tried to claim the land as her inheritance."

His eyes widened. "No shit!"

"God's truth." Kellie met his gaze with growing courage. "It cost me fifty thousand dollars to settle with her. This piece of the Sutton estate belongs to you, and I was damned if I'd let some gold-digger floozy have it."

Shaking his head, Travis leaned the rifle against the wall, but said nothing. The news had obviously affected him deeply.

She took advantage of the momentum. "I see you kept the buckle all these years."

He moved his fingers almost lovingly over the face of the design, and the tension on his face eased. "Yeah, it keeps him close to me all the time."

Kellie's confidence grew and her brain swirled with how next to proceed. Suddenly, Travis straightened up and a scowl furrowed his dark brows.

"Who the hell is *that*?"

She followed his gaze to the picture window, and she nearly fainted with relief.

Sara jumped up from the couch. "Uncle Hyde!"

Her friend's appaloosa trotted briskly through the long grass toward the house.

Travis snatched up the rifle and stepped back. "You listen up 'cause I'm only gonna say this once. I'll kill the Injun if you don't do exactly what I say. Go out there and tell him you found the kid here, and everything is fine. Nothing else. Then you get your horses and head for home at a leisurely trot. I'll be listening and watching, and if you try anything funny, I'll shoot your brat first, then your friend."

Travis's deep-set eyes darkened into bottomless pools. "And for dessert, I'll shoot *you*."

~ ~

Outside, Kellie shivered in the afternoon warmth, trying to handle the terror rolling through her insides. Why was Jethrow letting them go? The sickening truth almost overwhelmed her–he wasn't. Out there in the middle of nowhere, he'd use them for target practice, pick them off one by one. He was a Jekyll-Hyde, and all the family support in the world couldn't save him–maybe not even professional help.

Rage coursed through her heart. Knowing he'd destroyed her horses, all familial concern for his welfare disappeared.

She took Sara's hand. "You must do exactly as he said. He's sick, and he *will* kill us."

The child nodded solemnly, her eyes wide with fear. Kellie started toward the corner of the house to head off Hyde.

Sara whispered, "Mom, the horses are gone. What are we gonna do?"

Kellie's adrenaline kicked in and she turned back to the open kitchen window. "Travis, we have to go find the horses. I'll tell Hyde to go on home."

A long silence sent her fear into overdrive.

Finally, his blood-chilling voice drifted through the screen. "Go ahead, but remember this gun is long range."

Hyde rounded the corner and reined in. "Jeez, Kellie, what've you been doing out here all this time? You gave me a good scare."

Her mouth turned to cotton and she swallowed hard, trying to form a normal response.

His expression sharpened. "What's wrong?" He slid off the horse and took a step forward.

"Nothing! The horses got loose. You go on back, we'll follow."

His eyes registered disbelief, then his gaze moved past her to the pickup. Her heart hammered in her ears as she took his arm and pointed out toward a field, her whisper ragged.

"Please, go back. He'll kill us if you don't."

Hyde nodded and stepped away, speaking loudly. "Okay, well, hurry up–everyone's waitin' to eat."

In one graceful movement, he mounted his horse and reined around to the right. Kellie nearly threw up as he trotted back the way he'd come. She glanced at Sara, small and frightened. What could they do? Jethrow would just shoot them anyway–she knew it in her heart. Taking Sara's hand, she pulled her around in front, shielding the child with her own body. They started toward the field, Kellie wondering which step would be her last.

The grass swished against her legs as she walked around to the far side of the barn, out of sight of the house. The still afternoon air had grown muggy again, and the sky was a hazy ceiling. Her knees began to wobble and she leaned against the barn, gasping for breath to quell the panic.

"Will Uncle Hyde send help?"

A sob cracked Kellie's voice. "I think so, honey, but we have to do this right now."

She scanned the fields, a strange image forming in her mind. The haggard men and women of the land rush, huddled under makeshift shelters, doggedly guarding their piece of the promised land. She shuddered, struck by the reality of their sacrifices–all for the sake of a dream. Not too different from her own life. *Why am I thinking about this* now?

A light breeze blew from the south, and she looked toward the old windmill. The blades turned slowly, then another movement at the base caught her eye. The horses nosed through the grass, oblivious to the evil.

Sara called out to Juicy and his head came up. He watched them for a minute, neighed once, then dropped his head to continue pulling up clumps of grass. A booming thump stopped Kellie in mid-stride. Thunder? She frowned up at the cloudless sky. The hollow, resounding thumps increased in volume as they neared the windmill.

"Mom, what's that noise?"

Kellie squinted at the blades, trying to pinpoint the sound. It came again, but from a different direction. The heavy air buffered the thumps, the breeze hurling it around, playing tricks on her sense of direction.

"I don't know. Something is probably out of balance in the old shaft."

"Yeah, Cousin Travis said it needs adjusting."

An involuntary shudder shook Kellie's courage. Everything that had meant so much to her had become a deadly heritage.

She grabbed her gelding's reins and turned to Sara. "Now remember, act calm, stay right next to me, and don't go faster than a trot." She swung up into the saddle and tried to reassure her daughter with a confident smile she didn't feel. "It's going to be fine. Sheriff Campbell will take care of everything."

19

Travis watched his aunt through the kitchen window. She was dumber than he'd thought. A regular Pollyanna, thinking she could make everything right with words. And that's all they were–empty promises.

He stepped away from the window and glanced around. "Time to get ready for my party."

He pulled the last beer from the cooler, then sauntered into the living room. He pulled the dingy sheets off the overstuffed chairs, straightened some pictures on the wall, and collected the empty beer bottles. When he'd finished, he stood very still. Listening. Smiling. No echoes from the past, no stale whiskey and cigarette odors to bring back the memories. He picked up the rifle and headed out to his truck, a smile forming in his head.

He'd scared the shit out of Kellie and her kid.

He grinned at his reflection in the rearview mirror. "She ain't seen nothin' yet."

From the upper third of the field north of his house, Travis could see the barns and corrals of Kellie's ranch. To the east, a thick stand of pecan trees sequestered the estate farmhouse. Everyone would be there by now. He squinted at the scene. This would be one barbeque he'd never forget.

The old metal gas cans weighed almost eighty pounds each, but years of manhandling cantankerous steers had built enough upper arm strength that he barely grunted as he carried the containers through the grass.

A heavy rumble broke the warm air and he glowered at the gathering clouds. "Don't you dare fuckin' rain on my parade!"

The thunder growled and bumped while he worked and, twenty minutes later, he pitched the last empty can aside. He wiped the sweat from his forehead, and reached into his shirt pocket for a cigarette.

The wind had picked up, buffeting his back as he cupped his hands around the flame on the lighter. Then pulling a deep drag of smoke into his lungs, he gazed at the back of his hand.

"Yep, better get this looked at."

He stared out over the long brown grass bowing before the wind, and peace settled into his mind.

He took another long pull on the cigarette, then tossed it, watching it sail into the air and skid sideways on a gust of wind. In seconds, the dry grass exploded, flames racing away in both directions, licking at the trail of gasoline and igniting everything in its path. The wide arc of fire raced toward Kellie's ranch. Tension bordering on erotic excitement tightened his gut and he started to laugh, caught up in the intoxicating poetic justice of his deed.

"Th-th-that's all, folks!"

~~

Even with all the windows rolled down, the inside of the cruiser was sweltering. Ed removed his hat and wiped the sweat from his forehead.

"What the devil is taking Kellie so long?"

Danielle fanned herself with a newspaper. "Want me to go find out?"

"No, I'm not in any hurry to tell her the news." He glanced sideways at his deputy. "You didn't have to draw your gun on those two–I had it under control."

"What's the matter? Can't stand being protected by a girl?"

Her husky chuckle overrode the sarcasm, and Ed grinned.

"Are you a girl? Could've fooled me." He turned away and looked straight out the windshield. "You'll make a great sheriff."

A curtain moved at the living room window, and Clarke's face appeared. Ed opened the car door.

"I'm going to find Kellie. Tell dispatch we're still here."

Striding across the gravel, he replayed his earlier conversation with Kellie. He understood her resistance to the information about her nephew–her family loyalties had always been her driving force, sometimes to her detriment. If Travis Mack was the one responsible for the tragedy in the barn, could she distance herself from the blood ties? Once upon a time, Ed would have thought he knew the answer–now, he couldn't be sure.

Stepping into the cool interior of the barn, he exhaled with pleasure at the relief from the heat. The evening feed was underway, and he approached a young man tossing flakes of hay into empty stalls.

"Ms. Sutton around?"

"Dunno, ask Roy."

Ed continued down the aisle and saw the old man by the office, writing something on a blackboard.

"Howdy, Sheriff. You lookin' for Ms. Kellie? She and Hyde rode outta here 'bout an hour ago."

Ed's gut bucked. "Where?"

"Not sure, but they headed south through the fields. They was lookin' for Miss Sara." His wrinkled face moved into a frown. "Sumpin' wrong?"

"Can I borrow a horse?"

Terrible thoughts raced through Ed's mind as he followed the old man across the aisle. Roy tightened the cinch on a saddle, then turned to Ed.

"Anything I can do?"

Ed swung into the saddle. "Yes, go over to the house and tell the deputy to meet me at the old Randolph Sutton house."

He kneed the horse forward without waiting for a response, then urged his mount into a canter the minute they cleared the barn door. The big chestnut gelding gathered himself and Ed leaned forward as they sailed over the fence, landing with a hard thud. To the south, ominous clouds gathered, reflecting the fear growing in his chest.

He tried to remember the shortest way to Randy's place. The memories of horseback rides with Kellie merged with images of her in the clutches of a lunatic. His horse thundered over the hard ground, and Ed suddenly came to his senses and slowed the horse to a brisk trot. A second later, he heard a shout and reined in. He looked around, but saw nothing. Then he heard the voice again and turned toward the west. A lone rider approached. Ed started off in that direction and, in moments, recognized Hyde Browning.

"Ed, someone's got Kellie and Sara over at Randy's old place. I don't know who or any details, but she managed to tell me he's threatening to kill them."

"How'd you find this out?"

Hyde described the charade, and Ed took a deep breath. "It's her nephew.

"There was a green Ford pickup parked in the yard. Texas license plate started with AZ9."

Ed punched the radio button. "Danielle, where are you?"

Her voice sounded strange and tinny. "I'm parked down the section road from the house. I don't see any vehicles or signs of life."

"Can you see anyone on horseback?"

"Nope. What do you want me to do?"

"Stay put, I'll be there in a few minutes." He punched the button again. "All units. Sutton Estate quadrants. BOLO green Ford truck, Texas plates, AZ9. Owner Travis Mack. Consider suspect armed and dangerous. Over."

He turned to Hyde. "You go on back–"

"Forget that. Kellie's my friend too. And you shouldn't be out here alone in the sights of a crazy person with a rifle."

~~

Kellie jumped down and handed the sweaty horse off to Roy and moved toward Sara. She pulled the small shivering body close, terrified to ever let go again. Sara began to cry, and Kellie stroked her hair.

"It's okay, honey, we're safe now. I'll call the sheriff."

"Sheriff took off on one of the horses, Miz Kellie. He was goin' to look for you."

"Oh, my God! Jethrow will shoot him!"

She raced out of the barn, Sara beside her. A county cruiser was turning around in the driveway as she approached.

She waved her arms and yelled, "Wait! Hey!"

The car roared down the drive, lights flashing. Despair raged through Kellie's head. She turned and ran toward the porch where her brothers stood.

"Ed's in trouble! We have to call for help!"

Sara's voice shrilled from a few feet away. "Mom! I smell smoke!"

Kellie whirled around, automatically looking toward the barns. The acrid odor of burning vegetation filled her nostrils and she exhaled sharply, racing out to the driveway where she could see beyond the trees sheltering the house. Brown smoke rose across the horizon, enveloping the wide expanse of land. The dull rumble of thunder vibrated the air, followed by a jagged bolt of lightning to the west. A gust of wind blew the terrifying odor into her face and she took off at a dead run, while trying to pull her cell phone from the belt holder. Then, she stopped and stared at the display–she hadn't recharged the battery.

Cliff appeared beside her. "Tell us what to do!"

"Call 911!" She turned to look at the approaching bank of smoke, now punctuated by vivid orange flames. The haze settled across the late afternoon sun, turning it into a giant pulsing globe hovering at the edge of the horizon. Terror consumed her. The fire would race across the parched fields to claim the barns–nothing would stop it. And Ed was out there somewhere. Nausea slammed into the back of her throat and she drew a shuddery breath, trying to quiet her fear. He'd be all right–he'd probably been in worse situations.

She turned to Clarke. "We have to get the horses out of the barns before the fire gets there!"

He looked scared. "And take them *where*?"

"*Anywhere*–but for God's sake, don't turn them loose or they'll run back inside! Sara, you and Roy start pulling horses out of stalls and help Uncle Clarke get them into the field across the road–the one with the pond."

Terrified whinnies pierced the air and she wheeled around. Dark shapes raced back and forth against a fiery backdrop–her pregnant mares were trapped in the path of the inferno.

She pointed toward the south pasture. "Cliff, open that gate!"

She raced into the main barn, stopping only long enough to grab a saddle rag and tie it over her nose and mouth.

The gelding she'd ridden earlier rolled his eyes when she ran into his stall. She snapped two lead ropes to his halter and dragged him out into the aisle. With the sharp odor of smoke, panic had coiled through the barn, and the horse danced and dodged, tossing his head. Kellie scrambled onto his bare back and wrapped her legs around his barrel. She leaned forward and gave him a sharp kick in the flank. He galloped out of the barn, then reared and tried to turn back, but Kellie slammed her heels into his sides and he shot forward.

A dull roar inundated her senses, and determination replaced her fear. She raced through the open gate, the wind buffeting her as she tried to steer the horse toward the crazed herd in the middle of the field. Smoke burned her eyes and tears coursed down her cheeks. Even the cloth-filtered smoke seared her lungs, but the terrified cries of the trapped horses spurred her on.

Suddenly her horse planted all four feet, skidding into a perfect sliding stop. Kellie flew over his shoulder, hitting the ground with a bone-jolting thud. The herd's natural instinct to be with other horses sent them pounding toward her. She scrambled to her feet and grabbed the horse's lead rope, pulling him around to face her. The herd was closing in and Kellie began to run toward the open gate, dragging the reluctant gelding behind her. Twenty terrified horses thundered past her, and the gelding took off to join them, whipping the lead rope through her hand. Searing pain knifed through the raw rope burn and she stopped, gasping for what little air remained. The herd ran straight through the gate and headed for the main barn.

She started screaming, but Roy had already seen the problem. He pulled a blue plastic tarp off a pile of wood shavings, and flapped it at the confused horses. The herd stopped, then milled around. The dogs began working the frightened animals and, soon, Sara and Cliff were able to catch two horses and lead them down the ranch road. The rest followed, with the dogs nipping at the their heels.

Kellie's knees almost buckled with relief, then she looked behind her. The fire was closing in fast.

~ ~

Travis lit another cigarette and took a long drag on it. Narrowing his eyes against the brilliance of the flames, self-righteous satisfaction curled through his chest. The promise of revenge was intoxicating. The fire was out of control, the roar of the burning brush enhanced by booming thunder. Travis listened, orchestrating in his head the background music for a thrilling movie. He was the omnipotent director of this production. The wind picked up, sucked forward by the oxygen-gobbling flames that moved faster and faster. Over the din, he heard the distant wail of sirens, and he cackled.

"Too late!"

They'd be at it all day, but didn't have a chance of a snowball in hell of saving the barn and house.

"Okay by me. I always hated that fucking place."

The fire reached a hedgerow along a small dry stream bed, and the flames leaped higher as they fed on the brittle, water-starved brush. Sparks drifted through the air, whirling in the wind currents, landing in trees and igniting new blazes.

"Just like in the movies."

Banks of heavy smoke roiled in dream-like patterns, blocking out everything they touched. The hedgerow lit up like a fireworks display, the flames racing through the dry tops of the shrubs and forming a fiery fence along the gully. Travis looked up at the pale brown sky where heavy clouds scudded across the expanse, looking as though they carried rain. Frowning, he looked back at the inferno, which now obliterated his view of the ranch. He looked again at the hedgerow. The flames had changed direction, moving away from the target, eating their way toward his own house. The intense heat blasted him in the face and his eyes widened, his confused brain trying to focus on the moment. A gust of wind snatched the cigarette from his lips, and the temperature spiked around him.

"Oh *shit*!"

He grabbed the rifle and wheeled around to make a run for the pickup. Smoke burned his lungs and his heart pumped blood into his infected hand, throbbing through the painful wound. He stopped, blinking away the sting of smoke and trying to clear his vision, not believing what he saw. Someone was standing beside his truck.

Behind him, the crackle of burning grass drew closer. He raised the rifle and zoomed the scope.

"A sheriff's deputy. And it's a fuckin' broad!"

He focused on her dark eyes and centered the crosshairs between them, slowly squeezing the trigger. A hard gust of wind slammed into him as the gun exploded, but he saw her go down. Anger raged into his heart. *No* one was going to screw this up for him.

He glanced behind him at the advancing fire, then began to run. An excruciating pain crashed through his thigh, and his leg buckled. He dropped the rifle and threw out his hands to break the fall. Adrenaline surged through his system and his heartbeat raced. Smoke curled into his nose and lungs, the pain in his leg almost overwhelming. He began to crawl toward the truck, an image forming in his brain–his father, lying face down in the dirt.

20

Fire trucks roared up the drive as Kellie bolted through the pasture gate. One pumper stopped in front of the main barn and two others rumbled past her, headed for the burning fields. Cliff had closed the barn door, and was attempting to shoo away loose horses that wanted to get back inside. Sara, riding Juicy, tried to herd the frightened animals toward the safety of the pond pasture.

Kellie stopped to catch her breath. "Is the barn clear?"

Cliff nodded, out of breath. "Yes, we got them all out."

"What about the mare barn?"

"Clarke's over there now."

A fire truck engine revved to a high pitch as Kellie sprinted toward the small barn that held the future of Rocking S. Panicky neighs from the frightened mares answered the high-pitched squeals of the foals. Clarke led two mares out the door, and Kellie ran up to him, shouting over the din.

"Just turn the rest of them loose!"

It was a risky move, but they were running out of time. Inside, she began opening stall doors. At the last one, she buckled a halter on a chestnut mare, then looked out through the small window. The fire was approaching at breakneck speed, fueled by the wind. She led the horse out into the aisle, hoping the others would follow. Two mares ran back into their stalls, but the rest followed Kellie out of the barn. Clarke appeared and grabbed the mare's lead rope, and Kellie dashed back inside.

Belle cowered in her stall, nose pressed to the screen over the window. Her eyes were huge and her muscles trembled beneath the shiny coat.

"Come on, girl. Let's go." Kellie reached for the mare's halter, but the frightened animal dodged past her and ran out into the aisle. Kellie sprinted after her, but Belle was trotting briskly toward the door. Kellie stopped and turned back to the remaining two occupants. Moving as calmly as possible, she entered the stall and clipped a lead rope onto the big palomino's halter. A throaty nicker drifted from below, and Kellie stepped back to look. Bright eyes peeked from beneath the mare's tail.

"It's okay, baby. Follow mama."

She led the mare outside into the haze and headed toward the lane. A fire hose uncoiled like a huge serpent, and water roared over the roof of the main barn and, and, suddenly a streak of yellow shot past her. The mare reared, yanking the lead rope from Kellie's hand and racing after her foal who was headed straight toward the blazing pasture.

Kellie chased after them, but a fireman caught her arm. "Let us do that. You go on down with the others."

"No! You'll never catch her! Let me–"

The words died in her throat as Sara galloped past on Juicy. Kellie screamed as her own baby disappeared into the muddy brown smoke.

The fireman shouted into a two-way radio. "There's a little girl on a horse out there!" The reply was unintelligible over the noise of the fire and the equipment. "Damn! You *have* to find her!"

The searing wind swept over Kellie, snatching her breath away. She swallowed hard, tasting the smoky ash against her dry throat, her brain unable to comprehend the unthinkable outcome of the nightmare–losing Sara and Ed. The fireman looked up at the leaden sky, and Kellie broke away from his grasp. She ran toward the burning field, tears blinding her, but panic providing the strength she needed. Dodging hoses and people, she struggled to see through burning eyes, her sobs snatching what breath remained in her lungs. Suddenly, Sara and Juicy appeared against the fiery backdrop of the flames, and galloped through the gate leading the palomino mare. The tiny filly danced beside them, tossing her head as though she'd had a marvelous adventure. Sara was soaking wet, but her victorious grin outshone the flames.

Kellie wrapped her arms around her daughter's trembling little body, cradling her close, fighting the terror of almost losing her and, finally, absorbing the full impact of the child's courageous love for the horses.

Sara struggled free. "Are all the horses safe? Where's Uncle Clarke?"

Kellie looked around. "He was in the mare barn–"

She choked on the words as she looked back toward the small building. A blanket of flames covered the roof, the ancient wood giving no resistance to the merciless onslaught.

She raced toward the burning building. A burly firefighter snaked a hand out to stop her, but she leaped sideways and ran past him, screaming Clarke's name into the deafening roar. The fire licked around the silhouette of the building, forming an orange halo. The door loomed like a gaping black cave entrance, and the heat blasted her in the face. She gasped and stumbled, her lungs protesting against the deadly smoke. A series of loud explosions like gunfire resounded from inside the barn, and Kellie sank to her knees. If her brother was still inside, he was beyond help.

The east corner of the roof crumbled with an ear-splitting bellow. Huge jets of water pummeled the building, but the old wood was too hot, too willing to succumb to the seduction of the fire. Kellie sobbed, staring numbly at the death trap. The shimmering molten air tricked her senses, producing a mirage at the mouth of the cave, hovering just above the ground. She closed her eyes, took a deep breath, then opened them again as Grandfather Sutton's wood-sided station wagon rumbled into the yard. The tinny horn pierced the din, and Clarke's triumphant smile illuminated his sooty face.

~ ~

Frank stared at Rodriguez's dark features, eyes frozen in disbelief. A pool of blood widened around the man's dark hair, creeping across the dirt floor toward Frank's boots. Bitter defeat knifed through his chest. *It's over–they've destroyed me.* He could try to disappear, but these people were everywhere, their deadly network forming a web from which he'd never escape.

He gazed at the gun in his hand, wondering how he had come to this. *One lousy tough break at the track, that's how.* He stepped back from the corpse and Celeste's dancing blue eyes appeared in his mind. Would she stick by him through all this? Abandon her wealth and easy life to become a fugitive?

And what about Sara? His eyes burned. His little girl would despise him when she learned what he really was. He glanced down at the lifeless form at his feet, a silent testimony to just how low Franklin Frazier had sunk.

A deep rumble penetrated the silence and he listened intently. Another roll of bass tones sounded almost like stampeding hooves, and he noticed a wisp of gray smoke curling around the edge of the unlatched door. He moved closer, inhaling the distinctive odor of burning grass.

"Shit! The jerk must have dropped a cigarette."

He pulled the door open wide enough to slip through, then cautiously mounted the steps in the smoky stairwell. At the top, he peered around the bales of hay that camouflaged the entrance. Dense smoke obliterated everything but hay and one corner pole. The smoke burned his eyes and nose, and he coughed. Then a loud crack like gunfire echoed from somewhere. He grabbed the handle of the trapdoor and, pulling it shut, backed down the steps into the darkness.

~ ~

Ed reined in his horse and pointed toward the cloud of smoke. "Do you know another way to get to Randy's?"

Hyde nodded and turned west along the fence. Ed pushed the radio button. "Danielle? Come back." He waited, then tried again, but the radio was silent. He punched the button once more. "Dispatch, call the fire de–roger." He urged his horse into a trot and came alongside Hyde.

"Fire crew is on the way, but we have to get over to that house right now–I have a bad feeling about this."

"A farm track leads to a hay barn, then goes straight across the field to the other side. We can make good time that way."

He leaned down and unlatched a gate, and Ed trotted through. In less than a minute, they were galloping over a dirt road. Ed glanced at the pole barn as they flew past. No time to think about those memories right now. He smiled. But what memories! To the north, a heavy blanket of smoke obliterated everything, but its advance was measurable. In the distance, the faint wail of sirens sounded much too far away. The wind had picked up and Ed worried that they'd be hampered by limited visibility. A flashback to the desert slashed through his brain. Hiding anywhere they could find. Blinded and vulnerable by the vicious dust storms.

The loud crack of a gunshot vibrated through the thick air, and Ed's horse leaped sideways, almost unseating him.

Hyde turned and trotted back to him. "What's the plan?"

Ed squinted into the smoke. "If someone's shooting at *us*, then they have a vantage point that's not compromised by the smoke. But the shot didn't sound that close."

Hyde turned to look toward the south. "There's an old windmill on the property, but I don't see anyone up there."

Another shot rang out and adrenaline exploded through Ed's body. "Shit! Those aren't meant for us!"

The big gelding strung his neck out and pinned his ears, pounding over the red dirt as though the devil were after him. A gate suddenly appeared and before Ed could make a decision, the horse sailed over it, barely breaking stride on the other side. An ear-splitting explosion thundered through the air and the horse reared, tumbling Ed onto the hard ground. He rolled, then scrambled to his feet, yanking out his revolver.

"What the hell was *that?*"

He stared at mushrooming smoke and flames leaping a hundred feet into the air. Even from a safe distance, the heat was intense. He squinted against the hot wind, a familiar band tightening around his chest. The brown fields faded into gritty sand, and the roar of burning oil fields hammered his senses. Flames rocketing thousands of feet into the desert night sky. A glimpse into hell.

"Sheriff? You okay?"

Ed looked toward Randy's house. "Yeah. Let's go." He mounted his horse and took off again at a full gallop, praying like he'd never prayed before.

Minutes later, they rode into the barnyard and Ed swung down from the saddle. Adrenaline fueled his anger–the patrol car was empty.

"God damned independent cuss!"

Hyde looked around. "Who are you talking about?"

"My Under Sheriff. She's too macho for her own good."

Hyde dismounted. "I'll go with you to the house"

"No, you stay here and keep watch."

Without waiting for a response, he strode toward the side

of the house, his heart in his throat. If he pushed open that door and found Kellie dead, he'd...he'd what? It was too late to protect her like he should have. His damned pride and ego had steered him away from the only thing he'd ever wanted.

Releasing the safety on the revolver, his gut curled with the familiar sensation of walking into an ambush. Dark dusty huts. Abandoned streets. Children with submachine guns. An involuntary shudder passed across his shoulders and he shook off the images. Every muscle geared for battle, he pushed the door open with his foot.

"Logan County Sheriff! Anyone here?"

The silence filled him with dread and he moved into the living room. His pulse hammered with each step, just as it had on every mission in the desert, when he'd wondered if that step would be his last. The only difference was that these steps might take him over the edge.

He moved slowly down the hall, stopping to look through each doorway, his courage growing with each empty room. Madman or not, Jethrow Sutton was Kellie's kin. Maybe he wouldn't harm her. Ed snorted at his own naive optimism.

He strode out the back door and hollered at Hyde. "He's gone, probably took them hostage."

Hyde sat straight and still in the saddle, staring across the field at the single huge fire burning in the field. "I think I heard someone calling for help out there." He set off at a brisk trot through the long grass.

"Wait!"

Hyde kept going, and Ed kicked the front tire on the patrol car. "God dammit, why doesn't anybody pay attention to me?"

He barked into the radio. "All units, possible hostage situation. Suspect Travis Mack on the run, may have woman and young girl with him. Do not approach, but keep visual. Over."

His radio crackled with each responding unit's acknowledgment. While he listened, his brain pondered the situation. He felt useless out here in the middle of nowhere on horseback. The fastest way back to Kellie's ranch was the east section road. He should take the squad car. But where the hell was Danielle?

A heavy engine rumbled behind him and he moved out of the way for two heavy fire trucks. They bumped over the uneven ground and headed straight toward the head of the wildfire. With a final glance at the house, Ed mounted his horse and followed Hyde's tracks through the grass. The single fire now burned with less intensity, and he could make out the silhouette of a pickup truck. The acrid odor of burning rubber seared his nose and eyes. Just ahead, he saw Hyde's horse.

The vet was kneeling in the grass beside a body.

Ed jumped down. "Holy shit! Danielle, what happened?"

Her face glistened with sweat and black smudges covered her cheeks and forehead. A large gash over her eyebrow oozed blood, and one eye was swollen almost shut. Her uniform shirt was soaked with blood.

She managed a weak smile. "Sorry, chief..." Her eyelids drifted closed.

Hyde held her hand and stroked her hair, speaking in gentle tones. "It'll be all right. I'll take care of you."

Ed's radio crackled and he punched the button. "Get an ambulance out to this fire on the Sutton spread. Have them coordinate with the field crew!"

Hyde looked up. "She's been shot in the shoulder, and she's lost a lot of blood. I'll take care of it until we can get her to the hospital."

"*Shot?*" Ed knelt beside her. "Dani, who did this?"

Her good eye opened slowly and she winced. Her husky voice was thick with pain. "Don't know...someone out there."

"You mean, someone is in the field?"

Danielle's eyes closed again, and Ed leaned closer. "Dani?–"

Hyde's tone sharpened. "You can question her later. She's passed out again."

~ ~

The fire chief strode up to Kellie, pushing back his hat and wiping his forehead.

"I think we caught a break–the wind changed direction and the fire's headed south now. Anything out there besides grass?"

Her eyes brimmed. "Sheriff Campbell and Hyde Browning."

A thunderous explosion shook the ground, and everyone turned to look toward the burning fields. A fiery ball rose in the air, followed by another blast, and thick black smoke billowed around the core of the new fire.

The chief swore. "That looks like oil or tires burning!"

He raced off toward one of the trucks, shouting into his radio, and Kellie followed.

"Randy's barn still has an old tractor inside. Maybe that's what blew up."

A minute later, the chief gave her a thumbs-up. "Campbell just called for an ambulance."

"For who?"

The fireman shrugged. Kellie's knees wobbled and she closed her eyes. Ed was all right, but something must have happened to Hyde. *I can't stand another second of this nightmare.*

A hand touched her shoulder and Clarke's voice brought her back. "What happened out there with Jethrow?"

"He said he wanted to come back and connect with the family again, but I guess all he really wanted was to destroy me."

She turned to gaze at the soggy heap of charred wood that had once housed her mares. "My God, look at this"

"Your insurance will cover it."

"Nothing will replace the historic value of the original settlement barn." She squared her shoulders and gazed at her brother. "But it's only a building. The important and precious things in my life are safe, and that's all that matters."

Except for Jethrow. But perhaps it was for the best. He was trapped in the prison of his hatred, and his anger would never allow him to forgive and make peace with himself. Acceptance replaced her pain. She had to let go of her memories of who he'd been, and accept the man he'd become–a stranger.

She gazed across the blackened fields, thick with lingering smoke. The time had come to let go of the past and allow her brothers to get on with their plans.

21

Kellie trudged back to where the exhausted firemen were coiling hoses and stowing gear. A brush tanker grumbled through the pasture gate and rolled to a creaking stop, and the sooty-faced driver climbed down.

"Everything's under control. A crew is standing by at a pole barn on the southwest side of the property. We want to make sure that mountain of hay bales is fully extinguished." He shook his head apologetically. "I'm afraid the structure's a total loss."

"The fire got that far?"

"With thirty-mile-an-hour winds and these heavy drought conditions, grass fires can travel up to 15 miles an hour."

"There's a house out there. Was it...?"

"Nope, the guys set a backfire after we evacuated Deputy White–"

"Danielle? What was *she* doing out there?"

"Dunno, but Sheriff Campbell and Doc Browning were taking good care of her, last I saw. Anyways, the backfire burned up a hundred-yard-wide path that kept the wildfire from advancing when the wind changed. And we doused the building with retardant, just in case."

Kellie exhaled slowly, stunned by the overload of information. "I can't thank you guys enough.

He grinned and saluted. "That's what you pay taxes for."

Ed's patrol car eased up beside them, the door opened, and he leaped out of the car. "Kellie!"

He grabbed her, hugging her so hard she couldn't breathe. Her body trembled and the tears came, a lifetime of emotions returning all at once.

His husky voice rumbled through her hair. "Oh my God, I thought I'd lost you again."

"Eddie, just hold me."

Suddenly he cleared his throat and released her, stepping back and looking around in embarrassment. Roy, Sara, Cliff, Clarke, and several of the firemen were standing there, grinning at the spectacle.

Kellie started to laugh. "Don't you all have something else to do?" She turned back to Ed. "Where's Hyde?"

A wicked grin emphasized his answer. "He rode in the ambulance with Danielle...Did *you* know they had something going?"

"Hyde? And Danielle? Hardly!"

He chuckled. "Still waters and all that stuff."

She took his arm. "I have a lot to tell you."

"I'm going back out to your brother's house. You want to ride along? You can look over the rest of the property too."

She glanced back at the soggy scene. Roy and her brothers were hosing down some horses and Sara was helping. Things seemed under control. She climbed into the front seat of the cruiser, memories sending startling images into her head. When was the last time she'd sat beside Ed in a car?

Fighting the hard knot of apprehension growing in her chest, she stared out the passenger window as he backed the vehicle away from the barn. Where was her life headed? Confusion muddled her thoughts as they drove down the lane. So many things to think about, including an ex-husband wanted for assault and on the run. Through all this, he hadn't been there...he'd *never* been there, really. The painful reality washed over her. Sara was the only reason Frank stayed around.

The car turned onto the east section road and moved

along the rutted lane. Kellie stared through the windshield, struggling with the scene before her. The winter storage barn was gone, except for one pole at the far corner. Huge bales of hay glowed with the fires that still smoldered inside them. A full year's supply of feed destroyed.

Ed's tentative tone drifted in the close confines of the car. "Remember how we used to come out here?"

Her cheeks flamed, not from embarrassment, but from the heat of the memories. She nodded, but avoided looking at him. At that moment, her vulnerability would be her undoing.

A fireman flagged them down, then leaned in the window. His ruddy face glistened with sweat. Throwing a nervous glance toward Kellie, he lowered his voice.

"We found a body out in the field."

She gasped and leaned forward, craning her neck to see where the fireman pointed. *Who would be way out–?*

"Oh God!" She fumbled for the door handle, fighting the stomach-turning thoughts that crashed through her head.

Ed grabbed her arm. "Kellie Jo!"

His sharp tone pierced her rush of panic and she sank back into the seat. No one had called her Kellie Jo since grade school, and then, only when she was in trouble. She willed her trembling hands to still, then glanced over at Ed's face.

His stern expression said it all. "You stay put. I'll be back in a few minutes."

"Stop treating me like a child! I want to know who it is."

His gaze softened and he squeezed her hand. "Please, Kellie, let me check it out first."

Something in his tone calmed her reeling thoughts and she nodded. "Okay, but I'd like to take a look at the hay barn."

"Just be careful."

He left the car and headed across the field with the

fireman. She took a deep breath, stepped out onto the crunchy black ground, and surveyed the destruction.

Six workers moved through the rubble, shoveling burned material, and inspecting heavier debris. One of the crew stepped away from the group and approached her.

"Watch your step, Ma'am. This side took the brunt of the fire." He wiped his forehead. "I think some of the hay on the far side might be salvageable, but we won't know for a while."

Numbed, she watched the firemen hack open the bales and spread the smoldering hay over the concrete floor. Other workers covered it with sand to smother any hidden sparks. Seeing the bales destroyed, her thoughts traveled to another time, and images of the small love nest she'd shared with Ed in that very spot. What fun they'd had arranging the bales into a fort that couldn't be seen. Memories pressed against her heart–months of heavy petting, then the final consummation of their love on graduation night. A stronger heat than the fire scorched through her senses and she drew in a long breath, trying to obliterate all the years between those memories and this.

Ed's voice whispered close by her ear. "Come back to the car with me."

She turned, and her heart jerked at the sadness in his eyes. She started to ask, but changed her mind, suddenly sure she didn't want to hear what he had to say. He guided her gently into the front seat of the car. When he'd settled behind the wheel, he reached over and took her hand.

"...I don't know how to tell you this..." He stared at her for a moment. "That was Jethrow's body."

"No! It's probably some itinerant–how can you be so sure?"

"The belt buckle."

She recoiled, fighting the image of her nephew's burned body.

Ed squeezed her hand. "I'm afraid there's more–it looks like *he* started the fire. We found five empty gas cans close by...I'm sure sorry."

Grief stepped aside for disbelief. Jethrow was her kin, bonded through blood, thicker than water. Family was all-important–why would he do such a thing? His angry words rang through her head and she closed her eyes tightly against the truth. *This* was his revenge for all the imagined wrongs. But had he meant to die?

The dispatcher's voice crackled through the microphone, snapping her back to the present. Ed reached for the radio, giving her one more sorrowful look before his demeanor returned to an official one.

"Call the coroner out to the Sutton place. The southwest quadrant, Section Road 640...You have any news on Tina Brown?"

He put the radio back into its base and shook his head. "Tina didn't show up for her birthday party this afternoon. She left work early yesterday and no one's seen her since."

Kellie shrugged. "She's so unreliable, that means nothing."

"No, I have a real bad feeling about the girl. If your nephew could do *this*, he was capable of just about anything." Ed stared out the windshield for a moment. "I'll take you back. I need to get to town."

She grabbed his arm. "Take me over to Randy's. Please? I need some time by myself."

He considered her for a moment, then nodded and put the car into gear as one of the firemen ran toward the car, waving his arms.

"Sheriff, you'd better come take a look at this."

Kellie jumped out of the car before Ed could stop her. He glowered, but said nothing. Hesitating for only an instant, she caught up with him at the edge of the concrete slab that formed the floor of the pole barn. Stepping carefully through the smoldering hay, she focused on three men in sooty yellow gear who stood at the center of the destroyed structure, looking down at the floor. What had they found that was so important?

Ed turned to her, his voice hard as flint. "What is *this*?"

She gaped at a metal trap door in the floor. "I have no idea–a tornado shelter, maybe?"

Ed dropped to one knee and examined the large metal ring that had been installed as a handle. His hand moved to his belt, and he unsnapped the flap on his holster, then looked up at Kellie.

"Go back to the car."

Her pulse jerked. The sinister grey of the handgun made the scenario so much more frightening. She met his gaze and shook her head no, but did step back a few paces. His jaw tightened, but he let it go.

The iron hinges complained loudly as he lifted the trap door. A musty, slightly sweet odor wafted up from the pitch black hole. One of the firemen aimed a high-powered flashlight into the dark, the brilliant wide beam illuminating concrete steps descending into the dark.

Ed pulled out his gun, and his voice dropped to a stage whisper. "Someone's been here recently."

Kellie stared at the footprints on the dusty stairs, and her heart thumped against her ribs. Had Jethrow used this secret place as a hideout?

The firemen backed away from the opening, and Ed called out, "Logan County Sheriff Department. Anyone down there?"

A crow protested in the distance, emphasizing the heavy silence. Ed released the safety on his gun as he started down the stairwell, carefully avoiding the footprints. A second later, Kellie heard the scrape of wood on concrete. She held her breath, fear reaching into the corners of her mind. *Please don't let anything happen to him.*

A patrol car roared up and slammed to a stop. Two serious-faced deputies jumped out and hurried toward them.

"Folks, you'll have to move back off the concrete. This is a crime scene now."

"Crime scene?" Kellie felt rather than heard the waver in her voice. "What happened?"

The young deputy shook his head. "I can't say, Ma'am."

One of the firemen walked up to them. "We need to collect our gear and get back to the station. Is that okay?"

The deputy held up one hand, then spoke into the two-way radio on his shoulder. "Okay for the fire crew to leave?"

Ed's voice came through, loud and clear. "Affirmative, but we'll need to talk to them later."

Irritation snatched at Kellie's patience. "*What* is going on? This is my property, and I have a right to know."

The deputy's radio crackled again, and he stepped away as Ed emerged from the dark underground hideaway. Kellie searched Ed's face for some clue about what was going on, but she only saw disbelief in his expression. He spoke to a nearby deputy, then turned and headed toward her. A moment later, Frank emerged from the dark hole, handcuffed and head down.

Kellie gasped. "What was *he* doing down there?"

Ed blew out a long breath. "You really don't want to know." He took her arm and gently turned her toward his vehicle. "You still want to go out to your brother's?"

"Yes. And I *do* want to know about Frank."

The county coroner's van pulled up and a female technician leaned her head out the passenger window.

"Dispatch says you have two bodies. Is that right?"

Ed nodded. "One of my men will show you."

The woman climbed out of the van, and the driver steered the vehicle toward the center of the scorched field.

Fear curled through Kellie's chest. What had Frank done? Who was dead? She climbed into the car and waited, composing her thoughts and wording her questions. She wanted answers, and she wanted them now.

Ed slid behind the steering wheel and removed his hat. His face looked haggard, and she felt a sudden urge to reach out to him, run her fingers over his cheek, tell him how much she still loved him. But in the face of all that had happened today, she felt vulnerable and forsaken. This wasn't the time to do something emotional.

The car eased forward through the burned grass, and he cleared his throat.

"I know you want some answers, and I'll try, but we don't know much right now. Frank says one of his track thug-buddies came looking for him, that they were going to kill him. He's saying self-defense, and that's probably true."

"But why did they want to kill him? And how would they know to look in a tornado shelter that even *I* didn't know about?"

Ed's jaw hardened, but he didn't respond.

"*Tell* me!"

"There's a few million dollars worth of marijuana and heroin stashed down there."

She gaped. "Drugs? Frank, the health-nut athlete? Why would he do such a thing? He's always had plenty of money. And I think he's done pretty good at the track...or maybe this has something to do with that racehorse that died."

Ed reached over and grasped her hand. "It doesn't matter why–Frank's in a lot of trouble. He shot and wounded a law enforcement officer, he killed a man, and he's clearly involved in drug dealing. I can't come up with a good enough excuse for any one of those charges."

Kellie focused on the warmth of Ed's hand and the sensations it generated. In one long day, her life had been transformed forever. She didn't know how she would handle those changes, but one thing was sure–she needed some time to put the present and the future into perspective.

The car eased into the gravel behind Randy's house, and Ed turned to her, his eyes reflecting a lifetime of sadness.

"I think I understand how you must be feeling. A lot has happened, none of it good..." He took a ragged breath. "But I want you to know that I'll be here if you need me."

His vulnerability shook her confidence. She opened her mouth to reply, but he held up a hand. "Don't say anything right now. When you're finished here, call me and I'll come back to take you home."

"My phone battery's dead."

He reached into his pocket and pulled out a small white phone. "I keep this for emergencies."

She took the phone, then opened the car door and stepped out onto the land that had given and taken everything she'd ever wanted.

22

Smoothing her hand along the back of an armchair, Kellie gazed at the subtle changes in the living room. The protective furniture sheets were neatly folded in a stack on the end of the couch. The drapes had been opened wide. The morning newspaper lay on the coffee table, folded open to the latest story about the Sutton Ranch. Understanding hit her hard. *He was going to come back after he destroyed us. Live here like nothing happened.* Bile rose in her throat and she turned her back on the familiar room. Jethrow's rabid hatred obliterated all the good memories, leaving her with nothing but a sense of failure and loss. She never wanted to see this place again.

As she headed back toward the kitchen, her thoughts turned to Frank. Where had she failed as a wife and a partner? What could have driven him to get involved in something so dangerous? She closed her eyes against a new pain seeping into the outer edges of her mind. Sara would be devastated.

The red cooler still sat on the floor by the stove. Out of curiosity, she opened it. Soda, cheese, lunchmeat, apples–enough for several days. On the counter next to the sink, an ashtray overflowed with crushed cigarette butts. How long had he been out here? Stalking her, maiming her horses, plotting his wicked revenge. She stared at the smokers' debris and a prickle of apprehension crawled up the nape of her neck. She stepped closer to peer at the odiferous stubs. Bright pink lipstick stained two of the butts–Tina *had* been there.

Kellie spun around and scanned the room, looking for

more clues. Had the girl been there at the same time as she and Sara? She might have been hiding in the bedroom. Kellie hurried down the hall, glancing into the bathroom as she passed. The first bedroom was undisturbed, the bedspread faded, the top of the bureau clear. The second bedroom–Jethrow's childhood room–told a different story. The bed was rumpled and a dingy towel lay on the linoleum. The air smelled sour and vaguely familiar.

A square of paper lay on the floor under the edge of the bed, and she picked it up. Tina Brown gazed back from the snapshot, bare-breasted and smiling seductively at the camera. Ed's concern echoed through Kellie's thoughts and a chill ran over her skin. Would Travis Mack have trusted this girl with his plans? Not likely.

Tucking the photo into her back pocket, Kellie moved down the hall. Stopping at the bathroom door again, she eyed the shower curtain covering the tub. Heart thumping, she stepped into the room, terrified at what she might find. A deep breath, and she yanked aside the curtain. Only three mummified mice in the bottom of the tub.

She strode down the hall and out the kitchen door. Big gulps of air worked to cleanse her lungs and thoughts at the same time. In every direction, blackened fields shimmered in the heat, wisps of smoke spiraling up to join the blanket of haze that veiled the sun.

The pungent air burned her throat, but defeat burned her eyes. Her fervor to protect all the things she cherished had been for nothing. Touching her pocket for reassurance that the phone was still there, she crossed the yard and walked toward the barn. One last visit with the past, then she'd go home to Sara. And Ed? Her heart thumped gently at the thought.

The old barn smelled of warm wood and smoke from the fire. Light filtered through the sagging boards where the structure had given up the struggle to remain upright. Randy's old John Deere sat in the corner, encrusted with dust and cobwebs. His roping lariat hung on one wall next to a bridle and hackamore. In the eerie light, she reluctantly searched the dirt floor for the bloodstain, but the years had mercifully obliterated it. Her eyes burned with the pain of the past and the echoes of their happy childhood laughter.

A loud creak made her jump and she looked up toward the hayloft. *A perfect place for someone to hide–or to hide a body.*

The loft ladder rose straight up the wall into the dark. She hesitated, then slowly began climbing. At the top, she poked her head over the edge of the opening and squinted, waiting for her eyes to adjust. Several bales of hay were scattered about. A dark mound formed a silhouette against a small window. Hunching over to keep from bumping her head, she crept toward the lump. A tarp covered whatever it was. Her heart hammered so hard she could barely breathe. *Do I really want to do this?* She fingered the edge of the canvas, hesitated, then pulled it aside. A mouse squeaked and scurried over her foot. She leaped back in fright, banging her head on a rafter.

Dropping to her knees, she stared at Randy's old roping saddle, the sight bringing a flood of memories into her throbbing head. She reached out and ran her fingers over the smooth leather, worn dark by hours of hard work.

"Randy," she whispered. "Why did you abandon me?"

Never in her wildest dreams had she imagined that her strong, resilient brother could sink to suicide. Something stirred in the darkest recesses of her brain. She tried to bring it up, grasp the thought, but it faded, leaving an unsettled feeling in its wake. A vibration hummed against her breast, startling her. She pulled the phone from her pocket and peered at a series of letters and numbers on the screen.

"Hello?"

Silence pressed against her ear, a chill crawling across

her shoulders. "Ed? Is that you?"

A heavy voice rumbled back at her. "Who is this? Where did you get this phone?"

She stared at the display again, then pressed the disconnect button and frowned. More puzzle pieces.

She glanced at the saddle again, then her gaze drifted out the small window for another glimpse of the burnt grass. The smoke had thinned, cleansed by a brisk breeze that kept the windmill blades spinning. The peaceful scene calmed her turmoil, and she thought about Frank's secret activities in the underground shelter. In the old days, when the ranch employed dozens of wranglers, the pole barn would have been their only refuge during tornado season. She tried to remember if she'd ever known about the shelter, but nothing definite came to mind. Recalling her first experience with a twister, her pulse twitched. How she'd hated being in the small dark room under the big house. Sometimes she'd had nightmares about being trapped there, with no one to hear her calls for help.

She suddenly caught her breath and stared at the windmill, remembering the strange noises she'd heard. "Oh God!" Her gaze snapped to the pile of boulders east of the structure. "She's in there! I know it!"

Scrambling down the ladder, she jumped from the third rung, and raced out into the bright light. The long grass slowed her down a little, snatching at her jeans and tangling around her boots, but she kept jogging toward the boulders. She stopped at the corrugated metal door and leaned her hands on her knees, gulping for air. Another sound penetrated her ragged breathing, a buzz from somewhere close. She listened, waiting for the sound to repeat. The hollow warning came again, searing into her brain, and she instinctively looked first at her feet, then scanned the immediate area. Four feet away, a thick Timber rattlesnake lay coiled on one of the boulders, head raised. *My God, I ran right past it!* Taking a shallow breath, she held her body rigid and took one slow step back. The snake's tail shook again, his head came up a little more, and she froze. From the girth of the snake's body, she guessed he was over five feet long–plenty of length to connect if he struck. She slowly took another step backward, keeping him in sight. He didn't respond, and she backed up two more steps. The snake's head lowered back to the warm stone, and she took four more steps back, then turned and put another two yards between them.

Turning in a circle, she searched the ground for anything she might use to protect herself.

"How am I going to do this?"

A bare spot in the grass caught her attention and she investigated, finding a small pile of rocks. Selecting the largest ones that easily fit in her hand, she stepped back to a safe distance and took aim. The first rock sailed completely over the boulder, and she grinned.

"Baseball pitcher, I'm not!"

The second rock hit the boulder just inches from the snake, and he immediately slithered off the far side and into the grass. She cautiously approached the shelter doors again, listening for any sign of her new adversary or his relatives. The air was still.

Pulling the metal door open, she peered into the dim stairwell, littered with leaves and dirt. Fear crawled through her insides, and she scanned the corners for any sign of more snakes. Then, an icy lump moved into her stomach. The old wooden door to the shelter sported a shiny new padlock.

She sprinted down the steps, and pounded on the thick door. "Tina? Are you in there?"

Nothing stirred but the creak of the windmill above her. She hammered her fists against the oak planks.

"Tina! Answer me!"

Horror engulfed her thoughts–Jethrow had killed the girl, knowing her body would never be found in this deserted place.

A muffled wail came through the door. "Help me!"

"Tina! It's me, Kellie. I'm calling for help right now."

Her pulse thumped in her ears and her hands shook while she tried to dial the tiny phone. Ed answered on the first ring.

"Send someone out to the windmill right away. I found Tina!"

She pocketed the phone and turned back to the door, leaning close to be heard. "They're on the way. Everything is going to be all right."

She leaned her forehead against the musty old wood, listening to Tina's sobs from inside the shelter. *Would anything ever be all right again?*

The impact of Jethrow's actions stunned her. What had been his plan? Destroy the ranch? Kill them all? Just to recover what was already his? Prickles ran over her skin, remembering their conversations and his frightening personality swings. Would he really have left Tina to die slowly in this place?

She closed her eyes, shutting out the questions. No one would ever know.

Above ground, car doors slammed and men's voices rumbled. She started up the steps on shaky legs. A familiar silhouette appeared against the gray sky, and she reached for Ed's hand, grasping it as though her life depended on that contact. Two deputies charged down the stairwell and, in moments, the screech of metal against metal echoed in the hole.

Ed slipped his arm around her shoulders. "Are you all right?"

She nodded numbly, her gaze riveted on the shelter entrance. She couldn't stop wondering how Jethrow could kill another human being with no remorse. Her nephew had clearly grown into a deadly stranger.

A loud crunch reverberated from the stairwell, then the

sounds of splintering wood. Hysterical sobs preceded Tina's puffy tear-stained face. Supported by the deputies, she emerged from the cave, clutching a small black book against her chest.

Her face contorted into a snarling mask. "I hope you lock that bastard up forever!" she screamed. "He's a monster! He killed his own father!"

Ed threw a quick look at Kellie, then stepped up to the girl. "That's a pretty strong accusation, young lady."

She stepped back, flinging the black notebook to the ground.

"See for yerself! He kept a fuckin' diary, ferchrissake!"

~~

Kellie sat in the patrol car, fighting the nausea, struggling to quiet her trembling body. Several county cars rolled up and, in minutes, the field was filled with people. Watching Ed guide Tina into a patrol car, Kellie let her mind wrap around the horrible revelations. How had they missed Jethrow's possible involvement in Randy's death? Young sullen Jethrow had been questioned, but if she remembered right, his grief had been so heart wrenching that they'd discarded any idea he might be involved. Now it looked as though the Jekyll-Hyde personality had been honed at an early age.

Ed strode toward the car. She *had* to see what was written in that notebook. He slid into the driver's seat, and slipped the diary into a plastic bag.

She composed her tone. "May I look at that before you take it in?"

His expression softened and he gazed at her for a full minute before he shook his head. "I'm sorry, hon." He slipped the package into the glove compartment and locked it, then slouched back in the seat and groaned. "What a can of worms."

She gazed out the window, focusing on the investigators milling around the shelter entrance like hornets. It was probably just as well she didn't see the diary. It would be hard enough to sort through what she already knew. Voices brought her back to the present as Ed climbed out of the car and followed a deputy across the grass. She waited a minute, then followed, keeping her distance. A sturdy woman in field gear kneeled on the ground beside the shelter opening. Several boxes and containers were arranged over the grass, and Kellie squinted to see what they were. While everyone examined the display, she crept up close enough to see and hear.

Ed whistled. "Holy shit!"

The woman looked up. "This is about half of what's down there."

Kellie slipped up behind the group. She still couldn't see, and from everyone's reaction, she wasn't sure she wanted to.

A hand grasped her arm. "Ma'am, you're not supposed to be here."

Ed whirled around, his eyes widening. "Aw, Kellie–what are you doing?"

She wrenched her arm out of the deputy's hold and stepped up beside Ed. At first, her brain didn't grasp what she was seeing, then comprehension slammed through her. She was looking at mummified cat and dogs–headless or without paws. Two shriveled white mice were nailed spread-eagled to a board. A mockingbird stared with glazed eyes, its beak taped shut with electrician's tape.

Ed stepped in front of her, his voice returning to its usual authoritative tone. "Deputy Stark will take you back to the ranch. I'll be there in a little while."

Her strong will crumbled and she followed the officer to a patrol car, suddenly terrified to be alone with her thoughts.

23

"Mama!" Sara raced out of the house and launched herself into Kellie's arms. "Where've you been? I was scared!"

Cradling the small warm body, Kellie closed her eyes and struggled with her emotions. "I know, I know–so was I."

She hugged tighter, afraid to let go, consumed with the knowledge they'd been within arm's length of a madman. The front door opened and her brothers came out onto the porch.

Clarke's thin face was shadowy with stress. "God, Kell, we've been worried. What happened out there?"

"A purge."

Cliff stepped off the porch and put his arms around her. "I'm sure sorry about all this...anything we can do to help?"

She stepped back and smiled sadly. "You already have, just by being here."

She gazed at the brother she'd been so angry with earlier. Why had she believed her own desires and plans were more important than his or Clarke's? Or Ed's. Shame crept into her heart. Blinded by selfishness and resistance to change, she'd alienated the very people who counted. Had her oblivion made her as responsible for Randy's death as Jethrow?

She linked her arm through Cliff's. "Let's go inside."

Clarke pulled three beers from the fridge, and Kellie led the men down the hall toward the study. Though physically exhausted, her brain was afire with a dozen thoughts. Her brothers sank into the leather sofa and she settled behind the desk. Trying to calm the rush of thoughts, she contemplated the soft sheen of the knotty pine walls, letting the snug welcoming room surround her like a cocoon. The long history of the land, the ranch, and the breeding program filled the shelves of a floor to ceiling bookcase. With her at the helm, Rocking S Ranch had become one of the most successful Quarter Horse operations in the state. A deep stir of sadness moved through her heart. *Dad would have been so proud of me–but thank God he never had to witness this day.*

Cliff pointed at a yellowed plat map on the wall. "Hard to believe we only have a fraction of the original estate."

She gazed at the faded marks on the map. "Interesting how every generation tries to maintain control. Deathbed promises, clauses in wills–all attempts to dictate the future. But in the end, everything changes anyway."

The room became silent and she glanced at her brothers. Cliff's expression was guarded, but not unsympathetic. Clarke gazed at her through deep-set eyes, the dark circles beneath them stark against his sun-starved skin. She hadn't been a part of these men's lives for such a long time–would they let her step back in now? Family ties were fragile, at best, in need of understanding and nurture–something she'd neglected in the past. She'd paid for that today, but it would never happen again.

"I have some bad news–Jethrow died in the fire."

Cliff whistled. "Jeezus, you mean the house burned down?"

She shook her head, almost unable to tell them the rest. "He was out in the field...*he* set the fire." Cliff's face darkened into a scowl, but she held up her hand. "That's not the worst of it. He's probably the one who attacked the horses."

"Why the hell would he do something like that?"

"I talked to him earlier–he believed we were all responsible for Randy's death because we didn't help him, didn't recognize he was in deep trouble."

Cliff snorted. "That's bullshit! You bent over backwards for that loser. He did it to himself, then took the coward's way out!"

Kellie broke down, grief wracking her body. Clarke came over and put his arms around her.

"C'mon, Kell, it's over now. You're gonna be all right."

She struggled out of his grasp, choking on the words. "No! You don't understand! *Jethrow* shot Randy and made it look like suicide! Killed his own father for God knows what reason." She sank back into the chair. "Jethrow kept a diary of every evil thing he did out there. I wish the place *had* burned down."

Clarke stepped back, and Kellie took a deep breath. "There's more. Frank's been arrested for drug dealing. I don't know any details yet, but he's in a lot of trouble."

Cliff set his empty beer bottle on the floor and stood up. "This is definitely a two beer conversation."

Sara's voice echoed in the hall, then she appeared in the doorway. "The sheriff is on the phone."

Kellie gazed at her brothers. "I promise we'll talk about your land in the morning."

Ed's low voice crooned through her frazzled mind. "Listen, I'm sorry, but I can't get out there again until morning. It's a hornet's nest here and I can't leave."

She gripped the phone close to her ear, savoring his calm tone, but disappointment threaded through her heart.

"I understand. I'm exhausted anyway, and I still have to get the barns reorganized."

"I'm sending a deputy out to pick up my cell phone. He should be there any minute."

"Okay. It rang while I was out by the windmill. I answered, and some man didn't sound happy to hear my voice."

A tight silence rippled through the connection. "And?..."

"I just hung up. Who was it?"

"I'll tell you when I see you in the morning."

For a long time after saying goodbye, she stared at nothing, her mind racing with a kaleidoscope of images and impressions. She had to get some things prioritized, and first on the list were the horses.

She strode into the growing dusk, focusing on the main barn and avoiding looking at the destroyed mare barn. In the pasture across the driveway, a band of yearlings and two-year-olds nibbled their way along the fence as though nothing had happened. The broodmares had been put into the pond pasture, and the remaining horses were in the parched field behind the main barn. Roy hadn't missed a beat getting things back to some semblance of normal.

But the seven or eight official vehicles scattered over the property were not part of that normalcy. Most of them were Logan County, but a black sedan and grey van had no markings. A table had been set up at the side of the barn, and a crime scene investigator pored over items collected from the area. Kellie shook her head. With so many crimes in the same location, they'd be there all night.

Sara appeared in the barn door. "We got all the horses taken care of." She grinned. "And I gave Juicy a big red apple for being so brave!"

Kellie gently tugged a pigtail. "*You're* the one who deserves a prize for bravery."

Sara looked pleased at the praise, then shook her head. "Poor Daddy."

Kellie's stomach churned. "What do you mean?"

"He missed all the excitement! But that's what he gets for spending all his time at the racetrack." She turned and grinned. "He said he'd take me there some time. Can I go?"

Oh, baby, I can't bear what's coming. Kellie nodded and turned toward the house. "If he ever makes good on that promise, you may go."

~~

Kellie sank into bed, pulling the soft goose down coverlet up to her chin, her aching muscles crying for rest. Through the open window, the continuing sounds of the official investigation kept all her thoughts at the front of her mind. What did she want to think about, besides Ed? Nothing. This horrible chain of events had sucked him in, coloring everything they did, constricting every conversation they had. In the middle of it all, that brief time together in the kitchen shone as the only bright light in her future. Had he meant the things he'd said? In the aftermath of today, would anything change? Had it been only this morning when she'd worn his ring, that youthful declaration of undying love?

"Mommy?" Sara's soft whisper was close in the darkness. "I can't sleep."

Kellie peeled back the quilt and patted the mattress next to her. "Come snuggle, baby."

Sara crawled into bed and wiggled over against Kellie. "I'm not a baby."

"You're *my* baby."

"That's what Daddy said."

Kellie's throat ached. She couldn't put this off any longer. What better time than in the cover of darkness and the comfort of each other's arms? She stroked her daughter's cheek, delighting in the still-velvety texture of adolescence.

"I have something to tell you, honey."

Sara snuggled closer and a hollow feeling began deep in Kellie's chest. "Daddy's in some trouble."

Sara rose up on her elbow, but Kellie pulled her back down into her arms.

"He's gotten himself involved with some bad people, and he's been arrested."

Sara lay very still, her voice barely audible. "Is he in jail?"

"Yes, but I don't know any of the details. We'll just have to wait for Sheriff Campbell to tell us what's going on."

Sara relaxed. "Whatever it is, he's innocent–they'll see."

A hot tear trickled from the corner of Kellie's eye and rolled down into her hair. "Let's hope so."

A minute later, Sara's voice drifted sleepily through the darkness. "Sheriff Campbell likes you. I can tell."

Kellie smiled into the night. "Really? Well, I kinda like him too."

An hour later, Sara was sound asleep and Kellie was wide-awake. The sounds of outside activity had faded, and she slipped out of bed, turning to pull the quilt up over Sara's shoulders. Grabbing a sweater, she tiptoed out of the room and headed for the kitchen. For a few minutes, she milled around, unsettled and trying to corral the flood of thoughts roiling through her head. She stopped at the kitchen window and stared outside at the dark fields. *What I really need is a good dose of horse.*

Heading toward the barn, she inhaled the scent of charred brush now softened by the night air. The whole thing seemed surreal in the darkness, but morning light would bring back the stark reality. For now, she only wanted the reassurance of what she knew best. Lights glowed from the barn and she headed for that beacon of comfort.

Stepping through the open door, she inhaled deeply. The aroma of alfalfa and wood shavings and sweet feed and horse sweat almost obliterated the odor of burned wood. The palomino mare stuck her head over the stall door and nickered. A smaller voice echoed the greeting. Hyde's head appeared at the next stall door, and Kellie laughed.

"What are *you* doing here so late?"

"Just checking everyone out. You were lucky–only one minor injury in the melee." He pointed toward the last stall by the back door. "That gelding you rode this morning whacked his hind leg on the fence you jumped."

She gaped. "I jumped a fence?"

Hyde laughed and came out of the stall. "That's what they tell me."

She gazed at her friend. Handsome, skilled, intelligent, educated–she'd never understood why he hadn't married. Being a private person herself, she'd never asked. Now, she wanted to know.

"How's Danielle doing?"

His face lit up, and she grinned. Ed hadn't been kidding.

"She'll be fine. The bullet went through muscle, never touched a bone, or artery, or nerve. The spirits watched over her."

"How long have you known her?"

His self-consciousness kicked in. "Oh, I guess about–"

Kellie nudged his arm. "You two have a thing going?"

He stuttered, then laughed. "Not exactly. We've kind of been watching each other from a distance. She's a mighty handsome woman...I always told myself the right one might come along, but it never happened. 'Course, Guthrie isn't exactly a huge place and, with my job, the only people I meet are clients." He shook his head. "Couple of widows made it clear they'd like my company, but I don't believe in getting involved with the people who put bread on the table."

Kellie put her hand on his arm, speaking from the deep love she felt for him. "I hope it works out with Dani."

His craggy face broke into a boyish grin. "Me too...Now tell me how *you're* holding up."

She gazed at Hyde's understanding brown eyes. "Even with all the horrible things that have happened today, I somehow feel like I've been released from prison. A prison of my own making. All my life, I've thought my way was the best way, and to hell with anyone else's needs or plans. I don't know if becoming a caregiver and ranch owner at the same time was too much, too young, but all these years, I've convinced myself that what I was doing was for the good of the whole family."

She snorted and looked away. "*What* family? I was so busy doing my own thing that I never even noticed they'd all gone their own ways."

Hyde took hold of her hands. "I'm happy you've finally learned who you really are. Your strength is admirable, but when it manifests itself in stubbornness, you lose sight of the big picture."

Tears burned her eyes. "Why didn't you just shake me and tell me to get real?"

"A man can only know himself by looking inside."

24

The early morning air held a chill, and Kellie pulled her sweater closer. A car turned into the driveway and she squinted to see who would be coming to visit so early.

Cliff's round face beamed. "I knew you'd be up–wanna go get some breakfast?"

She stepped off the porch, shaking her head. "I want to be here when Sara wakes up–I told her about Frank last night."

Cliff's smile faded. "Ouch...We'll come back later."

"No, you come on in and I'll cook something. I'm hungry too. It's going to be a long day."

As the men followed her into the house, she pondered how she would begin the emotional discussion she'd promised.

Clarke whistled under his breath. "Holy cow, you made the front page!"

"Yeah, incredible photograph, huh?"

The butter began to sizzle and she broke eight eggs into the frying pan, one-by-one, focusing on the swirly design of yellow and white, and pushing away the front-page picture of the mare barn engulfed in flames.

She pulled the frying pan off the fire and set it aside. Steeling herself, she turned to face her brothers.

"I've been looking into having the land designated as national historical property."

Cliff's face colored with anger. "Bull-shit! That doesn't help *us*! You–"

"Let me finish." Her resolve strengthened. "I'm prepared

to buy you out. Tell me what you want."

His expression faded to astonishment, then chagrin. He glanced at his twin and shook his head, pain flashing across his features. "Clarke doesn't have a whole lot of time, Sis."

What she'd known deep in her heart now hung on the air, there to be examined and dealt with. She could barely meet Clarke's gaze, but she nodded, speaking softly.

"I will do everything I can to help–I promise."

~~

Kellie gazed through the kitchen window at Cliff's car as it reached the end of the lane. She slid the breakfast plates into the warm soapy water, thinking how un-traumatic the conversation had been. Her brothers were happy with the plan, and the Sutton estate would be spared the bulldozers.

"What smells so good, Mama?"

Sara's sleepy smile put the perfect frosting on the morning's cake.

"Eggs and bacon and cinnamon toast. Want some?"

She placed the frying pan back on the stove, humming a little tune as she pulled the eggs from the fridge.

"Can we go visit Daddy today?"

The eggs hit the floor with a slushy thump. "Honey, I don't know anything yet. But I promise we'll find out."

Sara turned to the funny papers, and Kellie faced the reality of her life as it was at that moment.

While Sara ate, Kellie looked up the insurance company's number. The only way she'd be able to make good on her offer to the twins would be if the insurance paid in full–and quickly. The agent's answering machine picked up, reminding her it was Sunday. She wandered back toward the kitchen, wondering if an arson fire would affect how fast the claim could be settled.

Sara put her dishes in the sink and skipped past. "I'm going out to see Juicy."

"I'll be out in a few minutes. We need to give everybody a good grooming."

She watched her daughter take the stairs two at a time, marveling at her youthful resilience. She would definitely need it for what lay ahead.

~~

Ed smiled, listening to his boss's praise.

"You did good, Campbell. Positive ID on the body in the shelter. Estevan Rodriguez–it doesn't get much better than that. We'll talk about a promotion as soon as you get back."

A deep thread of indecision moved through Ed's head. "Yeah, well, there's still a lot to do here."

"The Oklahoma City units can mop up. The Guthrie commissioners will be expecting your resignation by the end of next week."

Ed opened his mouth to protest, but the boss had signed off.

For a long time, he sat in the car thinking about the sharp turn of events. His time had run out with Kellie, consumed by his job and her situation. With only a week left, could he make things happen for them? He snorted and threw the car into reverse. He'd failed once, why should this be any different?

Sara's high-pitched voice echoed in the barn. "Hiya, Sheriff Campbell!"

Kellie's head appeared over the back of the horse she was brushing. The two of them together was like seeing double. His heart thumped. The girl was beautiful, just like her mother. A band closed around his chest. Sara should have been his child.

He stepped up close and grinned. "Looks like you have the cleanest horses in town."

Sara giggled, delighted with the teasing. "We have to do *all* of them–they got really dirty yesterday."

"When you're finished, you can come to town and do mine."

She laughed again. "Oh, sure!"

He turned to Kellie and the smile faded from his heart. "How are *you* holding up?"

She searched his face, a question in her eyes. He knew his attempt at a pleasant expression wasn't working.

She set aside the currycomb and wiped her hands on her jeans. "Pretty good. Come on over to the office."

Minutes later, he removed his hat and nervously fingered the brim. "Which do you want to hear about first–Jethrow or Frank?"

She moved to the door and checked that Sara was out of hearing range. "Start with Frank."

"Hard to believe, but he somehow got tangled up with a major Columbian drug ring that's been operating out of Remington Park race track in Okee City. He says they approached him after he lost a valuable racehorse."

Kellie's eyes darkened, and a warning flag went up in his head.

He tempered his tone. "You know anything about that?"

"Only that he turned down a huge offer on the horse before it broke down in a race." She tilted her head. "Now that I think about it, he changed dramatically after that. Our marriage went downhill real fast...I can't imagine Frank running drugs."

The buried pain surfaced and Ed turned away from her scrutiny. "From what we can gather, based on his testimony, he was afraid that his warehouse would be discovered during the investigation into the attacks on your horses. He was trying to get to Travis Mack before we did."

She frowned. "How did he know about the guy?"

Ed looked down at the floor. "He came to the station on Friday. I think he overheard me talking to the dispatcher.

With Frank's underground connections, I'm sure he had no problem finding someone to get the information he needed to find Mack.

"Another thing you might be interested in–we've confirmed that the construction companies operating here are fronts for money laundering. That's why they've moved so fast. I expect there's a tie-in to the drug group in the city. If we can close that down, we can delay the land gobbling."

He'd expected a positive reaction, but Kellie's tone gave no clue to what she might be thinking. "What happens next?"

"Frank will be charged with drug trafficking and homicide–I just found out that the guy he killed is the kingpin for the cartel. Actually, Frank did the world a great service, but the law is the law."

"Is there anything I should do?"

His confidence evaporated. She was ready to go to bat for Frank. The thought slashed through him like a knife.

"Celeste Harding was posting bail as I left the station."

"Oh. Of course."

Kellie's pain etched her features, an emotion he never wanted to see again.

"The good news is, I think we've solved the mystery of the horse attacks. The Perkins Police Department finally let someone search Mack's quarters at the ranch. They found a jar of live fiddleback spiders in the cupboard, a cereal bowl with pieces of smashed spider bodies, and some disposable syringes on the counter. I suspect we'll get a match to the substance in the syringe we found in your barn."

Her face contorted with horror. "Hyde was right! Those are the spiders he mentioned." Her eyes glistened with tears. "Jethrow must have done a lot of research to find out which toxins have no antivenin."

Ed nodded solemnly. "He was one sick son-of-a-gun...his diary proves it. He detailed every day of his miserable young life, describing how much he hated his mother, his contempt for his dad's cowardice and, worse, a detailed description of the day he shot Randy, then made it look like suicide."

Her expression was devastating. He touched her hand, wanting to pull her into his arms and tell her no one would ever hurt her again. But how could he do that when he'd been the first one to break her heart?

"I'm so sorry you've had to go through all this."

~ ~

Kellie couldn't allow herself to dissect Jethrow's crimes, or think about the hatred that had driven the macabre plans. The overwhelming scope of his revenge would haunt her often enough in the future, but right now she needed to distance herself from it.

Ed looked exhausted, and her heart thumped softly. Though nothing had been resolved between them, he'd been at her side through the whole horrible nightmare, supporting her with a love that had never died. Did she deserve such loyalty? Probably not, but perhaps she could use her new humility to build a positive future with him.

Love filled her heart and her smile. "With all that's gone on, you're sure to be re-elected."

Surprise widened his eyes and his jaw dropped. Then he pressed his lips together and looked away.

Dread crept into her chest and she touched his arm. "Eddie, what is it?"

"I haven't been completely honest with you...I'm not really the sheriff. I'm an undercover DEA agent. We've been after the Oklahoma City gang for almost two years."

Stunned for a moment, she finally found her voice. "So you didn't come back because of me."

"Yes, I did, but I never expected a major crime in the middle of my undercover work. I thought I'd have plenty of time to see if we could get back together." He shook his head and gazed down at her with sadness. "My track record for bungling is one hundred percent."

A parade of emotions passed over his face, this man she thought she knew. It wouldn't be easy, or happen quickly, but she would try.

She lifted her chin and met his gaze with courage. "We both have a lot ahead of us...but when the time is right, I'd like that second chance you talked about."

His eyes glowed with happiness. "I'll be here." He started toward the door, a jaunty spring in his step, his shoulders square and proud.

Her courage grew and she opened her heart. "Eddie?... I love you."

~~~~
~~~~

About the Author

Toni Leland has been writing for over 20 years. She has published four equestrian novels and two juvenile chapter books. Her short stories have appeared in *Arabella Romance Magazine, True Story,* and *Horse Tales for the Soul.*

Additionally, Toni writes a biweekly newspaper column on gardening as a spokesperson for the Ohio State University Master Gardener program in Muskingum County, Ohio; she produces articles for international gardening site, Dave's Garden (davesgarden.com), and writes feature articles for *Grit* magazine (grit.com) and a national trade publication, *Romance Writers Report*.

In her day job, she writes and edits books about caring for miniature horses, as well as scripting, directing, and producing educational DVDs about this unique height breed (smallhorse.com).

photo: Katie Angier

Toni Leland ~ Women's Fiction with Kick!

http://www.tonileland.com

Printed in the United States
204285BV00004B/70-78/P

9 781887 932202